R0700773021          04/2023

**PALM BEACH COUNTY
LIBRARY SYSTEM
3650 Summit Boulevard
West Palm Beach, FL   33406-4198**

D1516706

Also by Katherine Heiny

*Early Morning Riser*

*Standard Deviation*

*Single, Carefree, Mellow*

Games
and
Rituals

# Games
# and
# Rituals

*Stories*

## Katherine Heiny

Alfred A. Knopf · New York · 2023

THIS IS A BORZOI BOOK
PUBLISHED BY ALFRED A. KNOPF

Copyright © 2023 by Katherine Heiny

All rights reserved. Published in the United States by Alfred A. Knopf, a division of Penguin Random House LLC, New York.

www.aaknopf.com

Knopf, Borzoi Books, and the colophon are registered trademarks of Penguin Random House LLC.

Several stories originally appeared in the following publications: "Bridesmaid, Revisited" in *Narrative*, "CobRa" in *Grand Journal*, "Games and Rituals" in *Epoch* (February 2023), "King Midas" in *Meetinghouse*, "Sky Bar" in *Catamaran*, "Damascus" in *Narrative*, "Games and Rituals" in *The Cincinnati Review*, and "561" published as a novella by Fourth Estate Kindle Division in 2018.

Library of Congress Cataloging-in-Publication Data
Names: Heiny, Katherine, author.
Title: Games and rituals : stories / Katherine Heiny.
Description: New York : Alfred A. Knopf, 2023.
Identifiers: LCCN 2022023592 (print) | LCCN 2022023593 (ebook) |
ISBN 9780525659518 (hardcover) | ISBN 9780525659525 (ebook)
Subjects: LCGFT: Short stories.
Classification: LCC PS3608.E3823 G36 2023 (print) |
LCC PS3608.E3823 (ebook) | DDC 813/.6—dc23
LC record available at https://lccn.loc.gov/2022023592
LC ebook record available at https://lccn.loc.gov/2022023593

This is a work of fiction. Names, characters, places, and incidents either are the product of the author's imagination or are used fictitiously. Any resemblance to actual persons, living or dead, events, or locales is entirely coincidental.

Jacket illustration by Anna Parini
Jacket design by Kelly Blair

Manufactured in the United States of America
First Edition

for Angus and Hector

Love has gone and left me and the days are all alike.

—EDNA ST. VINCENT MILLAY

# CONTENTS

# Games
# and
# Rituals

# Chicken-Flavored and Lemon-Scented

COLETTE HAS BEEN A DRIVING EXAMINER FOR TWELVE YEARS—SHE'S thirty-six—and yet it only occurs to her today that Ted Bundy had had a driver's license. And that means that some driving examiner had taken him for a road test. Think about it: some driving examiner had willingly clambered into Ted's VW bug and driven off with him. Maybe the driving examiner had even been a woman. A woman who never knew she had ridden next to Death, never knew she had docked Death points for improper clutch control.

Why has Colette never thought of that before? But she thinks of lots of things lately that she hasn't thought about before.

IT IS EARLY FEBRUARY in Maryland, the day as bleak as a pen-and-ink drawing done on old gray paper—bare trees, muddy snow, the road clear but scored with white salt stains like the scars from old injuries. Colette parks behind the DMV building and walks up the sidewalk to the employee entrance.

She's a little late and the other driving examiners are already there: Vic, Gregg, and Alejandro. Vic is a pointy-faced man of about forty with slicked-back dark hair who looks like a weaselly sort of hood, or maybe just a weasel, with his small eyes and vicious smile. Before landing here at the DMV, Vic worked as a bouncer, a roadie, a security guard, a fitness trainer, an auditor, and a head cook—name a job where you got to intimidate people and Vic has held it.

Gregg is an older man with bushy salt-and-pepper hair, a bushy salt-and-pepper beard, and horn-rimmed glasses. He looks like a retired history teacher and is, in fact, a retired history teacher. He likes to do cryptograms between examinations. No one knows why Gregg works as a driving examiner instead of enjoying his retirement and doing unlimited cryptograms at home in his underwear. Colette worries that Gregg has been unwise with his pension and is short of money but Vic says it's undoubtedly that Gregg doesn't want to stay home with his wife. Gregg's wife packs him the most elaborate lunches Colette has ever seen, with all the food in undersized portions: tiny sandwiches, miniature quiches, itty-bitty salads in old baby food jars, cupcakes no bigger than a quarter. "Can you imagine living with the woman who packs those lunches?" Vic asked. "His choices are probably to come here or stay home and help her organize her toothpick collection." Colette thinks he might be right.

Alejandro is a compactly built man in his late twenties with close-cropped black hair, bright brown eyes, an easy smile, and chiseled features. Not chiseled as in especially strong or sharp, but chiseled as in some sculptor had apparently chiseled them especially for Colette, had known what Colette would find handsome before she herself knew it.

Alejandro had started work here six months ago. Colette had been out on a road test when he arrived—she'd come back to the office and there he was. He rose to shake her hand and introduce himself and Colette dropped her clipboard. "Sorry I'm so distracted," she said, leaning down to retrieve it. "My last road test drove the wrong way down a one-way street."

That was true. Colette had never been so grateful to have an excuse for looking flushed and out of breath.

e⁀

THE DRIVING EXAMINERS work at four metal desks in a room with cinder-block walls painted the color of curdled cream. The only window is one-way glass and the view is not of outside but of the four scuffed blue plastic chairs in the hall where test-takers wait to take their road tests. (The person who accompanies them—usually a parent—has to wait over in chairs on the other side of the building.)

A moment or two after the test-taker sits down, Trina or Gina from Written Tests pops open the door to the driving examiner's office, tosses the test-taker's folder into the tray on top of the filing cabinet, and retreats.

Vic always volunteers for the morning's first test, and today it's a burly guy in a maroon sweatsuit.

"Okay, I'm headed out for coffee," Vic says. What he means is that he's going to make the burly guy go through the McDonald's drive-thru as part of the road test. He does it every single day, and no test-taker has ever thought to complain, not even the lady who chipped the Ronald McDonald statue and had to pay three hundred dollars in repairs.

"None for me," Colette says.

Vic frowns. "Why the fuck not?"

"It gives me headaches."

"What, after decades of drinking coffee, it suddenly gives you headaches?"

"It's possible to develop an allergy at any time in your life," Gregg says.

Vic looks at him, annoyed. "Now you don't want one, either?"

"No, I want a premium blend, black with two sugars."

"Alejandro?"

"Americano, with an extra shot of espresso. I'll make up for Colette's lack of caffeine." He winks at Colette. The wink doesn't cause her heart to leap with hope anymore. She thinks that must be a good sign.

*e^

THE DRIVING EXAMINERS are supposed to work in strict rotation, like a batting order lineup: the first available driving examiner taking the next test-taker. But Colette and Vic and Gregg have long ago developed their own system where they assess the test-taker through the one-way glass (and study the paperwork in the test-taker's folder) and make their own assignments.

Rules apply, obviously. No one is allowed to strike every undesirable test-taker who comes their way because that would basically mean no one except pretty girls, men with kind faces, and librarians would ever get driver's licenses. But they can pick and choose to some extent.

None of them liked to take old people. The problems with old people were endless: hearing loss, vision loss, memory loss, slowed reflexes, confusion. It broke Colette's heart when she saw some elderly person shuffle out to take their test and knew that person had once been lithe and slender, brimming with intelligence and verve. And she knew that the old people still thought of themselves that way. They had no idea the younger, more capable versions of themselves had decamped decades ago. It was heartbreaking but it was also fucking *scary.* The old people led you out to their Lincolns and Buicks (they didn't approve of foreign-made models) and the cars would be ringed with dents and scrapes, little souvenirs of the places the old person had driven. And off you went on a hair-raising road test with someone who could barely see past the hood. They straddled lanes, ignored stop signs, braked abruptly (without cause), accelerated suddenly (also without cause), pressed simultaneously on the brake and gas pedals, drove over curbs, nearly drove over people. All of them—every single one—remarked without irony about how more drivers *honked* their horns nowadays, how there'd been a mysterious uptick in *honking* recently. The old men said it was because young people are so entitled they couldn't wait for anything; the old ladies said it just showed no one bothered to learn proper manners anymore.

No driving examiner liked to take teenagers, either. Teenagers were almost scarier than the old people. Teens had excellent vision and hearing, superb reaction times and hand-eye coordination, but their prefrontal cortexes were not fully developed. Teens were always speeding, running red lights, weaving in and out of traffic, tailgating, pulling out in front of oncoming vehicles—all this when they *knew* they were being tested. Shouldn't teenagers be used to taking tests and know how to concentrate? Weren't they beaten down by the educational system's focus on standardized testing? Apparently not. Colette had had teenagers behave in ways she at first took to be pranks: checking their phones in the middle of the road test, *answering* their phones in the middle of the road test, taking their hands off the wheel to do a little victory car-dance after turns, reaching into the back seat while driving to root around for a water bottle. Nerves accounted for some of the behavior but Colette thought most of it was just plain old terrible teenage judgment.

But the test-takers weren't all old people and teenagers. There were many other categories, and these were the ones the driving examiners were eager to volunteer for, depending on their own strengths and style.

Sometimes Colette thinks that Vic becoming a driving examiner had been like an artist picking up a paintbrush for the first time: that rush of exhilaration that comes from finding your calling. As a driving examiner, Vic can intimidate people full-time—and in the privacy of their cars. He breaks people down and enjoys doing it, like a professional torturer. He excels with aggressive test-takers: the impatient executives in power suits who carry briefcases to show how important they are, the medical professionals who wear scrubs or white coats to show how busy they are, the people who can't stop tapping their shoes and checking their watches, the awful and angry types who shout at DMV employees. Vic meets these test-takers with a shine in his small eyes, his sharp crooked teeth bared in a predatory smile. He takes them on the most challenging routes, requests impossible accuracy in parallel parking, asks them to read road signs that have already blipped by, shakes his head and clucks his tongue just to unnerve them. Vic is a bully and a tyrant, but sometimes when Colette watches him swagger out to meet a suited, loud-voiced man who has just yelled at Trina or Gina in Written Tests, her heart swells with gladness. Justice will be meted out swiftly.

Gregg's style is loose, casual, almost bumbling. He goes out to meet the test-takers still pulling on his coat, his clipboard fluttering with papers, a cup of coffee sloshing in one hand. He's particularly good with people on a deadline: the young mothers who check their phones for messages from their babysitters, the housekeepers and domestic staff who have obviously called in sick to work and won't be able to return if they fail, the anxious landscapers and construction workers whose livelihoods depend on them passing this test. They seem to understand that this cheerful, bearded man considers the test a quick disruption of ordinary life—the sooner it is over, the sooner they can get back to their jobs and he can get back to his cryptogram—and they adopt his efficient attitude.

Colette knows her own strength as a driving examiner is her ability to project calm. She's like a kind of reverse microwave—molecules slow in her presence. She approaches test-takers with a gentle smile and a measured step, her fine blond hair smoothed into a low pony-tail, her pale gray eyes free of makeup or judgment. She keeps her voice low, her gaze steady, her movements smooth. She volunteers for the extremely nervous test-takers (and all test-takers are nervous; it is just a matter of degree). She takes the teenagers whose hands shake so much they keep dropping their documents, the women who shred tissues compulsively and thin their lips into nonexistence, the men who grow unhealthily red cheeked and sweat huge amoeba-shaped stains on their shirts. And she takes the people who are not only nervous about the road test but seem nervous about *life*. People who come to the DMV wearing pajama pants and slippers, or cardigans with food dribbles and shoes without laces. Or—this is somehow worse—*people who have dressed up*. They wear clothing which has moldered unworn in their closets for years: shiny polyester blouses, corduroy blazers, mismatched suits, dresses bought on clearance with the price tag still attached. Men with crumbs in their beards, women with fearful white-ringed eyes, teenagers who swallow with loud clicks—all of them looking like they want to put their hands over their ears. Everyone hates going to the DMV but these people fear it. These people don't function well in the world for whatever cause—anxiety, illness, trauma, abuse, or just a lifetime of having been bullied by assholes. But they still need to get places, so here they are to get their driver's license, and Colette is here to guide them through the process as gently as possible.

"I know you're nervous but this is no big deal," she says to them softly. They look at her with mistrust—*everything* is a big deal to them. "I'm going to talk you through it. No surprises, okay? I'm not here to trick you. I'm here to help you. I *want* you to pass."

She does want it. She wants them to have this triumph, this shining moment of success in a life that, for whatever unfair reason, has held precious few such moments. Some of them still fail—no amount of gentle encouragement and patient reassurance could calm them—but a lot of them pass, and Colette can share in their victories. Those victories are why she stays at the DMV.

In the beginning, Colette and Vic and Gregg had been nervous about how Alejandro would fit in. He seemed competent but lots of driving examiners are competent. But would he actually add anything to their lives, would he lighten their workloads in any way, would he find his own specialty? The answer to all of these questions was yes. Alejandro steps up to every test-taker with a welcoming smile and a very small and courtly bow. (Yes, an actual bow.) He takes the entitled people—the soccer moms and the private-school kids and the expats and the impeccably dressed rich people who disdain the blue chairs as too down-market to even sit in—and he defuses their entitlement with his apparent delight in their company. He flashes his dazzling smile at the cross, cranky older people who bristle with defensiveness and makes them goggle at him with unexpected pleasure. Alejandro also takes the "Mouths." Mouths are people who talk so much in their professional and personal lives that they've forgotten how to be quiet even during a road test: hairstylists, bartenders, customer service reps, insurance salespeople, business recruiters, event planners, corporate fundraisers, backpackers who tell you how they've done Bangkok and it's way too touristy and how they're basically Buddhist now. No one likes Mouths because they talk all the way through the road test—usually they start talking before they even put the car in gear—and the test takes three times longer than normal. What's more, Mouths usually fail the road test because they are too busy talking to hear instructions—and that means they'll be back and the process will repeat itself. But not for Alejandro. He and the Mouth drive off and return precisely twenty minutes later, the Mouth having passed and Alejandro having somehow stayed sane. No one knows quite how he does it. He says it's just a matter of really listening carefully to the first story, of making the Mouth feel heard and understood, but Colette knows it's more than that. Alejandro genuinely *wants* to hear their stories (at least the first one) and this unfeigned interest makes the test-takers fall in love with him, just the way she had.

VIC RETURNS, HAVING FAILED the test-taker despite the drive-thru. "Sad sack didn't use his turn signal once," he says, setting a cardboard McCafé cup on Colette's desk.

"Vic, I said—"

"It's hot chocolate."

"Oh," she says, surprised. It's so rare for Vic to be thoughtful. "Thank you."

"You owe me two-eighty."

Colette sighs.

Beyond this, the morning holds few surprises: Gregg completes a cryptogram in ninety-seven seconds, his personal best. A soccer mom impresses Vic by expertly parking her minivan and he reluctantly passes her. A Mouth tells Alejandro that dogs use eighteen muscles to control their ears. Colette takes an elderly man out on a test and then has to urinate so urgently that she forces him to do an unannounced and tricky left turn into a corner gas station so she can leap out and pee in the gas station's horrible, sewer-smelling restroom.

ALEJANDRO HAD NOT ONLY lightened their workload, he had enriched their lives in a hundred ways. He was a saxophone player and he brought a portable speaker to work and played soft jazz for them from his iPod. He put up a whiteboard and wrote WE HAVE GONE ____ TESTS WITHOUT NEARLY DYING and they all changed the number after every test. (They never got higher than fourteen before going back to zero.) He printed out copies of a daily cryptogram and made all four of them solve it—the winner got whatever Gregg's wife had packed him for dessert. He talked to Gregg about bird-watching (who knew Gregg watched birds?) and the Battle of the Somme. He talked to Vic about workout routines and how he, Alejandro, could build more muscle, and about the Hudson Hornet that Vic hoped to buy someday. Once Colette had glanced over while Alejandro and Vic were talking, and Vic's pointy face had softened and his weaselly eyes had widened until he looked almost human, almost kind.

But Alejandro had changed Colette's life more than anyone else's. She realized that before he came, her life had been pedestrian—although could a driving examiner's life accurately be called *pedestrian*? Maybe it was more like she had been puttering along in a school zone at twenty-five miles per hour. But after Alejandro's arrival, her life—at least her work life—was full of excitement and adventure, great happiness and even-greater fear.

The fear came from knowing that Alejandro would move on, probably sooner rather than later—he was too smart, too ambitious, to work as a driving examiner forever—and also the constant worry that he would start dating someone. Colette learned from conversational crumbs that Alejandro had dropped (and she, mouse-like, had assiduously collected) that he was single, straight, lived by himself, and spent most of his free time playing saxophone in a jazz quartet called the Jazz Merchants. (Sadly, the Jazz Merchants mostly played at private events; Colette could not just happen to show up.) He was single now but he could meet and start dating some lucky woman at any moment! He could meet someone at a jazz rehearsal or the supermarket or the gym or—this last one was terrible to consider—*during a road test*. What if Alejandro drove off with some beautiful girl and came back twenty minutes later in love? And so many beautiful girls came to the DMV. Vic even had a code for them: "Chicken-Flavored and Lemon-Scented." *Chicken-flavored and lemon-scented*, a Chelsea, a pretty girl. Vic and Gregg had always volunteered to take the Chelseas, but last year, Gregg had been written up for asking a girl if she was on the pill—"It came up in conversation!" he'd told Colette. "It was perfectly innocent!"—and now he never takes one if he can help it. Pre-Alejandro, Colette had taken only the extremely nervous Chelseas and the ones who looked vulnerable enough that Vic might be able to bribe them into giving him a blow job, but now she takes those plus any Chelsea who she fears is Alejandro's type. Sometimes she thinks it might actually be easier if Alejandro had a girlfriend; it's horrible to feel you're competing with the world.

The happiness came from knowing that every weekday would

be spent in Alejandro's presence. Forty hours of pure pleasure— although minus time spent actually doing their pesky jobs, of course. Colette prepped for conversations with Alejandro nightly alone in her apartment: she researched jazz music, she signed up for an online class about craft-beer brewing, she watched professional hockey. (That's love for you.) But most of that was unnecessary because Alejandro was so easy to talk to.

"How are your neighbors?" he would ask. "Are they still watching *Calliou* every night at top volume?"

"Yes, but now I go salsa dancing most nights so it doesn't bother me," Colette said, although of course she didn't—she just put on headphones like a normal person. But it wouldn't hurt to have Alejandro think she was out dancing.

Or he'd say, "Tell me where you went hiking this weekend," and she'd say, "Cascade Falls," even though she'd really been hiking through Ikea, shopping for new sheets and throw pillows and framed prints to spruce up her apartment in case Alejandro ever came over.

And it seemed like he *would* come over; he *would* ask her out. He paid so much attention to her. "I watched *90 Day Fiancé*," he said once. "It surprises me that you like it—you're so levelheaded, so smart about everything, especially relationships."

"I've done my share of impulsive things," she said quietly.

Alejandro looked at her steadily, not smiling but looking like he wanted to. A bright, hot look. "Good impulsive or bad impulsive?"

The moment stretched between them like strands of spun sugar.

"*Guava!*" Gregg cried abruptly, causing them both to jump. "That's the word I couldn't figure out." He chuckled happily into his beard and Colette let out a long breath, trying not to sigh.

LUNCH ROLLS AROUND, and Colette realizes that salmon is just like the thought of Ted Bundy taking his road test: frightening and disturbing, and yet she's never thought of it until now. Gregg's wife has packed him a little Tupperware container of cold poached salmon and Colette can't imagine why anyone would make this, let alone eat it. The thought of biting into it, biting into a cool wet wobbly *fish,* its flesh on your tongue like a cold quivering glob of mucus—she pushes her salad away, half eaten.

Alejandro comes in, unwrapping a sandwich. Before he sits down to eat, he wipes the "2" off the whiteboard.

"What happened?" Gregg asks.

"A girl took her sweatshirt off over her head in the middle of an intersection," Alejandro says, writing a zero in the blank.

Vic leers around a mouthful of hamburger. "How were her tits?"

"I thought I was going to be *killed,*" Alejandro says. "I wasn't worried about her chest. And she had a T-shirt on underneath, anyway."

"What are you staring at?" Vic asks Colette.

"You really are reprehensible," Colette says to him.

"Don't be insecure," Vic says. "Your tits are great, and getting bigger all the time."

Unexpectedly, Gregg comes to her rescue. "I want to keep my dessert."

"Fair enough," Alejandro says. "You got the best time on the cryptogram."

"No, I mean I want to keep it every day."

"Gregg, man." Alejandro looks pained. "Have some decency."

Gregg clutches his lunch bag defensively. "You guys can have some other dessert. You can go get doughnuts or buy cookies or something."

"That's not the same," Vic says, and for once Colette agrees with him. She'll miss the miniature éclairs, the cheesecake squares the size of postage stamps. But that's February—all the joy leaks out of life.

℮

ALEJANDRO HAD HOSTED an office Christmas party at his apartment. He passed out the invitations, and Colette and Gregg and Vic had accepted. No one told Alejandro that their usual office Christmas celebration was ordering a party platter from Buffalo Wild Wings and having Vic bully his prelunch test-taker into picking it up—sometimes he even got the test-taker to pay for it. Instead they all said they'd be delighted.

Colette has a flat stomach and slender, shapely legs but square hips and no waist, which means that the khakis and green polo shirt the driving examiners are required to wear hide her body's assets and emphasize its flaws. But for Alejandro's party, she wore a short pale gold dress with bell sleeves and knee-high brown boots. She had wanted to wear makeup to work once Alejandro had started there, but she feared Vic's sharp eyes and sharper comments. She wore makeup to the party, though, and styled her hair in loose waves.

Gregg had come without his wife (but with a Tupperware tray of miniature strawberry tartlets she'd made). Vic was there with a date—a woman named Shelley, who seemed nice and normal but maybe she hadn't been dating Vic long enough to know how mean he was. Alejandro had invited Trina and Gina from Written Tests as well as people from Vehicle Registrations, Business Services, and Vision Testing. (Colette did not like the inclusion of Vision Testing, or at least not the inclusion of Lissa, with her platinum hair and low-cut blouse, but Lissa left early.)

Alejandro was as charming a host as he was a driving examiner. He circled among them with a wine bottle in his hand, topping up drinks, asking questions, loosening knotted conversations. When he got to where Colette stood listening to Bertha from Business Services talk about how she might update her phone's data usage plan, he winked.

Twelve guests, eleven departures. Colette waited the others out by lingering in the bathroom and then letting Alejandro refill her glass while they waited for Gregg's Uber to arrive. As soon as he was gone, Colette said, "I should call my own Uber," and Alejandro said, as she had hoped he would, "Why not stay for another drink?"

They sat on the sofa and Alejandro said, "Okay, now that I have you alone, tell me about Bertha's phone plan." They laughed and sipped their wine. They laughed and sipped their wine. They laughed and sipped their wine until there was no wine left. And then Colette leaned forward and kissed Alejandro. He kissed her back and she felt an actual thump as they crossed the barrier from coworkers to more-than-coworkers, just like the thump when a speed bump took a test-taker by surprise. *Thump,* the front wheels go up; *whack,* the back wheels come down; and the whole car shakes. The room shook, or at least Colette shook, and then they were undressing and then Colette was straddling him naked.

Alejandro said, "Is this okay?"

She sensed that a pause would be fatal. So she'd whispered into his ear, "It's perfect. Don't stop."

COLETTE IS BUSY ON HER computer when Vic says, "Look up. Chicken-flavored and lemon-scented."

Colette's stomach lurches again—she imagines chicken soaked in cleaning spray—but it's only Vic using the code. She looks out the window at the test-taker chairs.

The girl standing there uncertainly is definitely a Chelsea: very slender with tawny skin, light eyes in a small elfin face, and long light-brown hair that she has straightened and smoothed into shiny panels, like silk curtains. She's wearing black leggings and a gray sweater topped by a raspberry-colored down jacket that matches the color of her lips. But even through the window, they can all see the nerves rippling over her in waves. Nervousness is actually distorting her expression—it's like looking at someone on a television with faulty wiring.

"She's yours, Colette," Vic says regretfully.

"Yes, I guess she is." Colette checks the folder. The girl's name is Seraphina because of course it is. She turned sixteen in May and passed driver's ed back in August, so why is she here on a school day in February?

Colette walks out to the chairs and shakes hands with Seraphina. The girl's fingers tremble even when she's grasping Colette's hand.

"You look pretty nervous," Colette says. It helps if you can get them to admit that. "Is that how you feel?"

Seraphina's eyes are huge, like someone using the big-eyes filter on Instagram. *"Yes,"* she whispers.

"Everyone's nervous when they do the road test," Colette says. "It's totally normal to feel that way. Let's get started and you'll see that it's no big deal."

ON THE DAY AFTER Alejandro's Christmas party, Colette got to work early, wearing khaki pants but with a green silk polo shirt instead of her usual cotton one, and dangly gold earrings. She sat at her desk and tried to busy herself with paperwork but every time she heard voices in the hall, her head lifted as though pulled upward by strings. And yet Alejandro didn't show.

Finally, at ten, she said to Vic and Gregg, "Where do you think Alejandro is?"

"Took himself a personal day," Gregg said. "Gina told me."

"He's probably in bed balls-deep with Lissa," Vic said. Colette could not keep her gaze from flicking instantly to Vision Testing, but there was Lissa, working as usual.

"Made you look," Vic sneered. "I don't know where that bastard is. Aren't you cold as fuck in that shirt?"

Colette was indeed cold as fuck, and not just from the shirt. She shivered at her desk or else huddled frozen on test-taker passenger seats, breathing on her fingers to warm them, giving instructions robotically, staring out the window when she should have been watching the road. That day, a Thursday, wore on interminably, like some horror-movie monster who won't die. She replayed the moment of leaving Alejandro's apartment over and over: She had dressed quietly and leaned over to kiss him. "I'm going now." She was too hyped up to think about sleeping there.

Alejandro had stirred sleepily. "I should drive you home." His voice was slurred.

"Just rest," she'd whispered. "See you tomorrow."

"Safe journey," he said. He was asleep a moment later.

Should she have stayed? Should she have texted him when she got home? Should she have called him in the morning? Stopped by with coffee and doughnuts? Why didn't *Alejandro* call or come by with doughnuts? Why was she left to sort through every exchange for meaning, like a seventh grader?

Alejandro was there on Friday, same as always, friendly and smiling. But by then Colette understood that the previous day had been a buffer, a cooling-off period, a time to let her hopes diminish. Perhaps it had been a kindness; Alejandro had not seen the silk shirt, or the dangly earrings, or her eager face. Her fever had broken; she no longer glowed like a coal. Friday was just a day indistinguishable from thousands of others that had come before it.

But as she trudged through the snowy parking lot after work, Alejandro called to her. "Colette, wait a second!"

She stopped, heart rising like a balloon, and he caught up to her, pulling a wool hat on and hopping from foot to foot in the cold. He told her that he really liked her and valued their friendship enormously, but she had failed to use the mirrors correctly when changing direction and she had not responded appropriately to traffic lights and she showed confusion at four-way stops and she had driven too fast for the conditions and he was so sorry not to have better news, but she had failed to pass.

Or something like that.

e⁓

SERAPHINA LEADS COLETTE through the double glass doors to where a Subaru Forester SUV is parked. They get in and Seraphina grips the steering wheel so tightly that Colette thinks her hands might sink into it, that the steering wheel might puff up around her fingers like Play-Doh.

"You can relax a little, Seraphina." She wishes the girl's name was shorter. "We're not going to drive just yet. I want you to turn the headlights on. Can you do that? Good job. Now the hazard lights. Excellent. Now turn them off. You're doing really well. Now I want you to start the car and drive up to that stop sign and turn left."

Seraphina turns the ignition on and puts the Forester in gear. They drive up to the stop sign and Seraphina stops properly—which is excellent. Many, many people do a rolling or improper stop at this first stop sign and fail their test less than ten seconds after it had started. This stop sign has caused more tears and anguish than the ending of *Charlotte's Web*.

Seraphina turns left and Colette instructs her to follow the access road up to the intersection near the shopping plaza. Seraphina is doing well. She guides the Forester smoothly, following Colette's directions, and she's able to read the signs when asked. But she's still holding on to the steering wheel like someone clinging to the wreckage of a sinking ship.

"Now, make a right turn here at the intersection," Colette says.

Seraphina pulls to a stop at the red light, and looks to her left, where three lanes of traffic are coming toward them. The oncoming cars—two sedans and a pickup—are all red and Colette has just enough time to think the cars look bright and angry on the dull winter-gray road and then Seraphina pulls out into the intersection.

She doesn't do it slowly or hesitantly but she's not panicking or rushing, either. She just swings the Forester around the corner and into the right lane as though she has a green light and not a single care. The pickup truck is behind them in the right lane and the driver hits his horn and doesn't let up—an endless, furious howl.

*"Go!"* Colette shouts to be heard over the horn. *"Go! Go! Go!"*

Obediently Seraphina presses the gas pedal. The Forester surges forward but not fast enough. The pickup truck is closing up on them faster than an adrenaline rush. The snarling metal mouth of its grille is almost filling up the rear window.

Colette grabs for the steering wheel and pulls to the right, trying to get the car over to the right shoulder. Seraphina steers with her and presses even harder on the gas pedal and the Forester shoots across the shoulder and up the grass embankment. Colette sees white sky through the windshield and then abruptly black asphalt as they head down the other side of the embankment and then—shake, rattle, and roll, just like the song—the Forester comes to a stop in the (thankfully empty) outer parking lot of a shopping plaza. The wail of the pickup's horn peaks and then dies away as it races by on the other side of the embankment.

Colette yanks the emergency brake up, then she reaches over and slams the car into park and pulls the key out of the ignition. She leans back in the passenger seat, panting, her hand resting on her stomach. Not this. Please not this. She won't be able to stand it. But maybe it will be okay—it's not like they went on a roller-coaster ride. The impact was minimal. Their seat belts didn't even lock.

She opens her eyes and turns to Seraphina, who is trembling all over in a weirdly disjointed way—her head is shaking and her arms are shaking and her hands are shaking and her fingers are shaking, but all separately, all to an independent beat. She looks like she might jitter apart completely.

Her panic makes Colette calmer. She steadies her voice. "Are you hurt?"

Seraphina shakes her head. "I didn't see the cars," she says. "Just didn't see them. I mean, I saw them but they didn't seem real."

"That happens sometimes," Colette says. Amazingly, this is true. Sometimes test-takers get so nervous that they experience a sort of cognitive dissonance—they blow through very visible stop signs or make right turns from the left turn lane.

Seraphina moans. "I feel like I'm going to throw up."

That made two of them. "If you need to, just open the door. I'll check the car," Colette says. She gets out and walks around the Forester, looking for damage, but it seems to have emerged unscathed, and even the embankment doesn't look too chewed up.

She gets back in the car. Seraphina has stopped shaking and her color's better, but her eyes are still enormous. She pushes back the panels of her hair and Colette sees how small Seraphina's face is, how thin her neck. She's a childlike sixteen, despite her prettiness.

"I know that was really scary," Colette says gently. "But we're okay. The car's okay, I'm okay, you're okay."

Seraphina looks at her strangely, intensely, her eyes blazing, and shakes her head. "No, I'm not. I'm not okay. I'm pregnant."

"Ohhhhhh," Colette says slowly, making a number of mental adjustments. "I see. Are you sure?"

"Took three tests in the CVS bathroom last week," Seraphina says. She talks in a strangely precipitous way, like she's just filling in details of a story everyone already knows, and maybe she is. "I knew even before the first one but I kept taking them, hoping for, like, different results."

"How far along are you?"

"Seven weeks." Her tone is a little impatient, like Colette should know all this.

"And the father—"

"Brayden Shaw."

"Does Brayden know?"

Seraphina makes an impatient gesture. "Yeah, like I'll just call Brayden Shaw and say, 'Remember your little sister's caroling party? Well, I got some follow-up news for you.'"

"But isn't he your boyfriend?"

"Nope." Seraphina shakes her head at Colette's ignorance. "Because, guess what? He *has* a girlfriend."

"Oh, Seraphina, I'm sorry—"

Seraphina keeps talking, evidently warming to her story. "What happened was his mom hired my friend Tia to help her with her daughter's caroling party and Tia couldn't do it so she asked me. But when I get there—no mom, no kids, just Brayden. I didn't really know him. He goes to private school, so it's not like we've talked. Tells me the party's canceled because, like, the neighborhood association is against caroling and his mom is having everyone meet at the ice rink instead. I say, 'Okay, well, I'll just go back home,' and he's like, 'Aw, come in and have some cocoa first.' He said it like if I didn't do it, he would be so let down. He made it sound like he was lonely and wanted to have cocoa with someone, like cocoa doesn't taste good if you're having it alone, and that's true. Plus, you know Brayden, who wouldn't want to have cocoa with him?"

Colette doesn't know Brayden but she realizes she doesn't need to—she knows the type. Handsome, arrogant, charming when it suits them. The type who whistle at you and then give you a stupid *who me?* look. The type who cock an eyebrow sexily at the camera even for their driver's license photo.

"So in I go and we really did have cocoa because his mom had bought all these supplies for the party," Seraphina says. "Then we went down to the basement and played *Dark Souls III* on the PlayStation and then we had sex on this giant beanbag thing his dad bought when he had back trouble. Although, I mean, a lot of stuff happened between the PlayStation and the beanbag."

"What kind of stuff?"

Seraphina shrugs as though the details don't concern her. "Talking. Kissing. More talking. I mean, one thing we talked about was that I asked him if he wanted to have sex with me."

"And you, um, didn't use protection?" Colette asks gently. (So Gregg was right—this kind of conversation can happen organically!)

"Brayden said he didn't have any condoms," Seraphina says. "And *I* didn't have any—who brings condoms to a kid's caroling party? So then we heard his mom and little sister come home and we got dressed really quickly. His mom was super sorry about the mix-up and paid me for babysitting anyway. Brayden stood behind her and did this"—Seraphina holds a thumb-and-pinkie phone to her ear—"but he didn't call me the next day or the next. Finally I sent him an emoji of a penguin waving hello and he texts right back and says he has a girlfriend and can't be talking to me. Says 'I'm sorry if that wasn't made clear to you.' Those were his exact words. Like, you know, someone *else* should have made it clear to me. Like 'Oh, I thought the Department of Girlfriends had informed you.' When were they gonna inform me? When we were on the beanbag?"

Colette tries to steer the conversation back on track. "What about your parents? Have you told them you're pregnant?"

"Tell my parents?" Seraphina asks. "Tell my *parents*? Listen, I can only have thirty minutes of screen time a day. My mother has a boxed set of *Touched by an Angel*. I can never tell my parents. The only person who knows is Tia."

Colette is getting cold but she doesn't want to give the keys back to Seraphina or ask her to turn on the car. "Do you know what you're going to do?"

"I'm going to get an abortion," Seraphina says firmly. "That's why I need to get my license, so I can drive there. I can't take an Uber because my parents would see it on the credit card and none of my friends can drive me because they only just turned sixteen. I'm the only one old enough to get my license now."

How strange—the course of your whole life could hinge on your birth date, or a neighborhood association, or staying late at an office party.

"Seraphina, it isn't legal to get an abortion in Maryland without your parents' consent."

"It is in Connecticut," Seraphina says. "I googled it. I'm going to drive there and Tia's going to come with me. We're going next Wednesday when there's no school because of a professional day."

The madness of this plan fills the car like static suddenly, crackling and hissing. Colette pitches her voice low, in hopes of reaching Seraphina through it. "You can't do that, Seraphina. Even if you had a license, it's an extremely bad idea to drive yourself. Your reaction times could be very slow after the procedure, or you could even black out. They probably won't even let you leave if they know you're driving yourself."

"Tia's coming with me and we're going to say *she's* driving me."

"No." Colette sighs. She rubs her forehead, thinking. "No, you're not. Give me your phone and I'll put my number in it and we'll figure something out."

"Will you drive me to Connecticut?"

"No. But I'll find someone who can help you."

"Help me get an abortion?"

"Yes, if that's what you want." Colette has a friend who used to work at Planned Parenthood. She'll know where to refer Seraphina, and how to help her tell her parents.

"I want it."

"Okay," Colette says. "Give me your phone." She's never given her number to a test-taker before and supposes she might come to regret it, but what else can she do?

"Thank you," Seraphina says. She closes her eyes and whispers, "Thank you, thank you, thank you." She sounds like she's thanking the universe more than she's thanking Colette.

"You're welcome," says the universe in the form of Colette. (Because surely the universe arranged this particular road test.) "Okay, let's trade places and I'll drive you back to the office."

"Wait." Seraphina opens her eyes. "Did I pass or not?"

*℮⁀*

BACK AT THE DMV BUILDING, Colette parks the Forester and hands the keys to Seraphina. "Just tell your mom you didn't pass. Say you need to work on your left turns. Call me tonight."

"Okay," Seraphina says, reaching for the door handle.

"And don't drive anywhere. It's not safe." It occurs to Colette that Seraphina is probably more dangerous than Ted Bundy right now, at least as far as road tests go. Okay, so that's her new rule: no serial killers or insane teenagers, at least for the next few months. Vic and Gregg and Alejandro will have to take them.

They walk back into the building and Seraphina heads off to the waiting section. Colette goes into the driving examiner room where Alejandro and Vic are leaned back in their roller chairs, watching something on Vic's phone.

Colette looks at Alejandro. "We need to talk."

"About what?" Vic smiles like a velociraptor. "You pregnant or something?"

"It doesn't concern you, Vic." She keeps her eyes on Alejandro. "Are you free after work?"

He hesitates only a moment and then nods. "Sure. Let's go get a drink."

"Good." Colette feels the speed-bump jolt again as she passes from one part of her life to another. Bump up, bump down, a little shake, and the world changes. But it's no big deal, she tells herself. People do it all the time. She'll be a good mother. She just knows it.

# Damascus

MIA'S TEENAGE SON, GORDEY, CAME HOME FROM WORK LOOKING super baked and Mia thought to herself: He looks so happy! He loves his job! He's high on life!

And just like that, Mia turned into her mother.

BUT LET'S BACK UP A BIT. You have to understand that Gordey was the most exceptional of teenagers, not because of his intelligence or his looks—although he was very smart and Mia thought he was quite good-looking—but because of his kind and gentle nature. He was now seventeen and had almost literally never given Mia a moment's worry. How many people could describe their teenagers as *sweet*? He was the unicorn of teenagers, or perhaps a teenage unicorn: rare, magical, long faced but handsome, perhaps gifted with the ability to bless people with miracles.

SO WHAT HAPPENED: Mia was in the kitchen, opening her mail and feeding their elderly cocker spaniel, Warhol, when Gordey got home from his summer job at the supermarket.

Gordey poured himself a glass of milk and said, "This old lady came in and ordered *two* individual shrimps"—he worked in the butcher department and claimed that old ladies were the worst customers, always ordering itty-bitty cuts of meat—"and she says, 'One for me and one for my daughter.' When I told her that would be forty-two cents, she got this look like she was thinking next time she wouldn't include the daughter."

Mia gazed at Gordey, her handsome son with his sleepy smile and bright eyes and flushed face, and that's when she had that humiliating thought about Gordey being high on life.

*e⌁*

MIA'S OWN DRUG OF CHOICE in high school had been weed. She would come home late at night, more fragrant than a Christmas tree, glassy-eyed, loquacious, starving. Her mother would set aside her crocheting or her crossword puzzle and say, "Oh, hello, dear! Did you have a nice time with your friends?"

Mia's mother had a very round face, large hopeful eyes, and an eager smile. (She looked sort of like Frosty the Snowman wearing a curly black wig.) She was always up for baking, or quasi-baking, and she and Mia would make sugar cookie dough and eat it raw, or toast marshmallows under the broiler for s'mores.

Mia would tell her mother long rambling-but-intense stories. "So there was this girl there tonight with braces and nobody knew who she was or who invited her or why she wears braces if she's in high school but after Michelle left Scott got it on with her"—Mia had told her mother that *getting it on* meant kissing—"and, you know, I think that's completely bogus, and now I want to tell Michelle that her boyfriend has, like, a braces fetish but I know she'll have a cow."

"Oh, honey!" Mia's mother would say, her whole face quivering pinkly. "I'm so glad you tell me these things. I'm so happy we have this relationship!"

And Mia would say, "These are the best s'mores I've had in my whole entire life."

*e⌁*

IT WAS UNDERSTANDABLE that Mia's mother, who had worked the counter in a fabric store, wouldn't recognize a drug-addled teen, but Mia? Mia worked in the art world! She was the assistant director of a gallery in Georgetown and even though the gallery was genteel and somewhat staid, there were still drugs aplenty. Mia kept five pairs of sunglasses in her desk for artists who came to their shows with their pupils either pinned to nonexistence by heroin or dilated to the size of pennies by ketamine. Once Mia's sole chore for a four-hour opening was to hold back the hair of a celebrated sculptor as the sculptor vomited bath salts into the toilet. Mia was even mildly famous at her gallery for being the inventor of a walkie-talkie system (back in the nineties) that allowed the staff to stand discreetly in the corners of the showroom but still update each other on the movements of certain painters: "He has a drink in each hand . . . He's swaying back and forth . . . He just called Claudia Wolfe 'infantile' . . . He's trying to open a door in one of the paintings! He thinks it's the bathroom!"

And now here she was, thinking her own son was high on life! Mia groaned at the thought. But still—Gordey? That seemed impossible. When Gordey was a baby, Mia's mother had said earnestly, "I honestly believe that Gordon is the sweetest, easiest baby in the world. I know you're going to laugh at me, but I feel so sorry for all the other mothers who think *their* babies are the sweetest." And Mia *had* laughed at her, but privately she agreed. And Gordey had stayed sweet and easy through all the stages that followed.

Still, everyone tells you that love is blind. And Mia should have definitely considered that love is blind when she and her ex-husband were dating and she thought his habit of bantering with waitresses was a sign of how kind and caring he was. But no one tells you that parental love is also blind—at least no one told Mia. No one had even once suggested to Mia that she wasn't seeing the real Gordey. No one told her that when you looked at your child, love clouded your vision so much that you couldn't even picture them doing drugs—literally could not imagine it happening. Gordey smoking a joint? What would that even look like?

"Stop staring at me, Mom," Gordey said from the couch, where he sat scrolling through his phone. "It's freaking me out."

MIA KNEW HOW DRUG USE STARTED. It started for her when she got invited to a party. It was the kind of party that other kids went to every single weekend, but she only got invited this one time and she wanted to make sure she got invited again. So when someone passed a joint around this party and everyone looked at Mia expectantly, she took a hit, saw them still looking, and took another hit. (Mia really had been shit at resisting peer pressure in high school.) But over time, she began to think these other kids were onto something—being high made every cell in your body relax, made every social situation manageable. She became funny and extroverted, and suddenly she had tons of friends, tons of parties to go to.

She had begun to feel that stoned-Mia was the real Mia and sober-Mia was like someone with an unmedicated condition, an ulcer or a migraine. And nobody thought people with ulcers or migraines shouldn't be medicated. Everyone had the right to treat their afflictions! Soon Mia had to smoke in the morning before school and at lunch hour and during bathroom breaks in the afternoon (because the afternoons were just too fucking long without it) and after school and before dinner and after dinner and before bed, never mind the weekends where it was one long inhalation from Friday afternoon to Monday morning.

MIA CALLED HER EX-HUSBAND, Jack-Henry, hoping for understanding and reassurance, forgetting that these were not things he had ever provided and that this was one of the reasons they got divorced.

"Ah, Christ," Jack-Henry said when she told him. "I hope it's not weed."

Mia frowned. "I think weed might actually be one of the better possibilities."

"But weed just makes you want to lie around and do nothing," Jack-Henry said. "And Gordon already does plenty of that. He needs more ambition."

"Well, I—"

"Now the young people in my firm do coke when they need to stay up writing a brief," Jack-Henry said. "Coke, or else Ritalin."

"That's your advice?" Mia asked. "That he should switch to stimulants?"

"No, my actual advice is that Gordon should get out more. He spends too much time indoors," said Jack-Henry, who routinely worked ninety-hour workweeks and had once been diagnosed with a vitamin D deficiency from lack of sunlight.

"You could take him hiking this weekend," Mia said.

"Not with the Oberlin contracts exchange coming up, I can't," Jack-Henry said.

You can see from his attitude why Mia had divorced him. That, plus all the affairs he had.

ᘯ

ON TUESDAY, BOTH MIA and Gordey had the day off, so they drove over to Damascus to visit Mia's mother.

"She said she has a surprise for you," Mia told Gordey as they buckled their seat belts.

"It's probably an afghan," Gordey said. Mia's mother crocheted multiple afghan blankets for every friend and family member, and for many friends' friends and friends' family members. If afghans had been toilet paper in 2020, they'd all be millionaires.

"You never know," said Mia, who was one hundred percent sure it was an afghan.

"It's okay if it is," Gordey said. "I like afghans."

But when Mia's mother answered the door, her round face was flushed with the pleasure of a surprise greater than an afghan. She laid a finger to her lips and then stepped out into the hall and pulled the door shut behind her. "Hello, my darlings! Mia, you look so pretty and pulled together! And Gordon, you handsome devil!"

"Hi, Grandma," Gordey said. "Why are we out in the hall?"

"Benjamin's fallen asleep in my recliner," Mia's mother said. Benjamin was the retirement community's maintenance man, a blond, bearded guy in his thirties who'd once offered Mia a tab of Ecstasy. "He came over to set up the surprise and I made cocoa and we were having the nicest chat and then he fell asleep. It's an absolute shame how hard they work him here. But come in! I want to show you the surprise."

They followed Mia's mother back into the apartment and they all tiptoed past Benjamin, who looked like he'd been clubbed unconscious and thrown in Mia's mother's recliner. He smelled strongly of Budweiser. (Honestly, sometimes it was like the past crept right up behind Mia and cast a net over her, threatening to pull her back.)

Mia's mother threw open the door to the spare bedroom. "Ta-da!" she said in a loud whisper. "I bought you a PlayStation to use when you visit me!"

"For real?" Gordey looked dazed. "For me? Thanks, Grandma!"

He put his arms around Mia's mother's shoulders and she put her arms around his waist and they rocked back and forth a little bit. They had always been very intense huggers.

"Mom, wasn't that awfully expensive for something Gordey can only use once in a while?"

"Oh, Mia, you're such a worrier!" her mother said. "I split the cost with the Duckworths and the Morriseys, who have grandsons Gordon's age. It was hardly anything! Now, Gordon, will you teach me to play?"

"Sure," Gordey said. "What games do you have?"

"I have *Spider-Man 3* and Benjamin loaded it for me," Mia's mother said. "Maybe if your mother will put our lunch together, you and I can play a quick game. Everything's in the refrigerator, Mia."

Mia went into the kitchen, still worried about the expense. A third of a PlayStation wasn't "nothing." Mia paid her mother's rent and her mother had some savings but not a lot.

"What do I press to make him jump?" Mia's mother said from the other room and Gordey said something inaudible.

Mia opened the refrigerator and surveyed the contents: roast beef, focaccia bread, pasta salad, pita chips, a bowl of strawberries, and fresh cream for whipping. All of their favorites, and also not "nothing."

"I'm climbing a building!" her mother cried. "Look at me go!"

"You're doing really well," Gordey said.

Mia thought of how in high school she'd never questioned that they'd had money enough for Jordache jeans and movie tickets and spring-break trips with her friends. It wasn't until Mia became a parent that she ever stopped to consider the financial sacrifices her mother must have made to afford those things on a fabric-store salary and Mia's late father's pension. And now here her mother was, wanting to play *Spider-Man 3* with Gordey when Mia herself had never bothered to so much as pick up a controller.

Mia got the cutting board out but then she had to stop and brush a hand across her eyes.

In the recliner, Benjamin groaned and turned over.

MIA WOULD NEVER SEARCH Gordey's room, would never violate his privacy, so don't go thinking otherwise. She was merely tidying his room—putting away laundry and making his bed and vacuuming under the bed for dust bunnies. If you considered that sort of normal housekeeping "searching," then she'd been invading his privacy for the past seventeen years! Honestly, she wasn't looking for a bong or edibles or a baggie full of stems.

ℓ↝

(SHE DIDN'T FIND ANYTHING.)

ℓ↝

NO ONE KNEW THE DANGERS of drugs better than Mia, and she wasn't being melodramatic with the *dangers,* either, even if weed was legal now. She knew weed had made her do all sorts of things she wouldn't have done otherwise. Would Mia have ever, ever made out with Chance Dubose if he hadn't been her weed supplier? Would she have let Kirby Steele (who was kind of a loser) dry hump her under a pile of coats at a party if she hadn't been stoned? Would she have kissed that guy at the bowling alley who had such terrible teeth that it was like kissing George Washington while he was wearing his wooden dentures? Would she have scraped her mother's car on the edge of the garage while backing out and then painted over the scrapes with blue fingernail polish? Would she have bounced so many checks at Taco Bell buying late-night burritos that they blacklisted her? Would she have eaten Lisa Maupin's little sister's chocolate Easter bunny? Would she have gained fifteen pounds in a single semester? Would she have failed Music Appreciation? (Fucking *Music Appreciation?*) Would she have written a 1,000-word term paper on *A Tale of Two Cities* where 990 of those words were quotes from the book? Would she have made out with Chance Dubose again when he put his prices up? Would she have stolen five dollars from her mother's friend Mrs. Snell's embroidery bag? Would she have stolen ten dollars from the neighbors' garage-sale cashbox? Would she have stolen *fifty* dollars from Mr. Trice's desk drawer when she babysat little Trina Trice? Would she have fallen asleep while babysitting Trina and woken up to find the kitchen and Trina (who was thankfully still alive) strewn with flour? Would she have gotten fired from her job at City Dairy (before she even had a chance to steal from them) for spooning hot fudge into her mouth straight from the sauce warmer? Would she have blown off picking her own grandmother up from the airport? Would she have taken Coach Cowell up on his offer to teach her how to drive a stick shift in the back parking lot after school, when even the very freshest of freshman girls knew better? And when Coach Cowell unzipped his pants and reached for her hand, would she have stared straight ahead and let him guide her hand up and down, up and down, up and down? And when Coach Cowell put his hand on the back of her neck and pushed her head toward his lap, would she have only thought about how after this she could skip phys ed and get high whenever she wanted to, no note or anything?

ℯ↷

MIA WENT TO THE SUPERMARKET the next afternoon, ostensibly to buy supermarket things, but really to get a look at Gordey's coworkers.

Gordey was behind the butcher's counter, wearing a bandanna-patterned face mask and a white apron over jeans and a supermarket T-shirt. Next to him stood a young African American man with neat cornrows and sparkling eyes above a face mask that read: IT'S SUPPOSED TO COVER YOUR NOSE TOO. That must be Lazarus—Gordey talked about him sometimes.

Mia low-key waved at Gordey—a wave that said, Don't worry, I'll keep it professional and not embarrass you—and got in line at the butcher's counter behind an old lady.

The old lady said to Gordey, "Do you think you could cut a pork chop in fourths? And then cut one of the fourths in half?"

"You mean an eighth?" Gordey asked.

"Yes, an eighth of a pork chop," the old lady said serenely. "For my dinner tonight."

Lazarus and Gordey exchanged a look but they filled the old lady's order without comment. Then it was Mia's turn. "Hi, sweetie," she said to Gordey. She turned to Lazarus. "And you must be Lazarus."

"You Gordon's mother?" Lazarus eye-smiled at her. "Nice to meet you. What can we get for you?"

"I'd like five pounds of ground beef," Mia said in an effort to sound youthful. She'd planned on buying two small hanger steaks.

Obediently, Gordey opened the door at the back of the display case but Lazarus shook his head. "No, man. If it's you who's gonna be eating it, get the stuff from the fridge in back."

Gordey went off to the back room and Mia gazed at Lazarus, her eyelids flickering thoughtfully. If only Mia was in high school and still wearing frosted lip gloss! Then she could say, "Hey, Lazarus, you like to party?" (astonishing sentence) and Lazarus would say, "Duh, totally," and Mia would ask if he wanted to meet up near the bleachers.

Instead, she smiled weakly behind her mask and told Lazarus how much Gordey enjoyed working with him. She wondered what the fuck she and Gordey were going to do with five pounds of ground beef.

*e⌁*

AFTERWARD, SHE DROVE DOWN to the supermarket parking garage, looking for something, although she wasn't sure what—a group of seedy-looking smokers, a drug dealer checking his cell phone, a strung-out youth looking hopeful? But all she saw were a lot of parked cars and a beefy bearded man in a reflective vest pushing a broom. Could he be a dealer masquerading as a custodian? Mia drove up to get a better look at him and he banged on the side of her car with the broom handle.

"You just ran over a traffic cone, lady!" he shouted. "No Karens allowed!"

*e⌁*

MIA'S WEED USE ENDED when she got mono in the spring of her junior year of high school. She lay in bed for three weeks, her mother tiptoeing around heavily with the thermometer and cool washcloths and dishes of ice cream. Mia's head throbbed if she so much as moved her eyes, her throat was so sore she drooled on her pillow rather than swallow, and the lymph nodes in her neck swelled into such huge jowls that she looked like a 1980s version of Rembrandt. Smoking was not remotely feasible, nor was going out in search of something to smoke, so in addition to mono, Mia suffered all the symptoms of marijuana withdrawal: abdominal pain, tremors, insomnia, but mostly anger and irritability.

"Why do I have to have stupid mono? Mom, stop playing that dumb elevator music! Why are you always knitting? I don't want a new afghan! I don't want a milkshake! I want to die! Get out of here and leave me alone!"

"Poor Mia," her mother said affectionately. "Little grump."

When Mia finally recovered, she had a body that was twelve pounds thinner and a profound determination never to go through anything like that again. She didn't know which symptoms were caused by weed withdrawal and which by mono, so she gave up weed and she stopped sharing cups with people and figured that covered both bases.

She went back to school but she didn't go to parties. Her stoner friends called sometimes but she said she had to study. It was true. She had to. And she did.

GORDEY WORKED THE LATE SHIFT and Mia stayed up to wait for him, to assess his sobriety. But she fell asleep on the sofa and when she woke up, Gordey was covering her with an afghan. "Go back to sleep," he said softly.

THE NEXT DAY MIA'S MOTHER, who didn't know how to text, sent Mia a text at work: *heyyyyy, mia! hru? howz gordin? im keeblering with my bf jared ilusm lol mom.*

Mia stared at it, blinking rapidly as though a strong wind were blowing in her face. She called her mother. "Hi, Mom, it's me."

"Oooooh, hello!" Her mother sounded especially happy. "Did you get our letter?"

"I got your text, yes."

"She got it!" her mother said excitedly to someone.

"Mom, who's there?"

"An extremely nice young man named Jared I met in the jigsaw room," her mother said. "His grandmother lives over on the south wing and they've had a very small difference of opinion and he doesn't feel comfortable going back to her apartment right now, so I invited him to mine. We've had the loveliest time looking at my photo albums and then Jared offered to show me how to send you a letter on my phone."

"How old would you say Jared is, Mom?"

"He's a senior in high school," her mother said.

"What does he mean by 'keeblering'?"

"Jared told me it means baking cookies but we're actually making s'mores. Jared was feeling very peckish and you know how teenagers love to eat."

"What do his pupils look like?" Mia asked suddenly. "Does he smell sort of woodsy?"

"Now, I don't want to be rude, but I do have company," her mother said. "I'll send you another letter soon. Goodbye, my darling!"

The call ended but a moment later Mia's phone buzzed with another text from her mother's number: *o man packed dank bowl at my gmas houz and now im 2 shook 2 let her c me.*

*I believe this was meant for someone else,* Mia texted back coldly, assuming it's possible to text coldly. *Please stop using my mother's phone and leave her apartment. I am calling security right now.*

*K,* Jared texted back. *Sry.*
Then: *Killer smores.*

❧

GORDEY CAME HOME from work with the baked look again. Mia sighed and opened a bottle of wine.

❧

ON THURSDAY, GORDEY'S FRIEND Miguel came over. Gordey and Miguel had been friends ever since they had attended a bilingual preschool in Glover Park where everyone spoke exclusively English. Mia and Gordey lived in Bethesda now, and Miguel and his parents lived in Vienna, Virginia, so playdates or hangouts or whatever you were supposed to call them required pricey Uber rides and usually included a day or two of sleepover.

Mia never minded hosting. Miguel was a shy, dreamy boy, polite, slow moving, and even slower talking. But now Mia looked at him with new eyes. Was Miguel truly so dozy and good-natured or was he stoned? (Of course, if he was, that meant he'd been stoned since he was two years old, but still.)

She went into the kitchen. Gordey and Miguel were gathering water bottles and granola bars and potato chips to take up to Gordey's bedroom.

"How's it going, Miguel?" she asked.

Miguel looked startled—she didn't usually talk to him about much other than logistics and meal preferences. "Okay."

"Do you have a summer job?"

"Yeah."

"What is it?"

Miguel sent Gordey a look, seeking rescue. "Gas station."

"You work in a gas station?"

"Yeah."

"That sounds like a fascinating job," Mia said brightly. "Now, tell me, what do you like to do in your free time? Like, when your shift is over?"

"When my shift is over, I go home."

"Well, but—"

"The manager doesn't like us to hang around after our shifts."

"Oh? Why is that?"

"Because Duane used the radiator hose to write CAPITALISM KILLS on the sidewalk."

"Yes, but do you go directly home? Or do you and Duane go—"

"Duane got fired."

"Well, do you meet with other friends somewhere? Like somewhere outside? Maybe in a park? Maybe behind a building? Do they ever help you, um, relax or decompress? Do they ever give you—"

"Mom," Gordey interrupted. "You're being so weird."

"I'm not being weird, darling!" (Mia said this, although it sounded like Mia's mother was throwing her voice from her retirement community.) "I'm just interested in Miguel's life. I just want to get caught up on all his comings and goings."

Gordey rolled his eyes and grabbed Miguel's arm. They went upstairs to Gordey's room and Mia leaned her forehead against the refrigerator, her cheeks hot with shame.

SHE WAS IN BED LATER with Warhol and a huge glass of wine when Jack-Henry called her.

"Can I speak to Pablo Escobar's mother?" he asked in a deep, playful sort of voice.

Mia sighed. "I wish you wouldn't make jokes."

"Why? Has something happened to Gordon?"

"No, I just wish you wouldn't make jokes, period," Mia said.

"How *is* Gordon?"

"He's okay. Miguel is over and they're on the PlayStation."

"Gordon spends entirely too much time online. You don't know what sort of people he could be meeting," said Jack-Henry, who had a platinum membership on Tinder and had been on Match.com for so many years that Mia thought he could be considered one of the founders.

"Was there a reason you called?" Mia asked.

"Yes, I wondered if you could come over to the office tomorrow night and sign a transfer of interest for the Arizona property," Jack-Henry said.

Mia and Jack-Henry had been divorced for twelve years, but they still had a joint investment portfolio: stocks, bonds, properties, currencies, cash and cash equivalents, other . . . stuff. Sometimes Jack-Henry sold stuff and sometimes he bought stuff and Mia signed her name to all sorts of papers because Jack-Henry had been a terrible husband but he rocked it as a provider.

"I'm going to be at the gallery until at least nine," Mia told him. "We have a show."

"Come by the office afterward," Jack-Henry said. "You know how late I work."

Actually, Mia had no idea how late Jack-Henry worked. She knew how late he *said* he worked, but she had always assumed "staying late at the office" was code for "fucking the girl who makes the coffee here." (Jack-Henry had proven Mia's decoding skills to be extremely accurate in this area.)

"Okay," she said. "I'll see you tomorrow."

They hung up. Mia turned out the lights, put her arm around Warhol, and fell asleep, her head spinning slightly from the wine.

MIA WALKED OVER TO Jack-Henry's law practice at nine the next night, sending Gordey a quick text on the way: **Did Miguel get home okay?**

Gordey texted back, *I guess so*

Did you see him get in the Uber?

yeah

Did you check for the Uber sticker and match the license plate?

No we forgot

Mia sighed. She hoped Miguel had not gotten in some random car and been driven to an illegal work farm where he would labor out the rest of his days. *Please call Miguel to make sure he got home safely,* she texted. *I'll be a little late. Remember to take Warhol out before you go to bed.*

She paused in front of Jack-Henry's office building and slipped her phone into her bag. She pushed open the heavy glass doors, feeling very arty and bohemian in her short black skirt and leather blazer. She rode the brass-doored elevator up to the tenth floor where Jack-Henry was sitting in his enormous office behind his enormous desk.

Mia sat in the client chair next to Jack-Henry's desk and signed the papers. Jack-Henry had been drinking whiskey and Mia had been drinking wine and now they drank whiskey together. Mia looked out the office window at the city lights twinkling like a miniature Christmas village while Jack-Henry talked in an expansive voice about lifestyle funds and diversifying assets and his desire for them to buy an antiquarian bookshop in Cape Cod and a small fleet of snowplows. Mia yawned.

Jack-Henry said if she was that bored he'd show her something interesting. He pulled open the slide-out tray on his desk and said it was for cocaine. Mia said she thought those trays were actually just writing surfaces, and Jack-Henry said, "No, let me show you," and cut two lines of coke from a supply he apparently kept in a silver business-card holder. He snorted one of the lines through a rolled-up twenty and then held the twenty out to Mia and she said no thank you and he was like, come on, don't be so uptight, you've had a hard week, and so she took the twenty and snorted the other line because, really, she has always been shit at resisting peer pressure.

THE COKE MADE MIA'S HEART beat very fast. Jack-Henry took her hand and guided her to the leather sofa in the corner of his office and helped her sit down. First she felt hot, then she felt cold, then she had a profound idea that would revolutionize the way she did laundry.

"Give me a notebook," she said to Jack-Henry. "I need to write this down."

"Later," Jack-Henry said, sliding his hand up her skirt.

"I can take notes while you do that," said Mia, who now felt capable of anything, including multitasking.

So Jack-Henry gave her a legal pad and a fountain pen and put his hand under her skirt again and pulled off her underwear. Mia made a quick drawing of her laundry room with arrows showing the route dirty clothes would take on their way to sparkling clean in her new system. She sketched three laundry baskets and next to the third one, she wrote *VERY IMPORTANT! DON'T FORGET!* and circled it several times. (She would have no memory of the importance later.)

Then she put the legal pad aside, unzipped Jack-Henry's trousers, and they *got it on.*

THEY GOT IT ON like people of a certain age, of course, what with Jack-Henry's knee replacement and Mia's old shoulder injury and both of them wearing bifocals. But it was still good sex. Sex had always been their love language, or maybe just their language, since they continued having sex long after the love was gone. Maybe their bodies still loved each other? Maybe their bodies were separate entities from their minds? Maybe their bodies were like children, and Mia and Jack-Henry had brought their bodies together for a playdate? Maybe Mia's and Jack-Henry's brains were in some other room, drinking weak coffee and having passive-aggressive conversations about how many sight-words their bodies knew? This idea seemed very profound; Mia wished for the legal pad again.

There were bad parts, too, though, no getting around that. Like when Mia bent sexily over Jack-Henry's desk and he said, "Wait! Don't touch the Sanchez settlement!" And after they were done, when he patted her hip and said, "Thanks, honey," and she felt strongly that he had mistaken her for a paralegal wanting a promotion. And when Jack-Henry checked the stock market on his phone while Mia was still stepping back into her underpants. And when they walked over to an all-night convenience store and Mia bought every Twinkie they had (not because she was hungry but because their golden color seemed to her like sunshine) and Jack-Henry tried to flirt with the girl behind the counter. Mia could tell the girl felt very sorry for her, having a date who flirted right in front of her.

Mia wanted to explain to the girl that life was very complicated, that she and Jack-Henry shared a lot of things: an investment portfolio, and his pension, and a Bethesda Swim Club membership, and a love of cold spaghetti, and the memory of the time Mia had a nervous collapse in an overcrowded Ikea when she was six months pregnant and lay facedown on the floor in the Home Textiles department. And they shared a child. And enormous love for that child, even if Jack-Henry didn't always express that love the way Mia wanted him to. You didn't just walk away from that. (Also, no way was Mia giving up that swim club membership at this point.)

AFTERWARD, MIA AND JACK-HENRY stood on the sidewalk outside the convenience store and Mia looked at her phone for the first time in a long time and realized it was five in the morning. Gordey had sent her sixteen texts and there were four missed calls from him.

"Oh, my God!" Mia said.

"What?" Jack-Henry asked.

"Nothing," Mia said because once when Gordey was nine, Jack-Henry had forgotten to meet him at the bus stop and Gordey had stayed on the bus and wound up back at the bus depot in Silver Spring and had to be picked up there, bleating with fatigue and hunger, by Mia late that evening. It was the worst possible example of parenting and no way was Mia going to relinquish the Better Parent title at this late date. "I just should be getting home."

They shook hands like two executives who suddenly realized they'd forgotten to introduce themselves, and then Jack-Henry put Mia into an Uber. Right away Mia began worrying that the Uber driver thought she was a hooker.

"I'm a lawyer," she told him, trying to stuff Twinkies into her purse. "I'm just leaving a very intense legal deposition."

She wanted to keep talking. It seemed extremely important that the Uber driver understand that Mia was not the sort of person who did drugs and fucked lawyers and stayed out all night. She *did* that, yes, but she was not the *sort* of person who did it, or at least not the sort who did it regularly.

But then her brain reached some sort of railroad switch and began barreling down the track of wondering how to get back in the house without having Warhol bark and wake up Gordey. She checked her phone. The last text from Gordey—***Where are you?!!!***—was at two-sixteen. Surely he must have gone to sleep by now. Maybe if she unlocked the door quickly enough, she could throw Warhol a Twinkie and then tiptoe upstairs and put her bathrobe on and tell Gordey she'd gotten home at three, because coming home at three was just coming home *late,* it wasn't staying out all *night* and—

The Uber pulled up in front of Mia's house. Gordey was sitting on the front steps, his face pale and strained with worry. He jumped up as soon as she got out of the car and said, "Where have you been? You didn't even call!"

And so it was clear that Mia was still basically a teenager and Gordey was the one who'd turned into her mother.

℮

MIA WALKED ACROSS the lawn and sat down on the porch steps. Gordey sat next to her.

"Where have you been?" he asked again.

Mia felt strongly that the time for lying was past. She drew a deep breath and told him the truth. But she mumbled and paused and elided so much that what she basically said was "I did _____ and had _____ with _____ _____."

Gordey frowned thoughtfully. "You did fentanyl—"

"Not fentanyl. Cocaine." (A distinction good mothers made, evidently.)

"Okay, you did coke and had sex with the dog groomer?"

"You think I had sex with the dog groomer?"

"He left his card tucked in the door and you weren't here, so I thought—"

"Oh, God, Warhol's appointment!" Mia jumped to her feet. "I forgot the groomer was supposed to pick him up yesterday! Do you think we'll still have to pay for the appointment? What if he blacklists us?"

"Hey, Mom, relax," Gordey said.

The coke made Mia want to pursue the issue of Warhol's appointment for at least twenty more sentences, but she stopped and sat back down. "Sorry."

"Can we get back to what you actually did?"

"I did coke and had makeup sex with your father." (Her life was so full of astonishing sentences lately.)

"Oh," Gordey said. "What were you making up about?"

"Our whole marriage, basically."

"Is that something you do a lot, the coke?"

"No, I'd never done it before." She gazed at him, his dark eyes so like hers. Her sweet unicorn. "Is it something you do?"

"Coke?" Gordey looked genuinely horrified. "I've never even smoked pot! I don't even drink!"

"I just thought—"

"Legit the worst thing I've ever done is sometimes after work, Lazarus and I rope like ten carts together and ride them down the hill into the parking garage!"

"That's—" Mia stopped herself. She was about to say that sounded very dangerous, which it did, but it occurred to her that this might be the answer to the mystery of Gordey's bright eyes and flushed cheeks. Drugs could make you look that way but so could fun. She could imagine the thrill of it—the heavy carts clattering and picking up speed, the pillars of the parking garage flying past faster and faster, the sound of her own shouted glee. She laughed a little, just thinking about it.

"What are you laughing about?" Gordey asked.

"I'm just happy—" Mia said. She wanted to say "I'm just happy we have this relationship!" but she stopped herself.

The sun was rising. The sky was turning orange at the horizon and then shading upward to a creamy periwinkle and then darker cornflower blue and finally indigo with a few stars still visible. It looked as though God had made a chalk drawing and then smudged it with his thumb, thought Mia, who did not believe in God.

"Look!" she said to Gordey. "A shooting star! I've never seen a shooting star. Or maybe it's a satellite? Do satellites move differently from stars? We should look it up! We should find out! And—and— I really hope the coke wears off soon." She felt suddenly tired and leaned her head against Gordey's shoulder. Since when was Gordey tall enough for her to rest her head on his shoulder?

Gordey shook his head as though Mia was a hopeless case, beyond all understanding, and perhaps she was. But he put his arm around her.

Mia felt suddenly sure that she and her mother and Gordey were not replicas of one another, doomed to repeat the same mistakes. They were just rotating through the roles of parent and child, child and parent, taking turns at worrying and causing worry, at needing care and giving it. They would continue to do that for the rest of their lives, shining brighter and then dimmer. Yes, Mia thought (although maybe it was just the coke talking), she and Gordey and her mother were like lights on a satellite, flashing on and off by turns as it flew, tumbling, into the future.

# Twist and Shout

YOUR ELDERLY FATHER HAS MISTAKEN HIS FOUR-THOUSAND-DOLLAR hearing aid for a cashew and eaten it.

*e~*

THIS SIMPLE EVENT CONTAINS multitudes: sorrow and entitlement and love and annoyance. It also contains the *four separate appointments*—assessment, hearing test, fitting, programming—you made and took him to in order to get the hearing aid in the first place.

*e~*

HE'S NOT EVEN SUPPOSED TO be eating cashews! He has high blood pressure!

*e~*

YOU CALL HIM, dutiful daughter that you are, and say, Don't worry.
(Although, honestly, he doesn't seem all that worried.)
You say, I'll come take care of it.
What? your father says.
I'll come take care of it.
What? your father says.
I'LL COME TAKE CARE OF YOUR FUCKING MISTAKE.
He can't hear you anyway.

◦

YOU DRIVE THE SIX HOURS to your father's house. He still lives in the brick colonial house you grew up in, although now his bedroom is on the main floor because he can no longer climb the stairs. He's standing on the front porch when you drive up, leaning on his two canes. It's only been four months since you've seen him, but he's lost a lot of weight—his head looks like a downy skull, his arms and legs like pieces of kindling.

You feel a rush of tenderness. He's so frail, so fragile, so diminished—COVID has spared him, but for what?

You get out of the car and say, Hi, Dad.

What? he says. Also: You took forever to get here.

◦

LUCKILY, ARAMINTA IS THERE to smooth things over. Araminta is your father's housekeeper. She's in her sixties now but much the same as always: cheerful, freckled, short curly copper-colored hair (now threaded with white), muscles like tennis balls, her voice a baritone your father can actually hear.

She says, Edgar, you just hush.

She says, Erica, come give me a hug.

◦

YOUR FATHER FIRED ARAMINTA once for voting for Hillary.

And once for shopping at a food co-op.

Once for banking at a credit union.

Once for attending a Planned Parenthood march.

Once for using nontoxic oven cleaner.

Twice for buying organic milk.

Once for buying Ben & Jerry's ice cream.

Once (a separate incident) for buying Ben & Jerry's Cherry Garcia ice cream.

Once for making him watch a movie with Jane Fonda in it.

By now, Araminta knows to just go home when your father fires her and come back the next day. But your father won't go anywhere with her in her car (it's foreign made with a POLAR BEARS AGAINST TRUMP bumper sticker) and so she can't take him to the audiologist.

℮〜

WE HAVE AN APPOINTMENT with the audiologist tomorrow, you tell your father.

What?

WE HAVE AN APPOINTMENT WITH THE AUDIOLOGIST TOMORROW.

Okay. He shrugs as though this doesn't concern him. If you want.

℮〜

NIGHT FALLS. WELL, night falls in the sense that Araminta goes home for the day. As soon as she's gone, your father takes a package of cashews, a bottle of scotch, a family-sized bag of potato chips, and a sleeve of Oreos out of his big wooden poker box. Apparently Araminta has not thought to look for them there. It's clear that your father does this pretty much every night. It solves the mystery of why his low-sodium diet isn't working but creates a new one: Who buys this stuff for him?

Neighbor kid, your father says. Goes to McCormick's Party Store for me on weekends.

℮〜

YOU WORKED AT McCORMICK'S Party Store when you were a senior in high school and Mr. McCormick was forty but still sexy in a dissolute sort of way and sometimes you gave him a blow job in the back room. The older you get, the more shocking that seems. You let the owner of McCormick's Party Store come in your mouth and all you got out of it were stale pretzels! You didn't even get the coveted afternoon shift! Suppose one of your own daughters had done that. You might never recover.

And just imagine if your father knew. This news would probably kill him now in his weakened state.

e~

STILL, YOUR FATHER'S DEVIOUSNESS makes you feel better. There's still life in the old dog, at least where salty, artery-clogging snacks are concerned. You should take them all away and buy a relish tray, but instead you open the Oreo sleeve with a flourish.

Your father turns on Fox News, with the volume way up.

You pour yourself a scotch. A big one.

e~

BY THE TIME YOU GO to bed that night, you have acquired an unexpected companion: your teenage self. She has a tendency to show up around your father. She's the one who argues with him about immigration. She's the one who gets back out of bed to finish the Oreos. She's the one who says under her breath, I can't take so much fucking Fox News.

e~

IN THE AUDIOLOGIST'S waiting room the next morning, your father becomes suddenly—disconcertingly—interested in your life and starts asking questions. It's like he's (somewhat benignly) possessed and now you have to shout all your answers in front of the staff and other patients.

How's Jeremy?

Good.

What?

GOOD. BUSY.

Banking's such an interesting business.

Yes, it is.

How's work going for you? What's your title now?

Library—LIBRARY DIRECTOR.

Is that full-time?

YES, DAD. I'VE ALWAYS WORKED FULL-TIME.

How're the girls?

THEY'RE GOOD.

What's Jordan studying?

CRIMINAL JUSTICE.

Is that a real major?

OF COURSE IT'S A REAL MAJOR.

What's she going to do with it?

SHE WANTS TO GO TO LAW SCHOOL.

I guess she doesn't want to be an engineer.

NOT EVERYONE WANTS TO BE AN ENGINEER.

Not everyone is smart enough to be an engineer, I can tell you.

DAD—

Is Sydney still dyslexic?

YES. IF YOU HAVE DYSLEXIA, YOU ALWAYS HAVE IT.

I guess *she* won't be going to law school.

SYD CAN GO TO LAW SCHOOL IF SHE WANTS.

Don't you have to go to college for that?

SHE'S GOING TO GO TO COLLEGE!

Even with dyslexia?

PEOPLE WITH DYSLEXIA GO TO COLLEGE!

Regular college?

DAD! YES!

Well, good for her. Maybe she can be a nurse. I'm sure she can't be an engineer.

OH MY GOD! THAT'S SO SEXIST! SO PATRONIZING! GIRLS DON'T HAVE TO BE NURSES! NURSES DON'T HAVE TO BE

GIRLS! SYDNEY CAN BE ANYTHING! SHE'S PLENTY SMART ENOUGH TO BE AN ENGINEER! BEING AN ENGINEER WOULD PROBABLY BE TOO EASY FOR HER! THAT'S HOW SMART SHE IS!

Everyone is staring at you.

No need to shout, says your father.

᪥

THE AUDIOLOGIST SAYS the hearing aid was still under warranty. That's the good news. The bad news is that the replacement will require a further four visits. Time spins out in front of you endlessly.

᪥

YOU'RE WALKING BACK to the car when your father suddenly stops and says, They won't go.

What won't?

My legs. They just won't go another step. I need to sit down.

Dad, lean on me. Put your arm around my shoulder.

No, I really need to sit down.

You step close to him and put your arm around his waist—how insubstantial he is, how skinny! You try to take one of his canes away so that you can loop his arm around your shoulders.

What are you doing? Don't take my cane! I need to sit down.

DAD, THERE'S NOWHERE TO SIT. WE'RE IN THE MIDDLE OF THE PARKING LOT. THE CAR IS RIGHT OVER THERE.

What if he sits down? How will you ever get him up?

When you're with your father, it always seems like the world shrinks down to a tiny bubble and you and he are the only ones in it, but you're not. Two people appear next to you—a UPS guy and a woman wearing a white coat with DDS embroidered above the breast pocket. They must have seen you from the dental practice next to the audiologist's office.

Can I help you, sir? the dentist asks.

It's my legs, your father tells her. They've stopped working. I just don't understand it.

Happens to the best of us, fella, the UPS guy says. Give your walking sticks to this lady—she your daughter?—and we'll get you out of here in a flash.

Oddly, your father seems able to hear them. He hands his canes to you without complaint.

The dentist says, Now, sir, you just lean on us.

The dentist and the UPS guy bracket your father and haul him forward gently, like two movers shifting a fragile statue. His shoes barely brush along the asphalt. In moments, they've tucked him into the passenger seat of your minivan.

I just don't understand it, he says to them again. My legs stopped working. Why do you think that is?

I think you're just tired, sir, the dentist says.

Will they work again? your father asks her. Or is this it? Is this the end? Can you tell me?

His face is so pale, so bewildered—so lacking in dignity. You think that, really, telling him about Mr. McCormick might not be such a bad way for him to go.

❧

YOU HUG THE UPS GUY (who's kind of hot, your teenage self notices) and thank him profusely.

Girl, we gotta help each other, he says.

You hug the dentist, too, and ask her what to do. Should you take your father to the ER? To his regular doctor? He has high blood pressure and he eats Doritos. Could he be having a stroke? The dentist is at least ten years younger than you but your gaze clings to her hopefully.

He's probably just worn out, the dentist says. He looks exhausted.

If you have someone to help you at home, just get him to bed and let him sleep.

At home, Araminta comes out to the car to help unload your father, but his legs are working just fine. Well, sort of fine. Fine enough. Fine enough so you can try to forget what happened in the parking lot.

*e~*

IF THERE'S ANYTHING you hate more than gardening, it's gardening with your father. Rested from his nap, he sits in a deck chair and supervises while you labor in the heat with the pruning shears and a mustache of sweat.

Your father has a landscape service but he says they're lax. Cutting corners, is how he puts it.

Pruning's essential with heather plants, he says. You need to round and shape the plant.

I KNOW, you say.

Your shirt is stuck to your back. Your underpants feel like a piece of hot wet spinach wrapped around your hips.

You're making it lopsided, your father says.

The pruning shears are old, older than you, and very rusted. Probably too dull to kill him with.

HOW'S THIS?

Make it rounder.

Sweet baby Jesus.

What?

NOTHING.

I've always been partial to heathers, your father says. I named my daughter Erica, like the flower.

You sit back on your heels. Dad, I'm Erica.

What?

DAD, I'M ERICA. I AM YOUR DAUGHTER.

He squints at you. Yes, of course you are, he says. He shifts in his chair and leans his head back, eyes closed. Your mother wanted to name you Heather but I said no, let's go with Erica. More distinctive.

THE NEXT DAY, Mrs. Lightfoot, your father's friend for fifty years, stops over to see you. Mrs. Lightfoot is well over eighty but she walks without a cane and drives herself so when you open the door and see her standing on the porch, she seems to be bursting with youth and vitality.

This is how Mrs. Lightfoot talks: Hello, Erica, a little bird told me you were in town. I said to my husband, I hear Erica's in town. I said, you know she doesn't visit much, being so busy, but I sure would like to see her. My husband said, you should go see her then. So I thought, he's right, I should go see her. I got in my car and came on over to see you and on the way I passed Grant's bakery and I thought to myself, I ought to stop and buy a lemon-meringue pie. I said to myself, lemon-meringue pie is Edgar's absolute favorite and I ought to stop and buy one. I told myself, maybe Erica will like it too. I told the lady behind the counter, I said, I'm just on my way—oh, hello, Araminta! Where are you off to?

I got errands to run, Araminta says gruffly, pulling her purse strap higher on her shoulder. Araminta has disliked Mrs. Lightfoot ever since Mrs. Lightfoot offered to take her to a Color Me Beautiful session free of charge in 1997. She stomps off toward her car.

Come on in, you say to Mrs. Lightfoot, who is still on the porch, holding the cardboard pie box in front of her as though it contains a sacrificial lamb.

Mrs. Lightfoot walks through the house ahead of you, calling to your father. Yoo-hoo! Edgar! You won't believe what I brought you! It's a lemon-meringue pie from Grant's bakery. I was driving by on my way here and I thought to myself—

Is that a pie? your father asks.

—I'll just stop in all quick like and see if they have lemon-meringue because I know that's your favorite and I told the lady behind the counter—

Is it lemon-meringue?

It seems that Mrs. Lightfoot and your father are a perfect conversational match: he can't hear and she doesn't listen. You take the pie from Mrs. Lightfoot and carry it into the kitchen. You make coffee and cut pie wedges (taking as long as humanly possible to do so) and carry a tray into the family room where Mrs. Lightfoot and your father are sitting.

Now, there is one thing I promised myself I'd ask you, Mrs. Lightfoot is saying to your father. I said to myself, you must ask Edgar about his hearing aid. I told myself, don't forget to ask about his hearing aid because my husband is in the market for one. I said to my husband, I'll find out what Edgar uses. So I want to ask, what brand is your hearing aid? The very expensive one?

My what? your father asks.

YOUR HEARING AID, you say.

Well, funny you should ask about that—

I told my husband, we'll just find out what kind Edgar has and get the same one. I said to my husband, never mind the expense and don't worry about how it looks. I said, Edgar has one and it's hardly noticeable, looks just like a pencil eraser.

Actually, it looks just like a cashew, you say and hide your smile behind your coffee cup.

HONESTLY, HOW CAN ONE MAN in a ratty brown cardigan be so maddening? It's really sort of impressive.

You get home from the supermarket and find that Araminta has gone home. Your father has fired her yet again, this time for the double whammy of reading Michelle Obama's autobiography and carrying that autobiography in an NPR tote bag. You love

Araminta—you love Michelle Obama! you love NPR!—but you do wonder sometimes if she might be provoking him.

I was glad to see the last of her, your father says.

Dad, she's worked for you for almost forty years.

What?

SHE'S WONDERFUL.

She's an extreme liberal is what she is.

You sigh. It's four o'clock, the time Araminta reads the afternoon newspaper aloud to your father, whose eyes are apparently only sharp enough for tote bags and book titles. You were looking forward to having this hour to yourself. You could call your husband and daughters. Or you could practice some self-care: light an aromatherapy candle, drink mint tea, do some yoga, and maybe meditate. (It's also possible you might rest idly on your bed and stare at the ceiling.)

You sit down and open the paper. Your throat is beginning to feel like it's lined with a rough woolen sock.

Wildfires Rage out of Control, you read.

What?

WILDFIRES RAGE OUT OF CONTROL. FIRE OFFICIALS ARE ISSUING MANDATORY EVACUATIONS.

❧

FORTY MINUTES LATER, your throat-sock has holes worn in it. You refold the paper and set it aside.

That's odd, your father says. Not one single article about politics.

❧

THE NEXT MORNING, Araminta comes in as usual at nine o'clock while you and your father are finishing breakfast on the back deck.

Who are you? your father asks.

Don't you give me that, Edgar, Araminta says and bats him lightly on the arm. You know perfectly well who I am.

Who is that? your father asks you.

ARAMINTA. SHE'S HERE TO HELP.

Well, I hope she's better than the one who was here yesterday, your father says.

Araminta shakes her head, smiling, as though your father is joking. Look here, she says, setting a doughnut in a white waxed-paper bag in front of him. I got you a Bavarian cream long john from Dunkin' Donuts.

Your father beams at Araminta like a lighthouse.

You bought this for me? Is it Bavarian cream?

Yes, of course, Araminta says. And I got plain glazed for me and Miss Erica.

She sits at the wrought-iron table and hands you your doughnut.

I bought Dunkin' Donuts stock in 1979, your father says to her. Or was it Krispy Kreme?

Araminta puts her feet up on a spare chair and says, I get the lattes there, mostly.

Bought two thousand shares for three-oh-nine.

Pumpkin spice latte with whole milk, Araminta says. Getting so I can't start the day without it.

Sold it in 1989. Or maybe it was 1990. Price was then six-sixteen.

Girl knows me so well that I just walk in and she starts making it.

More than doubled my investment.

Me, I just like their coffee, Araminta says, and slaps at a mosquito on her neck.

Odd, how everyone can talk to your father but you.

FOX NEWS IS DRIVING you insane. You unplug the television just the tiniest bit, not enough to make the plug fall out of the outlet but enough to make the screen go dark.

TV's up and stopped working, your father tells you after his nap. I fell asleep in my recliner and now there's nothing.

Yes, I know, you say, I've already called the cable company. They say it should be back up on Friday.

What?

FRIDAY.

(Friday is the day you leave.)

SINCE HE CAN'T WATCH television, your father agrees (grudgingly) to go to the park with you. You and Araminta load him into the car, and you drive to the parking lot closest to the playground. You help your father stand up and walk slowly to a bench. (Your teenage self is quite excited about this bench. You and Tommy Hammond used to come here late at night. Tommy would drop his jeans and underpants to his ankles and sit on the bench, and you'd take off your tights and underpants and crouch on his lap. Your knees remember the feel of every slat.)

From here, you and your father can see the green grass of the park rolling away from you and, closer up, the playground full of children, shouting and laughing.

Your father inhales deeply. Beautiful afternoon, he says. Awfully hot even for August.

THANK YOU, GLOBAL WARMING!

(You don't really say that.)

Yes, it is beautiful, you say. YES, IT IS BEAUTIFUL.

Look, your father says, there's a princess right here at the park.

For a moment, you think he's straight-out hallucinating, but then he points with one of his canes: a little girl in a blue Cinderella costume (complete with elbow-length gloves and crooked tiara) is struggling to open the playground gate.

You and your father laugh together.

And yet, it's a little depressing.

This moment seems so sappy, like a moment from an overly sentimental movie or, even worse, a TV show. Like suddenly it will be over and one of you will turn off the TV and you and your father will go out for a beer and talk about how hackneyed the episode was. If only.

❧

YOU WON'T BELIEVE THIS, Araminta says when you get back home, but the TV wasn't plugged in all the way. It's working just fine now.

❧

CAFFEINE AND SUGAR, sugar and caffeine. It's all you ever seem to eat when you visit your father. Well, alcohol and salt, too. Perhaps if you ate more sensibly, you would not be so wildly irritable all the time.

Still, when Araminta offers to teach you how to make her extra-sweet brown-butter chocolate-chip cookies, you jump at the chance.

I love those cookies, you say. I always tell my husband they're the best cookies in the world—

You stop, realizing you have turned into Mrs. Lightfoot.

❧

WHEN YOUR FATHER told you a neighbor kid went to McCormick's Party Store for him, you figured he was talking about some stoned-looking guy in a hoodie. You're totally unprepared when the door-bell rings and a sweet-faced girl with short blond hair and the determined air of a mini-mogul is standing on the porch.

The girl is obviously surprised to see you, too. She says (very unconvincingly) that she's just there to see if your father has any books he needs returned to the library.

Don't give me that nonsense, you say.

You give the girl sixty dollars and tell her to get a bottle of whiskey, a six-pack of Guinness, two cans of ravioli, and a package of Chips Ahoy. (You are too tired to go out again.)

I can't buy alcohol, the girl says. If you want that, I have to get my cousin.

Then go get your cousin, you say. You peel off another twenty and hand it to her. But, remember, no more cashews.

Okay.

And stay away from Mr. McCormick.

Mr. McCormick died a long time ago, she says.

Of course he did. Time hasn't stopped. You're not really a teenager. Soon you'll be old.

❧

IT'S NOT EVEN EIGHT in the morning and you and your father are having a fight—not a debate or an argument or a heated discussion—but an actual *fight* about recycling. Because who in God's name is anti-recycling? Your father, that's who.

It just makes no sense, your father says.

WHAT ABOUT SAVING THE PLANET DOESN'T MAKE SENSE?

No economic sense.

OH MY GOD.

If recycling was a good idea, it'd be on the free market. It'd be like eggs.

EGGS?

Some company would make a killing. But you know why that doesn't happen?

SO YOU DON'T RECYCLE BECAUSE SOME CORPORATE OVERLORD HASN'T TOLD YOU TO?

BECAUSE IT DOESN'T MAKE ECONOMIC SENSE.

IT MAKES ENVIRONMENTAL SENSE! THINK ABOUT SOMEONE OTHER THAN YOURSELF FOR TWO SECONDS.

You're both shouting and not just because he can't hear.

❧

YOU GRAB YOUR CAR KEYS and storm out of the house, but once you get in your car, you're at a loss as to where to go. You're still wearing your pajamas so your options are pretty limited. In the end, you just sit steaming with anger in your car, the radio turned all the way up. This is exactly what you did after fighting with your father when you were in high school. Apparently you have not matured at all. But honestly, *recycling*?

Then, like a ray of liberal sunshine, Araminta's hatchback pulls up next to you, the polar bear on her bumper sticker gazing at you wisely.

She gets out of her car and comes around to the driver's side of yours. You turn off the radio and lower the window.

What are you doing out here in your pj's? Araminta asks.

You sigh and shake your head.

What was it? Araminta asks. Climate change?

No, recycling.

Anyway, she says, look here, I brought you a pumpkin spice latte.

Oh, Araminta, you are a good person, you say, and take the cup from her.

She pats your arm. She says, You just sit out here and listen to something soothing. You got any audiobooks? Relax and have your latte and come on in when you feel better. I'll give your dad his doughnut and get him started on animal rights. He's not too bad on that.

Araminta goes into the house and you turn the radio back up and sip your coffee.

You think of other times you sat in other cars, after teenage battles: missed curfews, torn jeans, the shameful D in algebra, the truly awful time you and Tommy Hammond rented a porn film and it got stuck in the VCR. But sitting out here was always voluntary, always your choice—you always knew you could go back inside. Your father was always there, waiting.

And then the front door bursts open and Araminta staggers out. She leans against the porch railing, panting. Her round face is pulled oblong by her open mouth, her eyes wide and frightened. Araminta was never meant to look like this. You can read her lips through the windshield: It's your father! Come quickly!

Adrenaline makes your body respond like an actual teenager's, faster than you've moved in years—in seconds you push open the car door, toss your coffee cup aside, and race up the driveway, your slippered feet driving you forward like a tiger's huge paws.

The teenage part of you still believes your father is immortal, but the adult part of you already knows the truth: the climate has truly changed. The atmosphere is heavier, the air is harsher, and you know why. Already you're struggling to breathe and it will only get worse. It will be so much harder to move through the world, now that you move through it alone.

# Turn Back, Turn Back

THIS IS HOW IT BEGAN. AT LEAST, THIS IS HOW IT BEGAN FOR LINDY. Like so many other nights, with Lindy getting home from the station as Rob was leaving for acting class. They kissed quickly and then Lindy began unbuttoning her coat while Rob zipped his up. A couple dressing and undressing in reverse.

"The girls are in bed—waiting for stories," Rob said, his sentences jerky as he wound a red scarf around his neck. "Maud skipped her nap—lunches are packed for tomorrow—chili for dinner."

Lindy wondered if the scarf was new. It looked expensive. Sometimes Rob went through little periods of buying himself luxuries—a cashmere scarf, a Muji turtleneck, a new watch strap—which they couldn't afford. But then it would be followed by a period of frugality, so maybe it worked out.

"Sorry I ran late," Lindy said. "This Sri Lanka story is a nightmare."

"No problem." Rob smiled. He was always happy and hyped-up when he went to class. "Fame can wait fifteen minutes. I'll be back late."

Then he was gone, the zipper on his leather jacket jingling, and Lindy shut the door quietly behind him.

❧

SHE WENT DOWN THE HALL to the girls' bedroom, dropping her coat over a chair on the way, and there they were, her daughters—snuggled in their twin beds, fresh from the bath and wearing matching pajama sets the color of honeydew melons. Georgia, eight, looked like a girl from a Hanna Andersson catalog: white-blond ringlets, pale blue eyes, nearly invisible eyebrows. Four-year-old Maud was pure Rob, with the same thick mahogany-brown hair, the same honey-colored skin and hazel eyes starred with dark lashes, the same perfectly symmetrical features that would someday make her as beautiful a girl as Rob was a handsome man.

Lindy never lost sight of what a privilege it was to read her daughters their bedtime story. Not even when she was so tired that she could only read Dr. Seuss and let the anapestic tetrameter carry her along. (And remember those dreadful Carl books, where parents were supposed to make up the words to go with the pictures? Parents who were often so exhausted that they didn't have two functioning brain cells to rub together?)

But Lindy knew no matter how weary she was from her job as a news producer, Rob was wearier. Or at least a different kind of weariness, the kind that comes from the sheer brute labor of caring for small children all day. And yet he always saved the bedtime story for Lindy, even when he was the one who'd struggled through dinner and bath and eardrops and toothbrushing and the endless delaying tactics.

The girls clamored excitedly when they saw her. "Mommy, I painted a turtle!" "Mommy, we drank out of the special glasses!" "I rode my bike—" "I rode my scooter—"

"Hello, dolls," Lindy said, laying a still-cool-from-outside hand on each of their faces and then kissing them in turn. "I've missed you today! But it's late, almost eight o'clock. Are you ready for a story? Which one would you like?"

"'The Robber Bridegroom,'" Maud said instantly.

Rob's mother had given the girls a copy of *The Brothers Grimm Fairy Tales* for Christmas last year and it contained a number of very disturbing stories that Lindy felt certain would lead to the girls having future abandonment issues. But Maud and Georgia loved the fairy tales. Especially Maud. Even at age four, Maud liked to live dangerously. Two weeks ago at the playground, she had begged an older girl to spin her on the tire swing, and when Maud got dizzy and vomited a steaming pile onto the bark chips beneath the swing, she was furious with the older girl. "I told you!" Maud had shouted. "Just to the edge! The edge!"

"Won't it scare you?" Lindy asked Maud.

"Yes," Maud answered immediately. "But in a good way."

"What about you, Georgia?"

"It doesn't scare me." Georgia sounded world-weary, or at least as world-weary as an eight-year-old can sound.

"Well, okay," Lindy said. She got the book from the bookshelf and sat in the rocking chair between the beds. She began to read. "'Once upon a time there was a miller who had a beautiful daughter . . .'"

She read aloud about the beautiful maiden's walk through the forest to her betrothed's house, of the bird who cried:

> Turn back, turn back, young maiden fair
> Linger not in this murderer's lair!

"She should listen to the bird," Georgia said. "It's told her twice already."

"Keep going, Mommy," Maud breathed.

So on Lindy read about the old woman who hid the beautiful maiden behind a large cauldron while the maiden's betrothed and a group of his friends murdered some other girl, and as they chopped up the girl's body, one of the girl's fingers fell off the table and rolled behind the cauldron and the beautiful maiden put it in her pocket and dear God, why *was* Lindy reading this to her daughters? But she was almost to the good part, where the beautiful maiden stands up at her wedding and describes the murder to the guests as a strange dream she had. The robber bridegroom gets more and more nervous, but every time he tries to interrupt, the beautiful maiden says, "It was only a dream, my love!"

"Only a dream, my love!" Maud whispered, pulling her covers up to her chin. This was her favorite part.

And then, finally, the beautiful maiden pulls the dead girl's finger out of her pocket and all the guests chase the robber bridegroom into the forest and kill him—no redemption arc for him.

"The end," Lindy said, closing the book.

"I don't get why she marries him," Georgia said. "She should have told everyone before the wedding."

"I agree," Lindy said. "Also she has a pocket in her wedding dress, which is very unusual." She thought of her own wedding. She and Rob in jeans and T-shirts at city hall. Rob had convinced her. "Let's just do it. Let's get married—let's *be* married—and have it be fun."

"I went to a forest today," Maud said.

"You did not," Georgia said immediately. "There aren't forests in New York City."

"Shut up! I did!"

Lindy touched Maud's arm. "Where did you go, Maud? To the playground?"

"No! It was an indoor forest!"

"Maud, just tell us softly," Lindy said. "An indoor forest? Like a play place?"

"No." Maud swiped at her nose with a chubby hand. "It was someone's house."

"Whose house?"

"I don't know," Maud said. "But it was huge."

"She means Ikea," Georgia said, shaking her head in disgust.

"Not Ikea!" The light of battle was back in Maud's eyes in an instant. "A house! And it didn't have cushions or rugs! And Daddy said I could pretend it was a forest and hide behind the trees."

"There were trees in the house?" Lindy asked gently.

"White trees! And Daddy said if I played quietly while he and the other man talked, I could have a chino."

Lindy knew what a chino was: a cappuccino minus the caffeine from Starbucks, called a babyccino.

Unfortunately, Georgia also knew. "You and Daddy went to Starbucks without me? Mommy, that's not fair!"

"Georgia, sweetie—"

"You were at *school*," Maud said with great satisfaction. "You were at school *learning* and so you couldn't come."

Lindy sighed. If the girls got emotionally revved up now, they'd never fall asleep. "It's time for lights-out."

"But Mom!"

"We'll talk about it in the morning, my loves. No more tonight." Lindy went to the doorway of the room and put her hand on the light switch. "Now go to sleep."

Georgia and Maud lay back down reluctantly. Maud's face was red and she was breathing heavily. Lindy turned out the light and said, "Don't say it, Maud."

"Don't say what?"

"Don't say 'It's too bad you couldn't come' or something like that."

"I wasn't gonna say that! I was gonna call her a loser!"

"Well, don't say that, either," Lindy said.

"I'd rather be a loser than a baby," Georgia said smugly, "who has to drink *baby*ccinos."

"I'm not a baby, loser!"

"Girls, please," Lindy said firmly. (It's what she always said. When the girls were younger and fought over control of the TV channels, Lindy had said "Girls, please" so often that Maud thought the word "girls" meant "TV remote.") "Both of you be quiet. Just go to sleep."

She closed the door almost all the way and waited there for over a minute. She heard some angry breathing and a couple of throat clearings, but neither girl spoke. Lindy stood on one foot and then the other, removing her shoes, and then she walked to the kitchen.

CHILI FOR DINNER, Rob had said, and the pot was on the stove, the glass lid foggy. On the counter, a plastic-wrapped plate held grated cheese and sliced avocado, a small pile of chopped cilantro. Dinner for one. Lindy turned the burner on under the chili and poured herself a glass of white wine.

She missed Rob on the nights he had acting class, but it was a pleasurable sort of missing, a soft miss, as they said in sales. She missed him, but she knew that he was working just as she had been working, that they were both working *toward* something—a happy future.

It had always been this way to some extent. They'd met in college—Rob majored in theater arts, Lindy in journalism—and they'd moved to New York shortly after graduation. They'd married two years later and lived in the smallest studio imaginable in the theater district—Lindy used to have to make a sort of three-point turn to exit the bathroom. Sometimes people saw the size of that apartment and said, "Wow, and you guys are still married!" in a wondering tone. But it was easier for Rob to audition (and sometimes perform! he was Sir Studley in *Once Upon a Mattress* and Trevor in *Thoroughly Modern Millie*) if they lived in the theater district, and it was a straight shot on the subway to Lindy's job as a glorified assistant at CBS. She had just become an assistant producer when they had Georgia. Lindy went back to work eight weeks later when her maternity leave ran out and Rob stayed home with Georgia. He still went to acting classes in the evenings. He and Lindy used to meet outside the Fiftieth Street subway station to hand over Georgia—Rob handsome in a sheepskin coat and watch cap, Georgia bundled to the point of immobility in a puffy pink snowsuit. The baby's cold cheeks were soft as water under Lindy's lips.

When Lindy was promoted to full producer, they had moved to Brooklyn, where miraculously—thank you, financial crisis!—they were able to snag this two-bedroom apartment in Prospect Park South. Georgia was such an easy, sweet baby that Rob could work again during the day, or at least look for work again, carting Georgia to open auditions and casting calls in her car seat. Once he even auditioned for a *Law & Order* episode with Georgia asleep on his chest in a Moby Wrap. He didn't get the *Law & Order* part but he landed a gig as a day player in a soap opera—he played a rich woman's chauffeur and they called him on set whenever the rich woman went to the bank or the hospital or her friend's house. And he did a lot of TV commercials: he was the husband doing the family laundry in a fabric softener commercial, and the jogger in a commercial for athletic shoes, and the train passenger in an ad for earbuds. He and Georgia even starred in a commercial for bath toys together, with Rob playing the handsome father bathing Georgia the beautiful baby—the *extremely* beautiful baby, Lindy had thought proudly—while the voice-over intoned: "Love prevents that sinking feeling."

But then Maud came along and it was harder for Rob to audition. Maud was a colicky baby and a difficult yet weirdly accomplished toddler—a master of the temper tantrum, an expert at the public meltdown, a virtuoso performer of howling outrage. It wasn't possible for Rob to take Maud to auditions the way he'd taken the pliant Georgia. His income from the soap opera and the commercials meant that they could—just barely—afford to live in Brooklyn on Lindy's salary as long as Rob stayed home with Maud.

Without auditions to go to, Rob grew moody and irritable. Lindy knew that Rob craved excitement and validation, and there was precious little of either when you spent your days caring for small children. Rob was locked into the routine of preschool drop-off and pickup, of making tiny bowls of alphabet pasta, of creating Play-Doh sculptures with a temperamental two-year-old sculptor who threw things when her statues turned out lopsided. Of course, that's parenting for you, and while it's immensely rewarding, no one has ever said parenting is fast-paced and exciting and spontaneous. But this was Rob. Rob, who drank pirate Everclear once in high school and woke up the next morning with no feeling in his fingertips. (The feeling came back later, fortunately.) Rob, who lost his virginity to a totally random woman who came to measure his parents' house for window treatments. Rob, who had kept an uncaged corn snake in his dorm room. Rob, who had once traded outfits with a man panhandling outside Key Food just for fun. Rob, who liked to skateboard on Fifth Avenue without a helmet. He was a good and attentive father but Lindy worried that it came at a high price.

He even grew bitter about acting, claiming that he had aged out of all the good roles, that he was not handsome enough to play a leading man but too handsome to be a character actor. Only his agent, Bennett, could pull Rob out of these funks. Bennett was a major agent and his continued belief in Rob's talent allowed Rob to believe, too.

Still, Lindy had begun to wonder if it would soon be Rob's turn to announce a job change on social media like so many of the other actors they knew:

*Becoming a yoga instructor is the most rewarding journey I could've ever hoped for personally and professionally . . .*

*I am truly happy to inform you all that I now have my residential painting license and I hope you will trust me with your renovation needs . . .*

*My most challenging role is now full-time landscaper . . . web designer . . . florist . . . auctioneer . . . clown . . .*

Clown was the most depressing job change, but they all struck fear in the actor heart. In other occupations, people could announce new career paths and have their friends congratulate them. But an actor giving up acting was always greeted with pity and scorn and a quick pulling away of friends. Failure might be catching; no one really knows.

But just when Lindy thought Rob might quit, he had thrown himself back into acting with new vigor. Georgia was now in second grade and Maud had started preschool in the afternoons. ("It's really called School for Babies," Georgia had told Maud and the resulting meltdown still haunted Lindy.)

Maud was not an early morning person, so most days, she slept in while Lindy took Georgia to school on her way to work. Rob got Maud up and dressed and fed and off to preschool (a challenge because Maud also wasn't a late morning person). Then Rob had the afternoon free to audition until he picked both girls up at four, by which time Maud was usually in a bad mood, not being an afternoon person, either. (Usually she had a brief cycle of sunniness after dinner.) And Rob was back taking evening classes at the Drama Spark Studio. At first it was just the On-Camera Technique class but then he added a Shakespeare class and one called Musical Theater Scene Study.

"Broadway beckons," he told Lindy with a laugh, and it was wonderful to hear him laugh, to feel his excitement again. Lindy had always loved how exciting Rob was.

Now, she stirred the chili and wondered idly where he'd gone this morning. Where was the "indoor forest"? She got out her phone and read back through their morning texts. Lindy had texted first, hoping to prevent Maud from having a wardrobe crisis—Maud refused to go to preschool unless wearing at least one article of purple clothing.

**Today 9:38 AM**

Forgot to tell you that M's purple tights and turtleneck are in the dryer.

**Today 10:12 AM**

Np.

Made do with purple hair ribbon.

**Today 10:39 AM**

Sorry. I was in the shower when you called.

**Today 10:54 AM**

I just wanted to say hi to M before she left for school.

She's not having a great morning but now she's watching Pete the Cat so let's not rock the boat.

Totally understand

**Today 11:25 AM**

Also can you pick up granola bars for G's lunches?

I'll run to the store later. Also, some of us are going out after class tonight.

Ok. See you later. Xxxx

So Rob and Maud were in the apartment today up until it was time to leave for preschool. No playdates or trips to the playground. But Lindy was puzzled. Maud was an imaginative child, but it was beyond the abilities of any four-year-old to fashion a story with so many details. Curious, she clicked on her banking app. She and Rob had individual accounts, but the joint account was the one they used most often. She scrolled through today's transactions and there was the Starbucks charge:

---

*DEBIT PURCHASE Mar 29#0456 -$9.09
At 10:49a TST* Starbucks Elmhurst NY

---

Elmhurst was in Queens—why was Rob in Queens? At 10:49 this morning? And—she scanned back through the texts—why was he *anywhere* when he was telling Lindy he was home, taking a shower, and watching *Pete the Cat* with Maud? Maybe it was a fraudulent charge on their debit card? But no, Maud had said they'd gone to Starbucks, and the debit card backed her up. Starbucks and the indoor forest.

Lindy studied the morning's text again and saw something she'd missed: **Made do with purple hair ribbon.** If Rob had "made do" with a purple hair ribbon, that meant he'd had Maud up and dressed for school before ten. Up and dressed and out the door to Queens, apparently.

But Queens meant taking the subway with Maud and that was something Rob and Lindy avoided. (Maud was hard to restrain and liked to lean out over the tracks to watch the train arrive, and once when Maud was two, she had placed her hand casually on the emergency brake handle and said "I pull?" and Rob and Lindy had been forced into the roles of hostage negotiators to talk her down. Even now, she would never sit in the seats but did stripper twirls around poles.)

Lindy frowned. Was it an audition that Rob didn't want to tell her about before he knew if he was going to be called back? But an audition in Queens? An audition he took Maud to? He's sworn he would never take Maud to another one after she had a spectacular diaper blowout at an audition two years ago—Rob not only failed to get the part but had to clean the theater floor afterward with spray disinfectant and paper towels. No, Rob wouldn't take Maud on a professional errand unless he had no other choice, and it seemed unlikely he'd take her on a personal one, either. Lindy could call Rob and ask him, of course, but he didn't answer his phone when he was in acting class. He said it was a new rule now—everyone had to toss their phones into a wicker basket on the front desk when they arrived. She could text him or call and leave a message, though, and that's what she should do. That would calm the faint panicked scrabbling sensation just below her rib cage.

Her phone rang and it was Drama Spark. Maybe Rob was calling to explain. "Hello?" Lindy said. "Rob?"

"Hello, this is Oona from Drama Spark Studio." Oona was the evening receptionist at Drama Spark and Lindy knew her well from Rob's early years at the studio when they'd all socialized constantly. Oona's words were normal enough, although spoken in a seductive but penetrating voice designed to be heard even in the last rows of a Broadway theater. Lindy had a theory that everyone in the acting world was always acting, especially out-of-work actors. No unemployed actors were receptionists or baristas—they were actors *playing* receptionists or baristas in an imaginary television series about a promising young actor who plays a receptionist or barista.

"Hi, Oona."

Oona Godfrey (real name Mary Fisher) had been the receptionist at Drama Spark sporadically for years. She was a tall, pretty girl with short dark hair, and sometimes she went off for a while to record an audiobook (Oona was very good at mimicking voices) or to shoot a pantyhose commercial (she had very long legs), but she always returned to Drama Spark. Oona was the most self-involved person Lindy knew.

"Oh, hi, Lindy!" Oona said in her regular voice (the one where she was just an actor playing a friend in a show about an actor playing a friend). "How are you? I haven't seen you in ages!"

"I'm good—"

"And how are the lovely young Miss Georgia and Miss Maud?"

(Oona had babysat Georgia for them once when Georgia was four months old, and Rob and Lindy had come home to find that Oona had taken the baby with her on a Tinder date *to a strange man's apartment* on the Upper East Side. "Don't you think that was a little dangerous?" Rob had asked. "Oh, no, I was very careful to mix my own drinks," Oona had answered.)

"They are very well, thank you," Lindy said, and then quickly, before Oona could start talking about something else, she added, "How can I help you, Oona?"

Oona's voice changed to slightly more professional tone, an actor playing a bookkeeper in a TV show about an actor playing a bookkeeper. "I was actually calling because Rob's card was declined for his March invoice and I wondered if I could put it on the card we have on file? I'm sure it's just a mix-up with expiration dates or maybe his card got hacked? My card has been hacked more times than I can count and it's almost always at the nail salon. It's like God doesn't approve of acrylic nails. Anyway, I left him a voicemail, but he hasn't gotten back to me."

"It's fine to use the card on file, Oona," Lindy said. The card on file was their joint card. Rob paid for acting classes from his personal account but maybe he was having trouble with his debit card. "But first ask him to try his card again when you see him."

"Well, the thing is, I won't see him until next week and once it's April, there'll be a late fee."

"But won't you see him tonight? Isn't he there right now?"

"Oh, no, Rob won't be back around until Monday."

"But he has class on Wednesdays and Thursdays, too."

"Rob only takes one class," Oona said. "On-Camera Technique with Winston on Monday nights."

An odd thing happened then—the kitchen went white for an instant. Lindy blinked and it was back to normal. She found her voice. "Are you sure? I know the other classes were add-ons, so maybe they're billed differently?"

"I'm looking at his account right now and he only takes the Monday class," Oona said. "And he's not here now."

"I'm sorry," Lindy said. "I—I guess I misunderstood."

"I'm sure that's it," Oona said cheerfully. "Everyone's lives are so busy! And sometimes he and Eliza use one of the spare studios to block her scenes, so maybe that's what you were thinking of."

"Eliza?"

"Oh, hey, Lindy, wait, my agent is calling me!" Oona said happily. "I'm up for a cat food commercial and I guess I got it!"

"Eliza?"

"Wish me luck, Lindy, and bring those beautiful babies around soon! Kisses! Goodbye!"

Lindy stared at her phone, the screen now blank. Eliza? *Eliza?*

LINDY POURED A SECOND glass of wine and paced up and down the kitchen, drinking. Her producer's mind was trying to sort out the facts. Never mind what she thought—what did she *know*?

She knew Rob wasn't at acting class tonight, even though he said he was.

She knew Rob had lied about his whereabouts this morning, his and Maud's.

And she knew Rob was spending time with someone named Eliza, was helping her block scenes.

She would wait until Rob came home. Hear his side of it. Sit and talk, really communicate—maybe they hadn't done enough of that lately. Rob could always reassure her, always soothe her fears—about money, about promotions, about Georgia and Maud—even if later Lindy spotted loopholes in his reasoning. He was an actor and he played the part of a caring, comforting coach very well. (He'd once had a nonspeaking role as a therapist in an episode of *Intervention*.) Surely, he would come home from class and say, "Oh, Lin, you worry too much, babe." He'd hold her hands with his warm ones.

"I'm taking the other classes at a different acting studio, that's why I wasn't at Drama Spark tonight. And I took Maud to Queens today looking for new rain boots, there's a discount shoe place there. I'm not helping Eliza block scenes—she's helping *me*. She's a fifty-year-old casting director." Lindy should just forget all this until she saw him. She should turn back before she found anything else.

Except—except Rob had told Lindy that all his classes were at Drama Spark. He even said he got a discount for taking three. And he wouldn't lie and say he was at home if he'd taken Maud shopping for rain boots. And he'd never mentioned any casting director helping him block scenes.

Lindy hurried into the bedroom and sat at the computer. This was their joint laptop, but Rob was the one who used it most. They had a joint email address too, but that was mainly for school and preschool correspondence, and Lindy didn't bother to check it. Instead she hit the mail icon and typed in Rob's personal email address, robert.brandenburg@gmail.com, and the password "Georgia&Maud."

Wrong password. Try again or click
Forgot password to reset it.

Lindy retyped the password and got the same message. Okay, he'd changed his password. But what about social media? Like most actors, Rob was active on Instagram, Twitter, Facebook, and SnapChat—you had to stay current, had to put yourself out there. Lindy had only a Facebook account, but she was "friends" with Rob on there, so she logged in now and went to his profile. There he was, staring at her soulfully from his profile picture, wearing a white T-shirt and the same leather jacket he'd left in tonight. His hazel eyes were solemn, his mouth unsmiling—he wanted serious roles. Lindy knew that Rob considered Facebook outdated and almost never posted anything—he just kept the account going. He had over four thousand friends, but when Lindy ran a quick search, she found only two Elizas and eight Elizabeths, and none of them had the kind of sharp professional headshot that signals a working actor. Still, Lindy took a closer look. One Eliza worked at "Happily Retired" and looked like Lindy's childhood piano teacher. One Elizabeth was the mother of nine-month-old twins. One was a Trump supporter (and surely Rob wouldn't stoop that low). And one was apparently not even a person, but a bichon frise, judging by her profile pic.

Lindy thumped the desktop in frustration. None of these were the right Eliza! She needed more information. She grabbed her phone and called Drama Spark again, but the line was busy—Oona had no doubt put the studio phone on hold while she hammered out the details of her cat food commercial. Lindy tried to remember what Rob had said about the on-camera class.

"It's one of Winston's classes," he had said that first night. Winston was a permanent fixture at Drama Spark, a distinguished-looking man with a headful of thick white hair and a lush beard. "Did you know Winston's hair went white in his twenties? He decided not to dye it and as a result, he's looked the same for, like, forty years." What else had Rob said? Lindy closed her eyes and concentrated. "Of course, Brad Barnacle is in it—he's been in every single class I've ever taken there. He says he's devoting all his weekends to vocal rest to preserve his voice for auditions."

Lindy opened her eyes. She knew Brad Barnacle, had sat by him at untold dinner parties, had shared cabs with him after late-night drinks with other actors, had attended the opening nights of Rob's performances with him. (That was life with an actor—you became part of their entourage.) Brad Barnacle was called that by everyone because of how stubbornly he clung to acting without any success at all. Brad had never acted in a film, television series, stage production, or commercial—he'd never even gotten a callback from an audition. His sole claim to fame was being the lead actor's dresser in a 2003 production of *Tartuffe* which closed after three performances due to the musicians' strike. Yet Brad Barnacle continued along, taking classes, going to open calls, updating his headshots—it was really very heartening in a disheartening sort of way.

Lindy didn't know Brad Barnacle's real name but that didn't matter because he was saved in her phone as BARNACLE, BRAD. She hit CALL and he answered right away. (Brad Barnacle always answered right away, Rob said, because you never know when Steven Spielberg might be trying to get in touch.)

"Hi, Brad. It's Lindy Kincaid."

"Oh, hi, Lindy," Brad said.

"I'm sorry to call you out of the blue like this," Lindy began, "but I'm planning a surprise party for Rob's birthday—"

"Put me down as a definite yes," said Brad, without knowing a single detail of the party's date, time, and location. But that was okay because Lindy didn't know any of those things either.

"I'm so glad we can count on you," Lindy said. "I wonder if I could ask you a couple of quick questions about the guest list?"

"Certainly," Brad said. "Are you inviting many industry people?"

"I was thinking—"

"Because if industry people will be there, I'd like to prepare some talking points."

"I thought I'd start with Rob's inner circle and go from there," Lindy said, and Brad Barnacle gave a little pleased-sounding grunt at the words "inner circle." "Of course I want to invite everyone from his class."

"I was very happy to see Rob back taking classes again," Brad said. "So many people in this business allow themselves to get discouraged if they don't make it overnight. Now back when—"

"I think I have everyone's names and emails from his current class," Lindy interrupted. "Everyone except Eliza."

"Rob would want Eliza there for sure," Brad said, and Lindy's heart lurched painfully. "But you know her name isn't really Eliza, right? We only call her that because she's trying to lose her British accent. Her real name is Alessandra Darling."

e⟋

LINDY WENT RIGHT BACK to Rob's Facebook friend list and there was Alessandra Darling, there she was. Lindy clicked on her profile. Alessandra's profile picture was a professional headshot. She looked to be in her midtwenties, maybe even younger, with wavy copper-colored hair and pale blue eyes under soft red-gold brows. She had a small, delicate face with small, delicate features, and the kind of very intense freckles that looked like she'd sneezed into a plate of crushed red pepper flakes and suffered the blowback. The kind of freckles that make you look twice: the first time thinking, *That girl would be so beautiful without all those freckles,* and the second time realizing she was so beautiful because of them.

Her bio contained a link to her showreel. Lindy clicked on it. The first clip was of Alessandra in a library, seated in front of a chessboard and wearing a strapless red ball gown that should have clashed with her hair (but didn't). "Hello, everyone," she said in a sweet, clear, and, yes, British voice. "In this video I'm going to teach you the basics of chess. We'll set up the chessboard, learn to move the pieces, explore the rules, and study the basic strategies."

The panicked scrabbling under Lindy's rib cage was sharp and powerful and all-consuming now—and yet she discovered she had room for one more emotion: scorn. Alessandra had put a *training video* in her showreel. No serious actor did, not unless they had no other clips at all. She clicked on the scrub bar and forwarded through the rest of the chess video and here was Alessandra again, in front of a bathroom mirror, wearing a loose white sweater and a hairband. "In this tutorial, I'm going to walk you through my morning skin care routine," she said. Lindy felt another surge of scorn. This wasn't even a training video—it was just a YouTube instructional.

She navigated back to Facebook and down to Alessandra's "About" info.

**Work**

**College**
Studied Channing School,
London, class of 2011

Lindy winced. Georgia was born in 2011. Alessandra was an eight-year-old? But no, that was just Lindy's overheated brain trying to process information. Alessandra must be twenty-five or twenty-six.

**Places lived**
Lambeth, England
New York, New York
Current city

**Family and relationships**
Giselle Darling
Sister

Just over a thousand friends. Under "Photos," more headshots but surprisingly few. Probably Alessandra, like Rob, was most active on Instagram and only kept a Facebook account in case some elderly casting director wanted to contact her. But Lindy didn't have an Instagram account, and her marriage was like a house being swallowed by a sinkhole—she didn't have time to set up a new account on an unfamiliar platform. She'd have to work with what was here. She scrolled back up to "Family and relationships" and clicked on Alessandra's sister's profile.

Giselle Darling—apparently Mr. and Mrs. Darling were into romantic names—looked like a bootleg version of her sister: wider face, thicker brows, larger freckles. Giselle lived here in New York, too, Lindy discovered. She worked as a realtor at Brightline Partners, and her Facebook feed was full of apartment photos and exclamation points: Now leasing! 2BR in Bedford-Stuyvesant! Complete renovation in Bushwick! Sun-drenched LR! Ultramodern kitchen! Diamond in the rough in Greenpoint! Huge open plan in Elmhurst! Sought-after neighborhood in Dumbo! Breathtaking views! Charming studio in Clinton Hill! Leafy garden space! State-of-the-art appliances! Perfect for the aspiring chef!

The truth slid into Lindy's mind, whole and incontrovertible, like a completed test sheet sliding under the door, like an answer whispered in her ear by an unseen person. Now she understood. Now she—

Just then the lid on the pot of burning, boiling chili in the kitchen flew upward with a hollow bonging sound, followed immediately by the shriek of the smoke detectors. Lindy screamed.

℮∽

LINDY LAY IN BED under the covers but she could not get warm. It seemed possible she would never be warm again.

She had run to the kitchen when the smoke detector went off, hardly seeing the chili sprayed everywhere, and turned off the burner. She heaved open the heavy kitchen window and flapped a dishtowel frantically under the smoke detector until it shut off in the accusing way of smoke detectors everywhere: *You want to burn up? Fine with me. I'll just stop saving your life.*

Then she raced to the girls' room. Georgia was shouting, "Mommy! Daddy! Come here!" Maud just screeched endlessly with a strange, throbbing beat, almost like the sound of the smoke detector itself.

"Shhh, it's okay," Lindy said to them, "everything's fine. I'm here. It was just the smoke alarm." Georgia had quieted quickly, but Maud would not stop screaming until Lindy lay down next to her and held her. That was when Lindy began to know how cold she was. She held Maud and tried her best to soothe her, but it felt as though her arms were too chilled to offer solace, as though her lips were too numb to speak.

When Maud fell back to sleep, Lindy returned to the kitchen. She filled a plastic bowl with warm soapy water and another with clear water and cleaned chili off the stove and wall and countertops. Soaping, wiping, rinsing—the timeless rhythm of cleaning had soothed her. Still, she had barely felt the heat of the water on her bare hands when she squeezed out the sponge.

Then she had gone back to the computer and her phone. When she grew too cold to sit anymore, she had crawled into bed and waited for Rob to come home.

And now here he was. Here he was. She heard him ease the apartment door open and shut it just as quietly—little girls were sleeping, remember—and then she heard the muted jingle of his keys as he hung them on the hook and his light footsteps as he walked up the hall.

Lindy rose to meet him. She had changed into yoga pants and a turtleneck topped by a sweatshirt. She was not dressed for sleeping because she knew that sleep would not come.

Rob was in the kitchen, just turning the burner on under the teakettle. The sight of him was achingly familiar to her: the short tousled brown hair, the sharp cheekbones, the slightly rounded nose that he claimed held him back from stardom, the five o'clock shadow that only made him more handsome.

"Hey," he said softly when he saw her. "Did I wake you?"

She shook her head.

Rob smiled. "Want some tea as long as you're up?"

She nodded.

He got two mugs out of the cupboard and two tea bags, then caught the kettle just before it whistled. Lindy sat at the kitchen table, and after a minute, he brought both mugs over and sat opposite her. The tea was peppermint; hot, fragrant. Lindy wrapped her cold fingers around the mug.

"You won't believe this," Rob said, his voice soft but vibrant. "The teacher's assigned us reverse-gender scenes to block and mine is 'She Used to Be Mine' from *Waitress*. Remember when we saw that? And Brad Barnacle wants us to do a sort of secret-Santa thing where we all write down our, quote, most treasured industry contact, unquote, and exchange them."

Rob was Fleshing Out His Character, Lindy realized. He was Building the Backstory. Creating an Identity. How many times had she helped him do this for roles—creating playlists and taking Myers-Briggs tests and choosing favorite foods for someone imaginary? Now Rob was fleshing out the character of Lindy's Husband, the one who went to acting class and lived in Prospect Park and made chili from scratch.

She realized he was waiting for her to reply. He was Reading the Audience. Waiting for Feedback.

"What's wrong, Lin?" Rob asked. "You look so pale."

Lindy had no idea of what she would say until she said it. "I had a bad dream."

"What was it?" Rob had been interested in people's dreams ever since auditioning for a part on *Falling Water*.

Lindy took a sip of tea. It burned her tongue. "I dreamt you were having an affair."

A tiny frown appeared between Rob's eyebrows. "That would be a bad dream, definitely."

"You know, I've always worried about you falling for another actor, a little bit," Lindy said, surprised at how calm she sounded. "I'm sure everyone who's married to an actor worries about that, given all the beautiful people in the business."

"Oh, Lin, you worry too much, babe," Rob said. "I know I've been out a lot with all these evening classes, but—"

"It was such a strange dream." Lindy blew on her tea. "It felt so real. So many people were in it. Even Bennett, although I only spoke to him on the phone."

"You called *Bennett*? Bennett my agent?"

"It was only a dream." My love. "I dreamed I called him at home. I said that I was sorry to bother him so late but we were just so excited. And he said he'd been happy to give us a glowing recommendation."

"Lin, please stop talking like this!" Rob's face was pale, anxious. "Please listen to me."

Lindy didn't stop, didn't listen. "Your debit card doesn't work because you went over the limit—I guess that's why you had to use our joint card at Starbucks this morning. After you and Maud looked at the apartment, I mean. The apartment with no furniture and white pillars where you told Maud to pretend it was a forest. The apartment where you and Alessandra are going to live."

"I didn't go looking for this—you have to understand that." Rob's voice was urgent. He leaned forward, as though sending his words toward her. This was Meisner Acting Technique, relying on your partner's reaction to strengthen your performance. "I really, seriously didn't go looking for it. I just wanted to take a class. But Winston kept assigning Alessandra as my acting partner and we began hanging out after class and—and we got to be friends. I've always had female friends, Lindy, you know that. It started off so innocently and then, the other part, it just sort of happened. We tried to fight it, but we fell in love, really in love. But I never meant for that to happen. I never meant for it to go this far."

Lindy said nothing. She turned Rob's sentences over in her mind, examining them one by one for truthfulness like a woman picking up grapefruit at the supermarket and checking each one for signs of softness and rot. She rejected all of them but the last. She guessed that was true. Rob probably *hadn't* actually meant to go so far.

"Lindy, babe—" Rob started again, but she wasn't listening. Her mind had turned from him toward the future.

She knew why she was so cold. It was because, finally, she stood where Rob liked to live, on the edge. Together they stood on the brink of the chill dark void of finances and custody and child support and living arrangements and stepmothers—everything that they would have to figure out now just because Rob had wanted to see what would happen. It was why Lindy had never wanted to live on the edge. She knew that if you weren't careful, you sailed right off.

# Games and Rituals

*The Relationship Game*

I play this with Harriet, my best friend in New York. Actually, she's the one who taught it to me. Right now we are on our way home from work. I'm exhausted, slumped in the hard orange subway seat, but Harriet looks perky and well rested, her ruby lipstick flawless, her pale blond hair sticking straight up in tufts that look sharp enough to draw blood.

She nudges me with her elbow and nods slightly at a couple sitting across from us on the subway.

"First date," she whispers right next to my ear, so close that I can feel her eyelashes when she blinks. "She ran out and bought those shorts today, and even though it's really not warm enough to be wearing them, she feels obligated because they're new."

Harriet pulls away from me and sits looking straight ahead. Then she swivels her head back and whispers, "Freshmen. Look at the big old high school ring on his finger. Who likes who better?"

I study the boy and girl. He seems very attentive, watching her face as she talks, but then she laughs and pats his knee.

"Aha!" Harriet is practically panting into my ear now. "*She* likes *him*. Oh, wow, they're getting off at my stop."

She stands up as the subway stops and the doors open. "I give them a month."

"Why a month?" I say. The couple is already off the train.

"Because," Harriet says impatiently, "she'll sleep with him and he won't respect her."

She's halfway out the doors, one foot in the train, one on the platform. The doors slam shut against her shoulders, jarring her words. Still she stands there a second longer.

"Men are pigs," she says.

## The Toothbrushing Ritual

Conrad, my boyfriend and reason for coming to New York, brushes his teeth with me last thing before he leaves to go home to his own apartment. This way it seems more like he's spending the night, which he doesn't do because he says he doesn't sleep well unless he's alone.

This ritual had considerably more charm last year in Kansas when he lived in the apartment above me and I knew that we were truly brushing our teeth together as the very last thing either of us did before we went to bed, that he would be in his bed just thirty seconds after I was in mine. These days, of course, he has to take a half-hour subway ride down to his apartment near NYU, where he's a graduate student in the International Affairs program. I didn't get into any New York City law schools, so I'm working as an office temp until I can reapply. Conrad has student housing but the only apartment I can afford is a studio on 130th Street.

Conrad puts his toothbrush in a Ziploc bag and slips the bag into his pocket. This bothers me. Surely he's not so broke that he can't afford to buy two toothbrushes and leave one at my apartment. Is my medicine cabinet that dirty? Does he think I will lend it out?

## The Memory Game

Zina, my best friend from Kansas, comes to visit. She's flying from Chicago, where she lives now, to New York, five times in the next two weeks so that she and her fiancé can get free round-trip tickets to Europe on some special frequent-flier deal.

Zina has permed her hair. It stands out from her head in thick coils, like a bunch of black Slinkys. It seems like too much hair for such a small person, but she's still the prettiest girl I know.

She's easy to entertain because she's content to lie on the extra mattress on the floor with a big bowl of popcorn and play the Memory Game.

"Remember when the gynecologist asked you if you were a virgin and you said no and he said, 'Are you sure'?" Zina asks, eating a fistful of popcorn.

"What a horrible thing to remind me of," I say, poking her with my foot.

"Well, remember when that one doctor had me put my feet on his shoulders during the exam because he said the stirrups weren't working?" Zina says. "*That* was horrible."

She has just violated a rule of the Memory Game, which is that we're supposed to take turns bringing up memories, but she's much better at this than I am.


## The Thursday Night Ritual

Because Conrad doesn't have classes on Fridays, I'm allowed to sleep over at his apartment on Thursday nights.

This Thursday, I get off the subway near his apartment and start walking. Conrad will be making dinner, wearing his moose slippers, his blond hair falling across his forehead, shuffling and singing. His roommate, who we nicknamed the Bird (he makes a clucking sound when he concentrates), won't be there.

I hurry through Conrad's neighborhood. Once a man cornered me down here and ran his hands through my hair before I could get away from him. Conrad was horrified when he heard the story and kept asking me if I wanted to take a shower.

Since then, I imagine myself hurtling through danger-filled streets toward Conrad on Thursday nights, as though I should always arrive with my color high and my blood jumping.

### The Scary New York Game

I play this with Jory, my downstairs neighbor. He had me over for dinner the first day I moved in and told me that the man who lives directly above me was stabbed on the street just outside our building.

"Not ten feet from the entrance," Jory said, licking his finger and pressing it against crumbs on the tablecloth.

I blanched.

"But he's fine," Jory added quickly. "Totally fine. He completely recovered."

And now whenever Jory and I see each other, we compare grisly stories.

### The Mating Ritual

"So," says Conrad, "do you still want to?"

This is typical. Here I am innocently cleaning out my refrigerator, trying to remember how long past the due date it's truly safe to drink milk, and Conrad's asking me if I still want to. What he means is, do I still want to have sex with him. Of course, there's no "still" since I wasn't even thinking about it to begin with, but Conrad likes to initiate this sort of thing indirectly. The first time he said he loved me we were having an argument about whether or not wine bottles were truly recyclable and suddenly he said, "Do you still love me?" I blinked and said yes and he said, "Me, too."

I'm wearing yellow rubber gloves and I have to brush my hair out of my face with my upper arm. I try to decide why I'm suddenly appealing to Conrad. I'm wearing my rain boots in case I spill anything. I probably look like I've just finished shoeing a horse.

"Sure," I say to Conrad.

## The Inquisition Game

Whenever I fly home to Ohio for the weekend, my mother spends the whole visit trying to get me alone so that she can ask me personal questions. She does the same thing to my brother Boyd. Once she cornered him in the attic and he had no choice but to talk to her or step backward and crash through the insulation into the living room.

Today, she gets Boyd and me together while we're cleaning out the pantry for her. When she appears in the doorway, looking too casual, Boyd yells, "We have the right to remain silent!" We have worked this into a routine by now.

"Oh, you children," my mother says. "What's so terrible? All I want to know is: Are you eating well, are you in love, are you happy?" My mother says "in love" because that way she can pretend that at least we only sleep with people we're in love with.

"Yes, yes, yes," I say.

"Yes, no, yes," says Boyd.

My mother shakes her head sadly. "It's just not the same," she says.

## The Telephone Ritual

I call Conrad that night at ten, eleven, and twelve. He doesn't pick up. At one, he sends a single text: *Study group running late.* I reply immediately: *Call me when you get home so we can say good night.*

I stay up late, watching Netflix with Boyd and drinking root-beer floats, until even Boyd is tired of me checking my phone constantly and goes to bed.

I'm legitimately worried, or at least I could be. Has someone broken in and killed Conrad? What if he tripped on his moose slippers and is lying dead at the bottom of his stairwell?

## My Own Inquisition Game

Conrad, as it turns out, is alive and well and lives to play this game.

"I hate this," he says.

"What?" I ask. I'm lying on my childhood bed with its prim white canopy.

"This where-have-you-been, what-are-you-doing routine," Conrad says.

"Well, where *have* you been?" I ask.

"Out," he says. "I'm allowed to have friends, right? We stayed out late. I didn't want to call and wake you."

"What friends?" I ask before I think. "Do I know them?"

Conrad sighs. "Look," he says. "This has got to stop."

He doesn't say, "You have to stop this," which is of course what he means.

## The Memory Game

"Remember the first time Conrad slept at your house and he turned out to be allergic to your sheets?" Zina says.

I'm beginning to seriously dislike this game.

"Remember when you climbed on that guy's lap in a bar and said, 'Santa, can I have *you* for Christmas?'" I say crossly.

Zina laughs, her new curls bouncing. "What about the time I dropped my blow-dryer in the toilet and called the fire department because I thought I'd get electrocuted if I touched it?"

I laugh too. After next week Zina will have her free tickets. I miss her already.

### The Adoption Game

"There's our son," Conrad says, pointing to his building's super-intendent.

This is a really idiotic game Conrad invented when he first fell in love with me. He picks out people he thinks are appealing in some way and pretends we're going to get married and adopt them. He likes his building's super because he's shy and sort of roly-poly and sometimes he invites Conrad down to his apartment to play check-ers and drink hot cocoa.

I nod. I like this game in spite of myself. I would like any game where Conrad at least pretends he's never going to leave me.

### The Lullaby Ritual

Last year when I couldn't sleep, sometimes Conrad would come out and sit on his balcony, which was right above my bedroom window. I would hear the scratch and creak of his lawn chair and call his name. We could talk this way, me in bed, Conrad outside.

The night was so still and thick in Kansas.

Here I sleep with my window open, but all I hear are car alarms and sirens. Sometimes I think that I should teach Jory to play this game but then I realize that I would never be able to hear anything he said.

### The Scary New York Game

At first I think it's some weird new twist to the game—that now Jory is acting like an intruder, not just talking about it—when I see his legs come in through the window off my fire escape. I know they are his legs by how hairy they are even before the rest of him follows. He's wearing boxer shorts and his dark hair is combed back off his forehead. It looks like he just got out of the shower, but it's sort of hard to tell since his hair is always combed back.

"Hello, Jory," I say, standing by the refrigerator.

He shouts with surprise and looks ready to climb back out the window.

"I didn't think you were home," he says.

"Then why were you climbing into my apartment?" I have a brief vision of Jory climbing in here every day when I'm at work, rooting through my medicine cabinet, smelling my nightgowns.

"I was shaking out my rug on the roof and the door swung shut and locked," Jory explains. He reaches back out through the window and hauls his rug in.

He sits at my table and I give him a glass of orange juice. He wraps the rug around his chest like a towel. "You should keep that window locked," he tells me. "A girl on Sixtieth Street was abducted out her window and kept as this man's slave in his basement for two years."

## The Snooping Game

Conrad keeps his phone in his pocket most of the time so I can only play this game when he's in the shower. I made the rules and I abide by them: I can only look at current emails and texts, no searching through the sent folder or call history. I am not totally without ethics.

I check his texts quickly; there is never anything new. Conrad doesn't like to text.

The emails in his inbox are a wearying jumble of class assignments and project reminders, the senders are nearly unbroken strings of repeating *sps.grad@nyu.edu*. It's easy to spot the one standout: an email from the University of Virginia. *We are delighted to tell you*—is all I can read before I hear Conrad turn the shower off.

## The Relationship Game

Harriet and I go see the Statue of Liberty because neither of us has ever been. I want to climb up to the crown, but she forces me to go to the top of the pedestal with her just so we can keep eavesdropping on the couple in front of us, or, more accurately, half of the couple in front of us, because the man is doing all the talking.

The man is about twenty, the woman over forty. Harriet thinks she's his boss, I think she's his teacher—but so far she hasn't been able to get a word in, so it's kind of hard to tell.

"This could go on for years," Harriet whispers, standing behind me in the elevator. People probably think she's a stranger making a pass at me. "He talks so much that she'll never get the chance to tell him it's over."

"Do you think she's married?" I whisper back. Harriet beams. She loves it when I participate in this game.

The elevator opens and we scatter out onto the pedestal. I lean against the wall and look out at the city. Harriet leans against the wall and looks the other way, toward the couple.

"No," she says finally, "I don't think she's married because I just can't imagine a husband who's more boring than this guy, although he must be terribly handy, working right in her office or whatever."

Harriet turns and rests her elbows on top of the wall. The wind whips her hair around, but since her hair always sticks straight up, she doesn't look any different, just sort of like she's in motion.

"In six months, he'll be gone," she tells me. "It'll break her heart. Let's wait here so I can drop my gum on his head when they come out below us."

## The Mating Ritual

I say, "Do you still want to?" to Conrad, only I don't time it very well and we happen to be moving the furniture around his apartment. "Definitely," he says. "That chair is just a waste of space."

## The Scary New York Game

I see Jory in my apartment lobby one day when Conrad is with me.

"Don't go to cash machines at night," he says, his gaze traveling between Conrad and me. "This guy I know was hit over the head with a lead pipe and had to have a contact lens surgically removed."

I want to tell him that I heard about a flight attendant who was kidnapped while getting her mail and they found her keys dangling from her mailbox. Instead I get in the elevator with Conrad, who is preoccupied.

"That was the Otter," I say. Jory does sort of look like an otter, but he's very handsome anyway. I can't believe I'm sacrificing him just to amuse Conrad.

It works, though. Conrad focuses on me and laughs, squeezing my shoulder.

## The Thursday Night Ritual

I know it is going to be tonight when Conrad opens the door wearing moccasins.

"What have you done with the moose slippers?" I ask suspiciously, making it sound as though they may be tied up in a closet with gags on.

"Nothing," Conrad says, "I just didn't feel like wearing them." He walks back across the kitchen and stirs the spaghetti sauce.

I sit at the kitchen table in my raincoat. Conrad has put out candles. I rest my elbows on the table and lean forward, my chin cradled in my hands.

"Conrad," I say, "are you transferring to the University of Virginia?"

He stops stirring but doesn't turn around.

"Yes," he says so softly that if I hadn't known what the answer was I would've had to ask him to repeat it. "I'm moving in ten days."

"But that's so soon," I say. "I can't possibly decide where to go by then."

"You should stay," Conrad says. He hasn't turned around yet. He's looking at the ceiling. I can see the very tiny spot where he's beginning to lose his hair. "You like New York."

"I don't like New York!" I say. I pause, thinking that I should've said, "I don't *either* like New York!" It would've had even more of that fourth-grade ring to it. Then it dawns on me what Conrad has truly said.

I get up from the table and go to Conrad, my raincoat rustling. I put my arms around him from behind, resting my forehead between his shoulder blades. Conrad is just the right height.

I guess I had always thought Conrad would say "This has got to stop" or "Do you still want to break up?" I have underestimated him. This was much, much kinder.


## The Memory Game

Zina calls me from LaGuardia. "Listen," she says. "I'm flying to Boston and then home because last week I flew to see my grandmother in Sioux Falls."

"Oh," I say, looking at the spare mattress already lying on my floor.

Zina's voice softens. "Remember the time I didn't pay attention to the flight attendant's spiel on safety and afterward she quizzed me on where the plane's exits were?"

"Yes," I say.

"What about the time the security guard x-rayed my purse and saw my bracelets and said, 'Honey, do you have handcuffs in there?' and everyone stared at me like I was a pervert?"

I reward her and laugh, imagining the sound of it barreling across the city toward her.

## The Inquisition Game

My mother calls me, but before she can say anything, Boyd shouts, "She's been quizzing me all weekend! She promised me immunity if I can trick you into giving details of your love life."

"Oh, hush," I hear my mother say. Because she's nearer to the phone and Boyd is screaming in the background, it does sort of sound like she might have him chained to the wall.

"No, no, yes," I tell my mother.

For a moment no one says anything. I imagine Boyd and my mother looking at each other, wondering if I've gotten the order of the questions mixed up. Then my mother says, "Well, as long as you're happy, dear."

I can hear the doubt in her voice. To her, eating well and being in love equal happiness, but she assumes it is different for us. She doesn't know that Boyd and I agree but that for her, we always make the last answer yes.

## The Adoption Game

On the day before Conrad moves, Harriet and I go to Asbury Park and spend the whole day there, so that I can't possibly be tempted to go past Conrad's house while he's packing. It doesn't work. As soon as we get back, I take the subway down to his apartment and knock on the door. He opens it in his pajamas. It's after midnight.

"Did I wake you?" I ask.

He shakes his head. "I was just lying in bed." He locks the door behind us and I follow him into his room.

Conrad's bed doesn't have sheets or blankets on it. Everything must already be packed away in boxes and crates. His alarm clock is perched on a box next to the bed. I'm surprised he's not sleeping in the clothes he plans to wear tomorrow.

He lies on the mattress and I sit on the edge.

"I saw our son today," Conrad says, holding my hand. I open my mouth to tell him that I don't want to play that game with him anymore. All that comes out is a harsh laugh.

"Shh," Conrad says, pulling me down next to him. He puts his arm around my waist and I can feel his breath on my shoulder as he whispers, "Just because you can't see the Bird's ears doesn't mean he doesn't have them."

I smile in the dark and Conrad touches my lips to see if he's made me laugh. Satisfied, he tucks me more securely against his chest, resting his chin on the top of my head.

I'm sleepier than I thought I could possibly be on this night, but I want to poke Conrad with my elbow and ask him to talk to me the way he did from his balcony. I'm hoping he will remember what he used to say, because suddenly I can't. All I can recall is the sound of his voice, muffled so that I can't make out the words, as though he has always been far away.

# CobRa

WILLIAM HAD BEGUN TO WORRY THAT HE NO LONGER SPARKED JOY IN his wife and that she would give him to Goodwill. It was alarmingly easy to picture. His wife would thank him for his service and then drop him off at the donation center, the one behind the store with the blankly sinister roll-up doors. Goodwill would take him in and William would live out the rest of his days there, among the old bowling trophies, the stained bedsheets, the too-shallow cereal bowls, and the stuffed animals with only one eye.

THIS BUSINESS OF SPARKING JOY had started with that Marie Kondo book, *The Life-Changing Magic of Tidying Up.* William's wife had read the book in a single weekend and then had begun Marie Kondo–ing their house. Only his wife had explained that William was wrong to call it "Marie Kondo–ing," that it was actually called the "KonMari method" because Japanese people reversed and combined their first and last names to create a nickname.

William's wife's name was Rachel Coburn, so her Japanese nickname would be (or could be, sort of) CobRa.

William told her this, however unwisely. He was trying to make jokes, trying to spark joy. It was in short supply lately.

THE NEW NAME SUITED his wife. She seemed like a predatory snake these days—cold, mean, ready to strike. She told William that it was because she was in perimenopause. She had given him a printed checklist of thirty-four symptoms of perimenopause: irritability, lack of libido, hot flashes, mood swings, headaches, constipation, gum problems, tingling extremities, fatigue, dizziness, burning tongue . . . She had checked every single box except incontinence.

Two days later, she asked him for the list back and checked the incontinence box, too.

FOR YEARS AND YEARS, they had been happy with their life. Or had it only been William who was happy? It seemed now that CobRa must not have been because she was bent on change. Big changes, like trading the minivan in for a hatchback, and deciding they should vacation in Tahoe instead of Breckenridge. But smaller ones, too. She had gone through an obsession with avocado toast and she had hired an outrageously expensive landscaper to create a "pollinator garden." She had joined AncestryDNA and found out she was mostly British, French, and Scandinavian and related to approximately half the internet. To William, this seemed likely to be the world's least surprising result. What had she been trying to find there? William wondered.

She had given up coffee, saying it worsened her insomnia. She had given up red meat, saying it made her sluggish. She had given up social media, saying it made her depressed. She had given up running, saying it hurt her knees. She had given up sex, though she didn't say why. (They didn't discuss it at all, actually.) She had given up alcohol, claiming it gave her headaches. Well, not *claiming*—William was sure it did give her headaches. It's just that it was hard not to take it personally. Some people called cocktail hour the "golden hour," referring to the last hour of light before sunset, but for William it had always been golden in that it was the hour he spent with his wife.

William wasn't sure there were many other things CobRa could give up and still remain the person he'd married. Already she seemed like someone else.

℮~

ANYWAY, BACK TO MARIE KONDO. It began the Monday after CobRa finished reading the book. She approached William that evening while he was reading the paper and told him they were going to start the tidying process and they had to begin by greeting the house.

"Hello, house!" William called. (He'd had a couple of whiskeys.)

CobRa gave him a stern look. "I'm serious," she said. "We need to thank the house for sheltering us, and tell it we appreciate its protection."

"The house knows I appreciate it," William said, opening *The Wall Street Journal* with a rustle and a snap. "I pay its mortgage. Tell the house *I'd* appreciate it not shifting around on the foundations anymore."

CobRa gave him a disappointed look and went off to another room, presumably to converse with the house in private.

This was not the beginning of William's realizing he no longer sparked joy, but a continuation.

℮~

FIRST COBRA ORGANIZED her clothes. She piled every piece of clothing she owned onto their bed and then shook her head. "I have way too many clothes."

Useless for William, who was standing by the dresser putting in his cuff links, to point out that he'd been saying this for years. Besides, he had a nostalgic fondness for some of those clothes: the coral-colored shell blouse she'd worn on their trip to Greece, the pale pink nightgown with the bow in front that was so much fun to untie.

"I haven't worn half this stuff in *years*," CobRa said.

But William knew she could still fit into all of it, every single item, even her premarital jeans. This seemed terribly unfair to William, whose own metabolism seemed to have turned on him, in much the same way the British tabloids had turned on Meghan Markle. For years, his metabolism had been adoring and tolerant, and now it was harsh and punishing—a single bite of doughnut could cause his stomach to strain against his belt the next day.

By the time William came home from work, CobRa had filled eight trash bags with clothes for Goodwill. But the bed was still heaped so high with garments that she and William had to stay in the guest room that night. The bed in there was slightly too small and they fought over the covers in their sleep.

NEXT COBRA TIDIED William's clothes, dragging him upstairs after breakfast to make decisions. She didn't bother with his suits and ties and dress shirts, only his casual clothes. On the bed were his corduroys with the frayed hems, his sweaters with the perfectly stretched-out necks, the flannel shirts worn soft as flower petals. William said it all pretty much still sparked joy in him, but CobRa said that it had to spark joy in both of them.

"You wearing it and me seeing you wear it," she said.

In the end, this left him with one pair of pants and four shirts.

So CobRa went shopping the next day and bought him some scratchy new polo shirts, stiff chambray oxfords, cotton-stretch chinos, a shawl-collared cardigan sweater. (Wasn't shopping the opposite of Marie Kondo–ing? William wondered, but didn't say.) She hung the new clothes in his closet, the hangers a precise inch apart on the rod. This made CobRa happy. Or, at least, it should have. But William saw her standing in the closet the very next afternoon, her shoulders slumped like yesterday's stock market index.

THE CHILDREN STILL SEEMED to spark joy in CobRa, but they were seldom home. Brittany was away at college and seventeen-year-old Nathaniel spent most of his time at his girlfriend's parents' house.

When she'd lived at home, Brittany's bedroom had been a sloping rubble of makeup and hairbands and earrings and bras and tights and red Solo cups. Brittany had somehow stuffed almost all her possessions into the four giant suitcases she took with her to Wellesley, although William had worried privately that one of the suitcases was so tightly packed that it might create a black hole in the trunk of the car. Her deserted bedroom presented CobRa with no real challenge, and Brittany wasn't there to protest anyway, so CobRa tidied it to Kondo standards in a mere four hours.

Nathaniel's room was already hyper-organized in a nascent-serial-killer type of way. CobRa bullied him into piling all his possessions onto his bed and sorting through them with her, but they wound up putting everything back pretty much the way it was before. The only thing Nathaniel said no longer sparked joy—he said it had *never* sparked joy—was an Irish fisherman's sweater CobRa had given him for his birthday last year. This made CobRa get all teary and Nathaniel was so guilt-stricken that he actually stayed home for supper that night, eating salmon and new potatoes off blue Wedgwood plates after CobRa had thanked the dishes for their service.

WILLIAM HAD ALWAYS LIKED that CobRa was an ER nurse. He felt that her schedule made them appreciate each other more. Couples needed to be reminded of the contrast between life together and life apart, he felt. The days that she worked a twelve-hour shift and he came home to an empty house—silent but for the ticking of the furnace—made the evenings she was home waiting for him feel like holidays, like celebrations.

They had met in the ER. She had been the petite blonde with the pixie haircut and eyes the same shade as her baby-blue scrubs.

(Think Sandy Duncan in those Wheat Thins commercials.) He had been the conservatively handsome young stockbroker who'd cut his hand with a box cutter while trying to slice bread. CobRa had cleaned his palm with Betadine while they waited for the doctor to come stitch up the wound.

The gentle smile, the burning sting, the anticipation of the follow-up appointment—their first meeting was like the very essence of love. A distillation of love. No wonder they'd gotten married. A whirlwind courtship; they were walking down the aisle less than six months after their first date. Yet no friend or family member protested or raised a single doubt—it was clear they were meant to be together.

William still had that box cutter—old now, and rust specked, its red handle fuzzy with grime—out in the garage somewhere. He still had the scar on his hand, too: an inch-long raised white line that always made the rest of his palm look a little dirty. The scar started below his middle finger and ran parallel to his Heart line, sometimes touching it. William sometimes wondered guiltily if this meant that he and CobRa were destined to divorce, and that he would remarry. But now he felt as though they already had, and it had happened without his even noticing. They had divorced and now he was married to Marie Kondo.

COBRA TOLD WILLIAM that she'd forgotten to do their dresser drawers and returned to the master bedroom. She folded all William's shirts and pajamas and underpants in a terribly complicated way that reminded William of swaddling newborns who then immediately started yelling.

Next CobRa unballed all of William's socks. She said the socks couldn't "rest" if they were scrunched up like that, and the socks deserved to rest after their hard service all day. "I need to rest, too," William said. "Not stand here talking about socks."

CobRa gave him an annoyed look and told him to go take a nap on the couch if he was as tired as all that.

Well, he was that tired, so he did go take a nap, or at least he tried to. He lay there, shifting uncomfortably on the narrow gold sofa, with a needlepoint pillow under his head. CobRa used to take naps with him here, the two of them twisting and turning to accommodate each other, and just when they were on the point of giving up, they would suddenly find the right position, like fitting the last few blocks back in the toy box and dropping the lid. Sadly, William realized they hadn't napped together for years. He sighed. He supposed his stomach would push CobRa right off the sofa if they tried that now.

He must have dozed off, because he suddenly became aware of a darkness in the living room and a dryness in his mouth. He found a note in the kitchen from CobRa, saying that she'd gone to yoga. He went upstairs and opened his sock drawer. He discovered that CobRa had smoothed and folded all his socks and poked them into the holes of a drawer divider.

How to describe the joy this new sock arrangement sparked in William from the very first? It's not possible; all descriptions fall short. He closed the drawer gently and then opened it again, just for fun. Picking out the day's socks would be a pleasure now, he realized. It would be like opening a brand-new box of Crayola crayons every morning: fresh, undulled, full of potential.

But when CobRa came home from yoga, he didn't tell her how much he liked the new sock drawer. He didn't say a word about it because, well, marriage.

℮

THEN CAME BOOKS. "I'M NOT going to give my books away," William said. "They all spark joy. No way am I going to cut down to thirty."

CobRa said that they could keep all the books that William liked—but first they had to haul all the books off the shelves and then clap at each volume gently to make it "conscious." This gentle wake-up call would determine whether a specific book was meant to stay in their lives.

"Wait a minute," William said. "I thought you just told me to clap at our books."

"I did," CobRa said.

Had perimenopause caused her to take leave of her senses? William had done many shameful things out of his love for CobRa—he had agreed turkey meatballs were as good as regular, he had watched all of Scandal, he had briefly grown a mustache which made him look like Dr. Phil—but he refused to do this. He told CobRa she had to keep all the books with his name written on the flyleaf and then he went downstairs to drink whiskey in front of the fireplace. But even drinking whiskey wasn't as satisfying as it used to be. For one thing, CobRa had donated their coffee table to Goodwill and he had nowhere to rest his glass. Also, he could hear CobRa clapping upstairs like someone having a very tentative seance.

So he bribed Nathaniel into going out for pizza with him by telling him that he'd order beer for both of them while Nathaniel was in the restroom. They went to The Dough Father and either their waiter didn't notice or didn't care—Nathaniel made trip after trip to the restroom, drank beer after beer.

After the fourth trip, he gave William a sideways look, and said, "What's going on with Mom?"

"What do you mean?" William asked, stalling.

Nathaniel paused. "She's different," he said at last. "It's like, you know, she . . ." He trailed off, frowning drunkenly at the wall.

William was suddenly sure Nathaniel was going to say that it was like CobRa was seeing someone else, or that it was like CobRa had fallen out of love with William, or that CobRa no longer saw the two of them growing old together. But how would Nathaniel know any of those things? Not even William knew. Not for sure.

The silence spread between them and just when William thought perhaps Nathaniel had powered down for the evening, Nathaniel reanimated himself and said, "It's, like, she used to be the first mom on the block who would let us go barefoot in the spring, and all the other kids thought I was so lucky, and now I don't even want to go barefoot, but I get the feeling she wouldn't let me."

William sighed with relief and understanding. "I know exactly what you mean. But it'll be okay." Wasn't that what you said to children? Always, over and over, until the end of time? "It'll be okay. Why don't you go to the bathroom and I'll order us another round?"

THE NEXT CATEGORY OF tidying was *komono*, which William assumed was Japanese for "everything you need to lead a happy and comfortable life." But CobRa told him it referred to small items that serve no purpose. She didn't come right out and *say*, "Like you, William"—it was more implied. Get ready, Goodwill, here he comes.

Lots of his possessions would be there to keep him company. Already dispatched were his dusty valet catchall tray, his fish-shaped ashtray, his wooden bottle opener. The ugly black-and-white triptych from his bachelor apartment was on the porch waiting to go, its face turned to the wall in shame. CobRa was marching through the house like a clutter-obsessed Sherman through Georgia, leaving scorched earth dotted with plump black garbage bags in her wake. She tidied the family room, then the den, the guest room, the bathroom, the guest bathroom, the downstairs bathroom, the bathroom William sometimes forgot they even had.

When she started on the coat closet, William stopped in the doorway on his way to the office.

"What?" CobRa asked, her arms full of plastic rain ponchos that had never once felt the rain upon their skins.

"I want to say hello to my old duffle coat," William said pointedly. "I also want to tell it that I hope it doesn't go anywhere. That applies to my hiking boots, too. Please tell them that I hope to see them again this very evening."

It did no good. They were gone by the time he came home. The duffle coat was a disgrace, CobRa said, and he hadn't hiked in years.

❦

THE NEXT DAY she tidied the kitchen. "Aren't you supposed to be going by category instead of by room?" William asked. "I mean, according to Marie?"

"Fuck Marie Kondo," CobRa said, wiping grime from her face with a dish-gloved hand.

William felt a spark of desire—finally, they agreed on something! It didn't last, though. When William came home that night, the kitchen was a harsh and alien landscape, bereft of the cheese board (seldom used but so pleasing with its stripes of walnut, cherry, and maple), the vintage FARM FRESH EGGS sign, the plump little coffee canister that was nearly impossible to spoon coffee out of but which had always fit in William's hand as sweetly as a woman's breast— a woman's soft, firm, round, holdable breast.

"Stop *touching* me," CobRa said, moving away from him on the couch.

❦

BRITTANY CALLED HIM at his office from Wellesley. "Mom's gone crazy."

"Ah, now," William said, "that may be overstating it."

"I just got off the phone with her," Brittany said, "and she was talking about something called a click point."

"What's that?"

"According to Mom, it's the point where you give away enough of your shit that there's only, like, essential stuff left. Then you feel a 'click' and realize you're happy."

"Is she there yet?" William asked.

"You tell me, Dad!" Brittany said, exasperated. "You're the one who lives with her."

He sighed. "No, I don't believe she's clicked."

"Has she been in my room?"

"Ah, well, I'm not entirely sure about that," said William, who was, of course, entirely sure.

"She didn't give away my American Girl Doll collection, did she? Because that's going to be worth a lot someday."

Normally the thought of Brittany's American Girl Doll collection filled William with a generalized sort of rage. The cost! The terrible "stories"! Their creepy teeth! The pilgrimage to the mother store in Chicago! But now he found himself unexpectedly sympathetic because recently he'd come home to find that CobRa had tidied the attic and thrown out their collection of porn videotapes from the 1990s. Didn't she remember watching them together? Or was it only William who remembered those stolen afternoons? (The VCR was in the living room; the tapes could only be watched while the children were at school.) William on his back on the Persian carpet, CobRa crouched on top of him, both their heads turned toward the flickering TV screen, their sounds mixing with the sounds of the porn couple—was William the only one who could recall that? He had felt at those moments, with the sunlight shining through the blinds to paint golden stripes on the floor, that he made love not only to his wife but to the woman in the video, to the neighbors, the whole town, the whole world. (The feeling had subsided instantly afterward, but still.)

WORST OF ALL, THOUGH, was when she did the garage.

The garage had always been a sore spot between them. CobRa had always called it a disaster area but William had preferred to think of it as pleasantly cluttered. You could find what you were looking for if you were really motivated, but more often than not, it was easier just to put the lawnmower away (the lawnmower was on the outer edge of the garage) and leave the rest for another day. William felt this kept him from doing all but the most necessary chores. It was not precisely a feeling CobRa shared.

He returned from an overnight business trip to find her standing in the driveway, waiting to show him the newly tidied garage. He knew instantly that she waited for him to leave, had looked forward to doing it without him there to protest. She showed the garage to him quite proudly.

The garage smelled less like a garage now, and more like lilacs, which seemed to William a disturbing combination. CobRa'd put up hooks and now the rake, shovel, hoe, and broom hung neatly on the wall, along with the wheelbarrow, though that looked a little precarious. The lawnmower and snow blower had been turned around so the handles faced the walls. (Inconvenient, William thought.) Plastic storage shelves lined one wall, holding bags of birdseed, carefully looped extension cords, plastic bins full of Christmas lights. She'd set up a worktable with a pegboard above it, each tool outlined like a dead body and labeled: hammer, wrenches, pliers, clamps. Even the box cutter. At least she hadn't thrown it out.

CobRa's eyes were on his face. "Don't you like it?"

William made a noncommittal noise. He knew he was being difficult and unappreciative—just imagine the work to hang that pegboard on the garage's unforgiving concrete walls!—but he couldn't seem to help himself. The worktable looked like a place where someone would be expected to do a lot of, well, work.

They continued the tour. Gone were the sticky paint cans, the cracked garden hose, the half-used bottles of motor oil, the empty flowerpots, the stacks of old newspapers, the deflated soccer balls, the sprung tennis rackets, the torn window screens, the broken dehumidifier, the dusty stereo speakers, the—wait a minute—ladder.

"How will we clean the gutters without a ladder?" William asked.

"That ladder was a death trap," CobRa said coolly. (True enough.) Something else occurred to William. "Where are the snow tires?"

"Those awful dirty old tires, you mean?"

"No, the new snow tires. They were right over here."

"Right where?"

"Right *here*."

You can see where this was going, and indeed it went there. William said the snow tires were less than a year old and worth over a thousand dollars. CobRa said how was she supposed to know. William said she was supposed to *consult* him, that's how. CobRa said she didn't like to consult him when she was tidying things because it always seemed to put him in such a bad mood. William said that this was why. He said that he was in a terrible mood now knowing that some lucky person who shopped at Goodwill would be driving around on *his* almost-new snow tires, wearing *his* soft flannel shirts and *his* duffle coat and drinking beer out of *his* Garfield beer mug, while he, William, was stuck here living with Marie-fucking-Kondo.

CobRa looked so angry that William thought she might actually hood, like a real cobra. Instead she stalked off to the house without saying anything.

William slept in the guest room that night and the too-small bed felt just fine.

WHEN WILLIAM GOT HOME the next evening, no garbage bags waited in the front hall to be taken to Goodwill. A first in at least two weeks. The wooden floor gleamed for miles, the tabletops were dazzlingly clear, the mantel above the fireplace shone white with blankness. The house was now picked clean as a bone; the very air William moved through was scrubbed of excess. But where was CobRa?

He found her in the bedroom, lying on her side on top of the beautifully made bed. She was still wearing her scrubs, and when she glanced over her shoulder at him, William gave a start: it had been so long since he'd seen her wear the blue color that made her eyes glow.

"Hi," she said softly, and smiled. Apparently she wasn't angry anymore.

Neither, decided William, was he. He crossed the room and paused by the side of the bed to remove his shoes. Then he too climbed on top of the covers to lie next to her.

"The house looks beautiful," he said softly, and even somewhat sincerely.

CobRa sighed. "I guess," she said. "It's just that I thought it would be different. I thought it would be life changing."

William waited a moment before he said, "And?"

"Oh, well, you know," CobRa said, her profile edged in sapphire by the twilight. Her voice had a slight quaver. "Life not changed."

William put his arm around her and gathered her close. He was willing, in this moment, to tell her how much he loved the new sock drawer, but just then CobRa held his hand and traced the old scar on his palm.

And suddenly he knew that he was wrong about that scar. It wasn't an interruption of his Heart line, as he always thought, but a broadening of it, a strengthening of it, two lines twisting together to form a new, stronger line. A new stage of their marriage—that's all this was. A new stage, to be followed by some other stage, and another after that. In all these stages, they would be together, entwined forever. The insight flared in him.

He took a deep breath, preparing to hail her from his island of discovery. Rachel! he would say. Oh, Rachel.

JUST AS JANE AUSTEN BELIEVED THAT FOUR PEOPLE CANNOT COMFORT-ably walk abreast, Charlene believes that three people cannot amicably move one person's belongings. Not when two of the people used to be married to each other. And especially not when one of those people had divorced the second person to marry the third person.

What's more, Charlie's husband, Forrest, had knee-replacement surgery six weeks ago and is still using a cane, and Forrest's ex-wife, Barbara, has some mysterious but convenient ailment—sciatica? nerve damage?—that prevents her from lifting things, so Charlie will be the only able-bodied one working today. This is the true price of infidelity, she thinks: twenty years later you and your husband have to help his ex-wife move out of the former family home. On a Saturday. In January. In D.C. It is fifteen degrees below zero with a sharp wind slicing through the air.

The wind hits Charlie as soon as she steps out of her front door, chilling her through. She waits for Forrest to make his way past her, then locks the door and helps him down the driveway and into the car. She hurries around to the driver's side, her breath pluming out in front of her like white feathers. Snow is piled high on either side of the damp asphalt driveway. The air is cold and flat and smells of nothing.

Charlie gets into the car on the driver's side and starts the engine. "Tell me why we're doing this again," she says to Forrest.

He buckles his seat belt. "Because we're all friends now."

"Barbara and I are not friends," Charlie says emphatically.

"Well, sort of friends," he says. "Friendly."

Charlie gives him a look as she backs the car out of the driveway. "She called me a cocksucking whore once."

"But that was a long time ago," Forrest says, smiling a little. "Now it's like you've reached a détente. You're more like North and South Korea."

Charlie frowns. "Would South Korea help North Korea *move*, though?"

"Well, it's more like premoving," Forrest says. "Barbara just needs someone to help her pack up the more fragile stuff before the real movers come tomorrow."

"But why *us*?" Charlie asks.

"I know it means a great deal to Stephen and Ross," Forrest answers, and a little silence falls between them because, really, that says everything there is to say. Stephen and Ross are Forrest and Barbara's twin sons, now all grown up and living in California. Forrest will do almost anything to stay in their good graces, and so will Charlie, actually, though she can't help thinking that if it means so much to them, maybe they should come do it themselves.

The heater isn't warming the car at all. Charlie blows on her fingers and wonders why Barbara and Forrest can't be one of those acrimonious divorced couples who spit when they say each other's names. They had done that for a while, in the beginning, with threats and insults and stormy phone calls. It had not been without certain satisfactions.

Charlie had met Barbara before she met Forrest, when she and Barbara had both volunteered at a suicide prevention hotline. Charlie had been a psych major at American University then, fulfilling her community-service requirements, and Barbara had been a volunteer, too, as well as a part-time fundraiser.

Charlie had met Forrest at a concert Barbara had arranged for the hotline. It was held in the back room of a Mount Pleasant music center, and folding chairs had been provided but not set up—Charlie and Forrest had done that while Barbara supervised the ticket table in the hall. (This is how Charlie knows about Barbara's nerve damage or whatever the hell it is that prevents her from lifting anything.) Forrest was then (and is now) the kind of person who is so smart and witty that he made setting up the chairs fun. During the concert, Charlie and Forrest had sat in the back row and whispered to each other, wondering whether the string quartet was playing in such a subdued way because that was their style or because they were afraid of their chairs toppling off the stage, which was on the small side. Afterward, Charlie and Forrest took much longer than necessary taking down the chairs—Charlie's love for Forrest would always be inextricably linked with an ache in her lower back—and she could remember standing next to him as they stacked the last chairs on the metal racks. Not even their shoulders were touching but she had felt as though their bodies were pressed together. Then she had glanced toward the hallway and realized that Barbara was watching them from behind the door, one eye visible, like a disapproving Cyclops.

Barbara lives way out in Falls Church, and it takes Charlie and Forrest forty minutes to get there. Charlie wishes it took longer. She drives as slowly as possible up the long, curving street to Barbara's home at the top of the hill.

The house is a white elephant in the figurative, financial sense— you wouldn't believe the mortgage, let alone the heating bills—and it *looks* like a white elephant, too, all sprawling white clapboard with gray flagstone paths winding across the big lawn. It has always seemed to Charlie like a stereotypical doctor's suburban home— Forrest is an orthopedic surgeon, somewhat ironically given that this is his second knee replacement—and she thinks the house is too showy and old-fashioned. (Forrest and Charlie live in a modern

brick house in Georgetown; second place must try harder, or whatever that expression is.)

They park in front of the house, right by the path so Forrest can
get out easily. Charlie sees that an orange-and-white U-Haul trailer
has been backed into the long driveway. She helps Forrest out of
the car and they walk up the steps of the large front porch and ring
the doorbell.

Barbara swings the door open right away. "Hello, Forrest," she
says. "Hello, 561."

Believe it or not, she's speaking to Charlie. At the suicide hotline,
the volunteers were known by number so that no caller could startle
a volunteer into revealing another's name. (Such a thing had happened. A caller had tracked down a volunteer named Bonnie at a
bus stop and given her a copy of *Looking for Mr. Goodbar*. It was very
upsetting for everyone.)

Charlie's number had been 561 and Barbara still calls her that,
possibly as a way to indicate that Charlie was merely the 561st in the
long string of Forrest's meaningless dalliances. ("I *wish*," Forrest had
said wistfully, when Charlie shared this theory with him.) Charlie
puts up with being called 561 because there are certain concessions
you make when you run off with someone's husband.

"Hello, Barbara," she says.

There is a long moment when Charlie and Barbara size each
other up, and Charlie wonders if Barbara is thinking the eye candy
isn't as sweet as it used to be, now that Charlie is in her forties.
(Although even in her twenties, Charlie wasn't what you'd call
*eye candy*: her looks had always been sharp edged and intense,
more like *eye tequila*.) On all of her own moving days, Charlie has
worn running shoes, sweatpants, a T-shirt, and a baseball cap, but
today she has on a clingy beige turtleneck and jeans tucked into
brown Frye riding boots and a buff-colored suede trench coat with
a creamy shearling collar. Her eye shadow could make a teenage

girl sigh with longing, and her short blond hair is carefully tousled because—because—well, there's payback for that 561 thing. Don't go thinking otherwise.

Barbara looks pretty much the same as always. Her thick ebony-colored hair is still on loan from Cleopatra, though surely it must be dyed by now—nobody's hair is that black in their sixties. And the pageboy cut is no longer as flattering as it once was: the short heavy bangs show too much of her eyebrows and her face is too wide for chin-length hair now. But she's wearing a turquoise-colored velour warm-up suit and chunky turquoise jewelry, and she looks short and curvy and ripe, which were always her strengths, in Charlie's opinion.

"Come in," Barbara says at last, standing aside, and Forrest shuffles in, followed by Charlie.

Of the many things Charlie dislikes about this house, she especially dislikes how *oversized* it is. Does anyone really need rooms bigger than playgrounds and ceilings higher than silos and floorboards wider than pizza boxes? (No, they don't, is Charlie's opinion.) The house also has an uncomfortable amount of dead, furnitureless space—like, right now, are they standing in a foyer or on the salt flats in Bolivia?

Barbara leads them down the hall toward the dining room. "How's the knee?" she says to Forrest, over her shoulder.

"Not bad," Forrest says. "I can get around now."

"Did Scotty Brannon do the surgery?" Barbara asks.

"No, it was Andy Wiggins," Charlie says immediately.

She assumes that Barbara asked about Scotty as a way of pointing out that she had been close to Forrest's colleagues, so it was necessary for Charlie to establish that times have moved on. (Between certain pairs of people, no conversational exchanges are ever neutral.)

Now they are all standing in the dining room. Charlie has been in this house officially—meaning when Barbara was present—on only a handful of occasions, but unofficially, during her affair with Forrest, she was here dozens of times. Barbara probably thinks Charlie has only ever seen the hall and the living room, the bathroom, and a glimpse of the kitchen, when in reality she has been upstairs, has had sex with Forrest in nearly every room, had actually *lived* there for sixteen days with Forrest while Barbara was off tagging sea turtles in the Galápagos. (Charlie has always felt slightly guilty that it was a turtle-tagging trip and not something less redeeming, like a knitting convention.)

"Now, Forrest, you sit right here at the table and help me pack," Barbara says. On the table there is a brand-new box of bubble wrap, two full rolls of sealing tape, and two pairs of shiny-bright scissors. Didn't Barbara own scissors with nicked blades and worn handles, and broken tape dispensers? Barbara's life has always seemed artificial to Charlie, like props and scenery on a stage set. She has never been quite able to believe it goes on when no one is there to witness it.

"Now, 561, you come with me," Barbara says to Charlie, and leads her toward the back of the house. "The U-Haul man backed the trailer in last night, so if you could just carry these boxes out and put them in there."

She says this as though there are a couple of boxes—a few boxes, maybe four or five boxes, a *limited number* of boxes—but when Charlie comes around the corner and sees the mountain of boxes stacked outside the kitchen (in another of those dead zones with no furniture), she's appalled.

There are dozens upon dozens of boxes—small ones, about the size of shoeboxes, and wrapped with layers and layers of slick carton tape. A person could carry only one, perhaps two, without dropping them. Of all the times for Barbara to give up her stagelike presentation! These are a real person's boxes: soft, bendy, grubby cardboard.

"I'll be in the dining room if you have any questions," Barbara says brightly, and goes back along the hall.

Charlie pulls a soft ribbed hat with a fake-fur pom-pom from her coat pocket and puts it on. (She didn't put it on before because she wanted to present her prettiest self to Barbara. But she's vain, not stupid—of course she needs a hat.)

She carries the first box out of the back door and realizes that the thing she hates most about this house is not how oversized it is: the thing she hates most is the back porch stairs. The steps are too steep, the treads too narrow, the risers too short—perhaps a goat or other animal with very small hooves could navigate them safely, but not Charlie. Why the stairs were constructed this way, and why they have never been replaced, she can't imagine.

But her only choice is to go up and down these awful stairs, or go all the way through the house and out of the front door, then down the flagstone path and up the driveway, which would be about ten times longer. Clearly this move is going to be like pitting cherries, or doing long division, or traveling with children: difficult and unpleasant however you do it.

She sighs and descends the back porch stairs, her free hand gripping the railing, and opens the door of the U-Haul trailer. She puts the box on the metal floor and pushes it toward the back. In the thirty seconds Charlie's been outside, the insides of her nostrils have shriveled with cold and her lips feel stiff and waxy, like they would stick to her teeth.

She goes back up the stairs, placing each foot sideways on the narrow treads. She's in the warm house only long enough to know how cold she is, and then she grabs another box, goes down the stairs, puts it in the U-Haul trailer, slides it to the back, climbs the stairs, feet turned sideways, into the warm house, grabs another small box—

When Charlie was twenty-seven, she'd had electrolysis done on her bikini line in a dodgy downtown salon owned by a severe-looking Korean woman. Having one hair follicle destroyed is not too awful—but having one destroyed every eight seconds for an hour made Charlie nearly gibber with pain. Zap. Zap-zap. Zap.

ZAP! ("Tough one," the woman had said, clucking her tongue and reaching for a bigger epilation needle.) This move is like electrolysis; it is the unending nature of it that Charlie can't stand. Zap. Zap. Zap-zap. Zap. On and on.

By the tenth trip, Charlie's nose has begun to run, and her feet are numb. Also, something is wrong with her hands—even inside the gloves they seem to be made of metal, like the skeleton hands of the cyborg in *The Terminator*. Surely there is no flesh on her fingers, keeping them warm.

Zap. Zap. She decides she will make the next trip out of the front door just to stay inside a little longer. She takes a small box labeled BRANDY SNIFTERS—it couldn't possibly hold more than three glasses—and walks down the hall past the dining room, where Barbara and Forrest are.

Right away she wants to kill them. They have turned on the fire (yes, there's a fireplace in the dining room), put on a Johnny Cash CD, and are sitting at the table—looking warm as toast, warm as tea, warm as fucking hot sake—and slowly swathing jade figurines in bubble wrap.

"Remember that first house we lived in on Jefferson Street?" Barbara says to Forrest fondly. "Where we woke up one morning and found a mouse had died in the candy dish?"

"And Stevie got so upset," Forrest says, smiling, "because he wanted to keep it as a pet."

"We had to bury it in the backyard," Barbara muses, "with a lemon drop still stuck in its mouth."

"I never felt the same about lemon drops after that," Forrest says, and they both laugh softly.

Really, it's a good thing that at this moment Charlie is carrying a box of glassware and not a bunch of steak knives, because otherwise she'd end up serving a double life sentence for murder in the Fluvanna Correctional Center for Women (and serving it proudly).

She stops in the doorway to the dining room. "I didn't realize I'd be outside so much," she says pointedly. "Barbara, do you mind if I borrow a coat?"

Barbara frowns, and Charlie can almost hear the low whirring buzz of Barbara's brain as it tries desperately to manufacture some valid excuse for not lending her warmer outerwear. But there is no excuse. When someone is making a hundred trips outside with your belongings, you can't withhold all favors, much as you'd like to. It's like having to let a certain kind of lecherous workman use your bathroom, even though you know they're going to leave the door open a crack.

"Why, certainly," Barbara says at last, pushing back her chair. "The coat closet is—"

"I saw it," Charlie says, turning. "Don't get up, I'll help myself."

"The blue wool is especially warm," Barbara calls.

So, clearly, any coat but the blue wool. Charlie steps into the coat closet, which is of course bigger than most people's kitchens. But like all coat closets, it's reassuringly jumbled, and smells of athletic socks and wet wool. Charlie chooses a puffy white down parka that looks warm and also like it might stain easily and have to be dry-cleaned, all of which are positives in her book. She pokes through a basket of gloves until she finds a nice pair of fur-lined deerskin ones and pulls them on. Her fingers are too long for the gloves, as they are for all gloves, everywhere. No one has fingers as long as Charlie's. She puts her own gloves in her pocket.

She makes a few trips out of the front door and down the flag-stone paths, but it's even worse than the slippery back stairs because she's out in the cold longer. She begins alternating, first the long route, then the short one. Zap. Zap. Zap. (Actually, not even elec-trolysis was this bad.) By late morning, Charlie is so cold that her teeth hurt. It feels like the fillings in her molars have been dipped in liquid nitrogen. Zap. Zap-zap. The mountain of boxes doesn't seem to be getting any smaller.

Charlie hopes that she and Forrest will go have lunch somewhere by themselves, somewhere nice and cozy where they can say bad things about Barbara, but on one of her trips past the dining room, she sees that Barbara is setting the table for three. On her next trip, Barbara tells her that lunch will be ready in five minutes. Charlie takes off her coat and hat and gloves, and goes into the bathroom to wash her hands. In the mirror her eyes are bright with tears from the cold; the skin across her cheeks is raw and chapped-looking. Her nose is as pink as a rabbit's.

For lunch, Barbara serves salmon burgers on brioche buns and a green salad drenched in balsamic dressing. Charlie is dismayed: first, everyone knows you have beer and pizza on moving day, and second, well, *salmon burgers.*

"Now tell me," Barbara says to Charlie, as soon as they are all seated, "how is your daughter?"

Charlie glances at Forrest, who is—damn him—giving her a look of polite interest as though Davina were her daughter, not theirs.

"She's good," Charlie says, and smiles a little as an image of Davina flits through her mind. Davina is thirteen but so far untouched by teenage acne or personality rot. She is perfect. "She works at a food pantry on Saturdays."

This is a lie. Davina is almost certainly still asleep and will probably remain that way for at least another hour. If Charlie suggested to Davina that she spend her Saturdays working at a food bank, Davina would be shocked and disbelieving. But Barbara doesn't need to know that.

"And your work?" Barbara inquires politely. "Are you still an addictions counselor?"

"Oh, yes," Charlie says.

"What type of addiction do you specialize in?" Barbara asks.

"Meth and heroin mainly," Charlie says.

Barbara's nostrils flare slightly. "That's an—"

"And many of my clients are sex workers," Charlie adds. "All of them, actually. With hepatitis."

This is also a lie, although at one time, when Charlie was younger and worked at a welfare detox clinic, it wouldn't have been. But now she's the after-care coordinator at a luxury rehab center in Virginia, and the closest thing she knows to a sex worker is a woman named Aileen who works in the massage therapy department and once got written up for failing to change the sheets between clients. But she can't resist trying to one-up Barbara: *You* may have tagged a few turtles, but *I've* touched people crawling with infectious diseases.

"I know addiction is an illness," Barbara says thoughtfully, "but it is so terribly hard on the families."

"How *is* your cousin Paul?" Forrest asks.

Barbara seems disappointed by this question. No doubt she was looking forward to talking about how Charlie enables addicts to torment their loved ones. "Paul's doing very well," she says. She turns to Charlie. "My cousin has been a recovering alcoholic for twenty-five years now."

"I seem to remember Forrest talking about him," Charlie says coolly. "Wasn't he always taking impromptu hikes carrying a thermos?"

Barbara frowns. "It was a very small thermos—"

"I always liked Paul," Forrest says. "Where does he live now?"

"On Long Island," Barbara says. "Garden City. I have his email address if you'd like to get in touch with him."

"He and I played golf at Deepdale once," Forrest says to Charlie, as though she could possibly care. "It was a great course."

Charlie doesn't reply. Her gaze is flicking over Forrest critically, and she's thinking that if she and Barbara really are like North and South Korea, she would just as soon they dropped this pretense and North Korea took Forrest political prisoner. There's always the worry of starvation and reeducation, of course, but maybe he'd be detained in one of the nicer camps and not for too long. Right at this moment, Charlie thinks it might be worth it.

Suddenly Barbara looks pained—that is, even more pained than usual in Charlie's presence. "I think I'm getting a migraine," she says. (She doesn't say that having Charlie in the house is the cause but it's sort of implied.)

She leaves the table for a moment. She returns with her purse and rummages through it for a bottle of pills. She swallows one and dons a pair of oversized sunglasses that make her look like an insane welder. "There," she says. "Perhaps that will hold it."

"It's such a shame the way you suffer," Forrest says, shaking his head and taking another bite of his salmon burger.

But Charlie doesn't say anything because the rattle of the pill bottle has touched a memory deep inside her mind, like a scalpel touching one tiny cell on a sheet of bubble wrap and making it pop.

TWENTY YEARS AGO, the suicide crisis hotline had been called Hopeful Place, a name Charlie found deeply ironic, since the call center was so grim, so dingy, so depressing that anyone who went there automatically felt like killing themselves. (It was a good thing they didn't offer in-person sessions.) The call center consisted of two rooms on the third floor of an office building on G Street in Southeast D.C. One of the rooms was an office, with filing cabinets and metal furniture, where the administrators sat in the daytime. The other room was for the volunteers, with two battle-scarred desks and squeaky roller chairs, a small refrigerator, and a table with a coffee machine and a microwave on top. Both rooms had chipped lime-green walls and wooden floors dark with the dirt of a hundred thousand shoes. In the winter, the pipes clanked, and in the summer, an inadequate window AC unit buzzed so loudly that it was hard to hear the phones. The volunteer room smelled predominantly of whatever takeout the previous shift had ordered—on this particular hot August evening when Charlie showed up to work an overnight shift, that smell was of pepperoni-and-onion pizza.

Charlie's usual partner on overnights was a statuesque African

American woman named Dominique. Dominique's voice sounded like glass beads rolling on a snare drum and she had the demeanor of a seasoned homicide cop or waitress at a truck stop—someone who has seen a lot and risen above it. She could soothe the most troubled caller seemingly just by laying her hands on the receiver. She ended every call by saying, "Now, dear one, you rest easy tonight." (A technique Charlie had tried to imitate with deeply unsatisfying results—"Rest easy?" a caller named Georgina had repeated doubtfully. "With my acid reflux?") Dominique was a real-estate agent and she'd helped Charlie find an unlisted apartment; she'd told her to carry her cash around in a sanitary-napkin wrapper where no thief would think to look for it; she'd taught her how to break in new shoes with a hair dryer and a pair of thick socks. And to every overnight shift, Dominique brought homemade red-velvet cupcakes with butter-cream frosting. (There were many, many fine things about Dominique, but the cupcakes might have been the finest.)

That night, though, Dominique had called Charlie to say she had bronchitis and wouldn't be in. Instead a woman of about forty sat at the other desk. She was just the right side of plump, with glossy black hair cut in a pageboy, and a nose so snub it made Charlie want to slide a ruler under it. When she smiled, she showed square white teeth, like children draw. She wore a ruby-red peasant blouse and a denim skirt. In the dingy room, she was as lush as a hibiscus, as opulent as a tropical bird.

"Hello," the woman said. "You must be Charlie561. I'm Barbara383." (She'd been into the numbers thing even back then.)

Charlie's hair was a dull, dirty brown, but since high school she had bleached it a fragile ash blond and worn it in a sleek pixie cut. She was wearing jeans and a thin white tank top with a leather vest over it. Normally her own looks pleased her well enough, but suddenly she felt tall and overly lanky, oddly spiderlike.

"Hello," she said. Her gaze flicked past Barbara to the small table next to the fridge. No cupcakes. She sighed.

Charlie and Barbara said good night to the outgoing shift— Mario699 and Susan302—who told them that a regular named Hilda had called to say she'd watched a documentary about the *Mary Celeste* and it had stirred up her annihilation fears, and she might call back.

Yes, well, those regular callers. Hopeful Place had a lot of them— so many that there was a whole three-ring binder with notes on them called the Regular Book. New volunteers were supposed to read through it and familiarize themselves with the regulars so that they could be handled in a time-efficient manner. Otherwise a volunteer might spend two hours talking to Maureen about her feelings of worthlessness, for instance, only to have Maureen say at the end, "Well, I guess I'll give you a call again next week when my husband is out at his poker game." There was Hank with his disabling insomnia, and Clive, whose emphysema kept him housebound, and Ruth, whose daughter never called, and Abe, with his addiction to lottery tickets, and Florence, with her crippling fear of cockroaches, and Mose, with his ailing basset hound, and Leon, who had paid $6,300 for a used Ford Escort in 1992 and later found it listed in the Blue Book for $5,900 and never got over it.

Some regulars called pretty much every day, as a sort of check-in: "Not too badly, thanks, though they were clean sold out of Grape-Nuts at the supermarket." Some called weekly: "Well, just thought I'd let you know I'm still upright." Sometimes they disappeared for months or even years. Charlie always wondered what happened to the regulars during these hiatuses. Did the regular get more functional, go out into the world, and live life for a while? Or did they get *less* functional and spend time in a mental-health facility where phones were not allowed? Or did they take up with some other, more desirable hotline and only return to Hopeful Place when the new hotline stopped taking their calls? (In nearly all respects, the regulars mirrored Charlie's romantic life up to that point.)

Volunteers were encouraged to work the assessment algorithm with the regulars. It was supposed to go more or less like this: "Are you thinking of suicide?"

"No."

"Have you thought about suicide in the last two months?"

"No."

"Have you ever attempted to kill yourself?"

"No."

"Oh, well, thanks, goodbye." *Click.*

But it didn't really work like that because the regulars had gotten wise to it, and if they felt like talking, they answered yes to one of the questions and that prompted the volunteer to ask, "How often do you think of killing yourself? Do you have a plan? Do you have access to pills or weapons?" And then the regular would say yes to one of *those* questions, which would prompt others, and the call might go on pointlessly for half an hour when, really, all the regular wanted was a little sympathy about how Rite Aid had declined their coupon for shampoo.

The good thing about the overnight shift was that there were no pesky administrators sitting in the next room, listening to the calls, and the volunteers were free to chuck the algorithm out of the window and say, "Oh, hi, Stanley, how's your hypertension?" And similarly the regular could abandon all pretense and say, "When's 495 scheduled to work? I want to tell her about how they over-charged me for coffee at the office." It was tons more satisfying all around.

Mario and Susan left. Charlie sat at her desk with a Diet Coke and a small packet of Cheetos; the overnight shift was all about over-eating. She pulled her *Visual Anatomy & Physiology* textbook out of her backpack and opened it with a small sigh. Barbara took a copy of *Good Housekeeping* from her bag and began flipping through it. Occasionally the phones rang and they took turns answering.

By pretty much any standard, it was a slow shift. A regular named Dolly called to complain about construction on Military Road. A dancer called to say she'd failed an audition. A man called to say he felt suicidal about the Orioles' performance against the Yankees. A regular named Frank called to ask if he could substitute pretzels for graham crackers in a pie crust.

Charlie put her hand over the receiver and consulted Barbara, who said, "I don't see why not." She turned a page in her magazine. "As long as he ups the sugar. Though I wouldn't recommend it if he's making a key lime pie, or any pie in the meringue family."

Charlie recorded every call in the logbook, as did Barbara. The date, the time, the duration of the call, the caller's complaint, any referral given. Charlie always wondered if anyone ever looked back through the log or whether it was a sort of busywork.

Around midnight, Charlie and Barbara decided to order takeout. Charlie said she was really craving chicken fried rice at the same exact moment that Barbara said Chinese food was for those with unsophisticated palates, and then the conversation was sort of like a frog that jumped off a lily pad and disappeared underwater. After a moment, Barbara said Indian food was always a good choice, so they went with that. (They couldn't order separately because they wouldn't meet the ten-dollar delivery minimum.)

The food came, and while they ate, Barbara asked Charlie what she was studying, and Charlie asked Barbara where she'd been on vacation. Then they ate mostly in silence, except for Barbara saying she believed the Indian place had used too much turmeric in the chicken pasanda. Charlie looked at her thoughtfully, recalling the night that she and Dominique were high on chai tea and butter-cream frosting, and Dominique had said that anal sex made her hemorrhoids flare up, and Charlie had said that she'd gotten trichomoniasis from masturbating with a dirty carrot, and Dominique had said, oh, yes, that thing about washing fruits and vegetables didn't apply just to tossed salads. Truly, Barbara couldn't measure up to Dominique in any way.

The shift continued. A woman called to say she'd been evicted and Charlie referred her to a homeless shelter. A regular named Ollie called to complain about the political unrest in the Middle East. A girl called to say she was going to drink a cup of bleach and changed her mind when Charlie told her that wouldn't be fatal. A regular named Fritz called to say that he was ninety-eight percent sure he had mad cow disease. A woman with a gravelly smoker's voice called and claimed to be seven years old. A man called to say he was going out to get an overdose of heroin just as soon as the late-late movie was over. "Well, unless I fall asleep first," he told Charlie. "It may be that I'm just sleep-deprived."

The phones went silent for a while. Charlie ate a Snickers bar and touched up her fingernails with the bottle of bronze-colored polish she kept in her purse. Barbara finished her magazine and started on the *Washington Post* crossword.

A call came in and Charlie took it. A man with a querulous, agitated voice said, "Who's this?"

"Hello, Emory," Charlie said, and sighed. Emory was perhaps her least favorite regular, and that was saying something. He was a fretful, suspicious man in his sixties and his page in the Regular Book dated back over a decade. He lived in a drafty duplex in Brookland with his mother and at first he'd called to complain about barking dogs and construction noise and his mother's hypochondria. His mother had died three years ago (apparently she wasn't faking that coronary artery disease after all) and Emory's calls to Hopeful Place had increased dramatically. Now he was lonely and sad and worried about intruders, and he'd turned all his underpants pink in the wash. His one remaining pleasure in life seemed to be collecting stamps with the money his mother had left him. He liked to quiz the volunteers on stamp trivia, and once he'd called Charlie an idiot for not knowing that Great Britain is the only member of the Universal Postal Union not required to name itself on its postage stamps. (Not like Charlie gave a fuck, but still.) Emory was always threatening to overdose on his dead mother's Seconal.

"Who's this?" he said again.

"You know I can't tell you my name, Emory," Charlie said.

"Well, I know your voice. Tell me your number."

Technically they weren't supposed to give out their numbers, either, but sometimes it was just easier. "My number is 561," Charlie said.

"Oh," Emory said, in the tone of someone who has just tried unfrosted Pop-Tarts for the first time. Apparently he and Charlie felt the same way about each other.

"How are you feeling, Emory?"

"Just terrible."

"Would you like to talk about what's going on?"

"That's why I'm calling, you moron."

Charlie gritted her teeth and forced her voice into a gentler tone, the way she'd stuff a cat into a pet carrier. "Why don't you tell me about it?"

"Tell you about what?" Emory said aggressively.

"Why you're feeling so terrible."

"Okay. You know what eBay is?" He was not asking this politely: his voice was a challenge.

"Yes," Charlie said.

"Well, today I was all set to buy a 1957 Argentina Railways Centenary stamp on eBay for eight dollars," Emory said. "Normally I don't bother with South American stamps but I have a fondness for trains."

"I can see this means a great deal to you," Charlie murmured. It was the sort of all-purpose answer you learned in hotline training.

"And at the very last second," Emory said, his voice rising, "some sneaky bastard jumps in ahead of me and bids eight dollars and one *cent*. And he gets it! Meanwhile, I'd been up all night, making space in my stamp book. And then that lowlife runs off with my possession."

Charlie thought of the vintage crocheted poncho she'd bid for once on eBay and lost to a last-minute bidder. Her sense of loss had been so keen she'd almost felt the poncho's fringe flipping over the ends of her fingers. For the briefest of moments, her heart and Emory's touched, two wires closing the world's smallest circuit.

"I'm so sorry to hear that," she said softly.

"Also, I miss my mother," Emory said.

"I know it's been hard without her," Charlie said.

"How do *you* know? Your mother die?"

"It's hard on anyone when they lose a parent, Emory."

"At first, it wasn't so bad," Emory said, "because she was sending me messages, but now that's stopped."

"Messages from, um"—Charlie paused delicately—"from the afterlife?"

"Do I sound like some fool who believes in the afterlife?" Emory snapped. (He sounded exactly like that but Charlie didn't say so.) "I mean, messages that she left for me before she died. That's what I mean."

"Tell me about the messages, Emory. Please. I really would like to know."

"Well, the first one was about a week after she died," Emory said grudgingly. "Out of nowhere, the mailman delivered this package and I opened it and it's a box of the soap she liked, Camay. Must've been ten bars of Camay in there. And I realized that she ordered that soap, thinking to herself, 'What a comfort this will be to Emory when I'm gone.'"

Charlie seemed to recall that Emory's mother had died some-what unexpectedly, in what was supposed to be a routine hospital visit. It seemed unlikely that she'd been thinking ahead to her own death that very week.

"And she was right," Emory said. "I smelled the Camay and I felt better. And then I kept finding *more* messages. Like one night I wanted a snack and I went to the pantry and there was a package of M&M's. My mother never bought M&M's, not once in her whole lifetime. She preferred cakes and cookies and such to candy. But she must have bought those M&M's, thinking, 'Emory has such a sweet tooth, these will perk him up no end when I'm not here to bake for him.'"

"That sounds very nice—"

"And there were little Tupperware containers in the freezer, labeled CHICKEN A LA KING, ONE SERVING and like that. Now my mother hardly ever saved leftovers—generally she ate whatever food was left on the plates and in the pots and pans as she was doing the dishes. She said that was the cook's privilege and also that it prevented wastefulness. She would never save one serving of anything. But there were five or six meals for one in there. It was like she knew I'd get tired of canned soup and she planned ahead. Other stuff, too, like planting perennials instead of annuals and signing a two-year service agreement with the boiler company."

Charlie cleared her throat softly. "I'm glad she thought to do those things."

"And once I was sorting through some old papers and photos and things," Emory said, "and I found a picture of me as a little boy, maybe two or three. I flipped it over to see if there was anything written on the back, like *Emory, age two* or *Emory, 1940*. But there in my mother's handwriting, it said *Emory, I love you!* It was like my mother knew I'd read it someday and she was speaking directly to me."

Charlie imagined Emory's mother sorting photos more than sixty years ago, of a young woman so moved by a picture of her baby that she recorded her feelings in that moment. "Oh, Emory," she said softly. "Your mother loved you very much."

"But I haven't found a message in at least a year," Emory said. His voice had lost its fretful edge. He sounded humble, confused. "And

I've been thinking, maybe she didn't want me to live so long without her. Maybe she thought I'd have joined her by now."

"Emory," Charlie said firmly. "I think your mother would want you live your life to the fullest."

"You didn't know my mother." Emory's voice was querulous again. "And you have no idea what it's like without her." He hung up.

At four thirty in the morning, sleepiness washed over Charlie, like a giant wave, sucking the oxygen out of her lungs and threatening to slam her to the floor. She looked at Barbara groggily. "I think I need to rest."

"Me, too," Barbara said, yawning.

On overnights, the volunteers were allowed to turn off the phones and sleep for an hour. The idea was that an hour of sleep allowed them to go to work the next day with functional brains. It wasn't enough—it wasn't *nearly* enough—but it helped.

They put the phones on hold—callers would hear a busy signal—and wheeled the two rollaway cots out of the closet. These were beds whose sheets had never, ever been changed so far as Charlie knew, whose pillows were flat and musty smelling, and whose blue blankets were pilled with lint. They were the most welcoming sight in the world.

Barbara went into the bathroom with a small cosmetics bag and a bundle of clothing, but Charlie was the veteran of many spontaneous, alcohol-fueled, sex-related sleepovers. She merely kicked off her jeans and put a drop of Visine into each eye before she lowered herself carefully onto one of the cots—both cots were unsteady on rusted casters and lying down on one was something like trying to mount a skittish horse. Barbara emerged from the bathroom, smelling of Noxzema and wearing a long white nightgown with puffed sleeves. Charlie was almost asleep and could only think wearily that Barbara looked like the kind of prissy guest at a slumber party whom the other girls would want to beat the shit out of.

The hour of sleep slipped by, as it always did, too quickly, and seemingly in just a moment, Barbara was turning off the alarm clock and shuffling back to the bathroom. Charlie pulled on her jeans, folded up the rollaway beds, and slid them back in the closet. She got a Diet Coke out of the fridge and sat at her desk.

Barbara came out of the bathroom, dressed again in her blouse and skirt, ruby-red lipstick applied, hair brushed. Now Charlie understood the value of the whole nightgown routine because Barbara looked fresh as a strawberry daiquiri while Charlie felt like a grimy burlap bag.

"Good morning," Barbara said. "Shall I make coffee?"

"Not for me, thanks," said Charlie, who felt that coffee breath on top of her wrinkled shirt and smudged mascara would push her too far over on the spectrum of personal grubbiness. She glanced at the clock. It was almost six. They had one hour to go.

She punched the hold button on her phone and a call came through at once.

"Hopeful Place," Charlie said, her eyes still bright with sleep.

"Hello, 561."

The skin on Charlie's scalp crinkled and she gasped. She could not have been more spooked if a caller had stepped out of the supply closet. "Who is this?"

"Now *you're* the one asking," said a sourly triumphant voice.

"Emory?" Charlie said doubtfully.

The not-quite-Emory voice snorted. "Just thought you'd want to know, I finally did it."

"Did what?"

"You-all never believed I'd do it."

Charlie was sure it was Emory now, but something was wrong with his voice. "You did what?" she asked again.

"Took my mother's Seconal," Emory said, and suddenly Charlie felt as though her esophagus were filled with sawdust. No air could get in or out. That's why Emory didn't sound like himself; the Seconal had slowed his speech.

Charlie blinked and heard the tiny clicks of her eyelids. "Emory," she said carefully, making sure to speak loudly enough for Barbara to hear, "I believe you. I absolutely believe you. How many Seconal did you take?"

She was aware of movement behind her, then Barbara standing next to her desk, her expression full of urgency. Charlie nodded emphatically. Barbara picked up the phone on the other desk and tapped the button for an outside line.

"Listen to me," Charlie said to Emory. "There's another volunteer here with me and she's going to call you an ambulance. I need you to give me your address."

"I don't want an ambulance," Emory said pettishly. "I want to die."

"I don't think you do," Charlie said, "because you called me. Now let me help you. Emory, what is your address?"

"I told you, I want to die."

"Dying is a big decision," Charlie said. "And I want to talk about it. But first I need your address. Can you give it to me, Emory?"

Silence.

"Emory? Can you give me your address?"

Emory sighed, a long, guttural sigh that sounded as though it started at the soles of his feet. "Seven forty-five Locust Street."

Charlie scratched it on a piece of paper and put it on Barbara's desk. Barbara gave the address to 911 and then reached over to take Charlie's hand. Charlie gripped Barbara's hand gratefully.

"Okay, that was excellent, Emory, really, really good." Charlie tried to think about what came next. "Can you get up and unlock your front door so the EMTs can get in?"

"No," Emory said, sounding strangely matter-of-fact. "I tried a little while ago and I can't stand up."

"Don't worry about that, then," Charlie said. The EMTs could break down the door. "How many pills did you take?"

Emory yawned hugely.

"How many pills?"

"There weren't but twenty in the bottle," Emory said slowly. "I took fifteen . . ."

"Emory?"

"Just to be . . . on the . . . safe side."

The safe side of living or the safe side of dying? Charlie was suddenly terribly sure Emory had gambled and lost. "How long ago did you take them?"

"Don't rightly . . . know," Emory said. His voice was slowing more, distorting, the words twisting unrecognizably.

Charlie met Barbara's eyes and they exchanged a long look, frightened and helpless.

"Emory, I know you're feeling sleepy but I need you to stay awake for me."

A pause and then Emory said, "I . . . can't."

"The ambulance is on the way," she said. "I need you to stay on the line with me, okay?"

Emory didn't say anything.

"Emory?" Charlie asked. "Just stay with me, all right? You stay on the line with me until the EMTs get there. One of them will take the phone from you and speak to me."

That was how it was supposed to work, at least in theory.

"Mmmm," Emory said.

"I know you're getting sleepy," Charlie said again, "but I need you to stay with me here."

"Here?" Emory asked thickly. "Where?"

"Where you are," Charlie said firmly. "Just stay right where you are, but don't hang up. I'm there with you, Emory. Do you understand? I'm not going to leave you. You and me, we're waiting together."

Silence. Then Emory said something that might have been "No."

"Emory," Charlie said. Then more sharply, "Emory!"

Charlie looked at Barbara. "Go to him," Barbara whispered urgently. "Go to him with your voice."

Charlie's voice leapt from her as though it had been awaiting Barbara's odd command. Her voice was no longer in her throat, it was a missile speeding madly down the line, trying to reach Emory. Her voice was spinning through tunnels, flashing through wires, until suddenly Charlie was in a room she'd never seen before—sitting in an armchair with an orange floral design and she could see her legs in gray corduroys and her chest in a faded plaid shirt. She felt a hand holding a phone receiver to her ear—to Emory's ear! She had found him, she was with him, she could hear his breath.

"Emory!" she cried. "Stay with me!"

But Emory said nothing more.

It took the EMTs eleven minutes to get to Emory's house. They were the longest eleven minutes of Charlie's life, of anybody's life. They had to be.

She kept the receiver pressed to her ear the whole time, but she couldn't feel it or anything else. Her essence, her *self,* had flown to Emory and remained there, leaving behind a phantom girl—a nebulous, pixelated, slowly dissolving husk. Only Barbara's strong, warm hand in hers kept her anchored in the chair until the unstable feeling faded and Charlie slowly grew whole again.

TOWARD THE END OF LUNCH, Charlie finds an inch-long bone in her salmon burger. Substandard cooking preparation or murder plot? Impossible to say. Charlie uses her thumb and finger to remove the bone from her mouth and sets it on the edge of her plate—the edge facing Barbara.

Forrest knocks over his iced-tea glass, making an amber puddle on the table. He tries to mop it up with his napkin but that just causes a stream of liquid to run between the leaves of the table and spatter on the floor.

"Stop it," Barbara snaps. "You're dribbling all over!"

That's what she said, Charlie thinks. (And according to Forrest that is *exactly* what Barbara said, or at least the kind of thing she used to say.) She decides this would be a good time to go back outside. Better physical suffering than emotional torture. "I'll keep packing," she says, pushing back her chair.

She walks into the coat closet and shrugs into the down parka, which is still chilly to the touch. She pulls on her hat and the deer-skin gloves. She picks up a box from the pile and opens the back door.

Outside, the cold bites right through the parka like an actual animal, teeth tearing at Charlie's vitals. She gasps and steels herself to keep moving, squinting against the afternoon sunshine as it bounces off the U-Haul van in sharp, dazzling points, reminding her suddenly of how G Street looked on the day Emory died.

Charlie's memory of that morning is patchy. She remembers an EMT picking up the phone and telling her how sorry he was. She remembers Barbara crying softly into a paper towel from the roll on top of the microwave. She remembers leaving the call center and how the world—even G Street, with its chain-link fences and broken sidewalks and garish storefronts—looked clean and washed of color. She remembers stopping to buy a jelly doughnut on her way to the Metro, how sweet the doughnut tasted, how the sweetness lasted much longer than the doughnut; all day, in fact.

Charlie tucks her chin down from the wind. Her shoulders ache from being tensed against the cold. She will never be warm again, never. She's sure of that.

Zap. Zap. Zap-zap. After an hour, the pile of boxes is noticeably smaller and then suddenly it is almost gone. Only five remain, plus whatever Forrest and Barbara are packing now.

She picks up one of the last cartons and walks through the house to the dining room. Barbara and Forrest are bubble-wrapping a series of cups and saucers. Charlie, pausing in the doorway, sees that the little gold-embossed footed teacups are all the same soft lemony color, but each is decorated with a different floral pattern.

Barbara sees her looking and says, "Forrest gave me these cups and saucers on our wedding anniversaries."

Forrest looks up thoughtfully. "Could be."

"I didn't know then that each anniversary has a flower," Barbara says to Charlie. "But Forrest did, and every year, he gave me a different antique cup and saucer with that year's flower." She touches one teacup lightly with a finger. "I'd always thought by this point I would have thirty-five teacups. Sometimes I wondered where I would put them all. I was sure we'd get to nasturtium or even rose on our fiftieth." Her eyes are not visible behind the dark glasses, but her mouth has taken on a pouty look. She turns her head toward Forrest and says dryly, "I guess that wasn't your plan, though."

"At least you're not bitter about it," Forrest says cheerfully, and suddenly Charlie's love for him is like a ripe melon in her hands, that sweet, that full.

Charlie smiles at him. "Almost finished," she says. "I'll be back for that box in ten minutes."

She carries the last four boxes out in a double handful, daring Fate to make her slip on the porch stairs. She retrieves the box of teacups from the dining room and carries it out the front door. She slides it into the U-Haul trailer and grabs the handle. The icy feel of the metal sinks right through her glove. It's as though she and the trailer are going to be cold-forged into some sort of deformed centaur. She swings the trailer door shut, yanks her hand free and stumbles up the back porch steps one last time. She bursts into the house, slamming the door behind her.

In the coat closet, she hangs up the down parka and changes back into her suede jacket. She walks to the dining room. Barbara and Forrest have put away the packing supplies and Barbara is using a sponge to sweep all the bits of paper and torn bubble wrap into a wastebasket. In a moment, the table is restored to gleaming emptiness except for Barbara's water glass.

"All set?" Charlie says to Forrest—unnecessarily, since he's standing there in his coat with his cane in his hand.

"Just a moment," Barbara says. She starts rooting around in her purse and, for a long happy moment, Charlie is sure Barbara is going to get out some cash and tip her. How wonderful, finally, for everyone to acknowledge that a transaction has taken place here! But Barbara is only getting another migraine pill. She pops it into her mouth and takes a sip of water.

How bad is her headache? Will she lie down for the rest of the night after they leave? Or does she have plans? Maybe as soon as they leave, Barbara will take a quick nap and then meet friends for dinner, where she'll talk about how her ex-husband and his slut wife helped her move. But if she had friends, wouldn't they be the ones helping with the move? More likely Barbara will eat a solitary supper tonight, here, in the dining room. Charlie can almost hear the click and scrape of a single fork, a lone knife. It must be the loudest sound in the world.

Barbara follows them to the door and out onto the porch. "Thank you both so much," she says.

"Good luck tomorrow," Forrest says as he grips the porch railing and begins navigating his way down the steps.

"Good night, Forrest," Barbara calls. "Good night, 561."

From the bottom of the steps, Charlie gives Barbara a big smile, but she doesn't wave: if she took her hands out of her pockets, Barbara would realize that she is still wearing those nice fur-lined gloves. Who cares if they don't fit very well? Payback is endless, endless. Karma is not a bitch, Charlie thinks—it's more like an eternal unwelcome gift exchange.

She trots along the flagstone path in front of Forrest and opens the passenger door for him. He drops awkwardly onto the seat and she scurries around to the driver's side. She gets in and switches the heat on full blast, aiming all the vents directly on her. She supposes

Forrest would like some heat on his side of the car also, but she is too cold and preoccupied to worry about that too much.

"Shut the door," she says impatiently to him.

She's thinking that they're going to have pizza and beer for dinner—Charlie will show Forrest how *civilized* people live. (She has forgotten momentarily that she and Forrest are married, that they already agree on pizza and beer and the importance of democracy and art and education and heated floor tiles and all that.)

Barbara is no longer on the porch. She's gone inside, because guess what? *It's fucking freezing out here.* Forrest shuts his door. Glancing over, Charlie sees that he's gazing at the house, his eyebrows drawn together. Until this moment, Charlie has not realized that this day might be sad for Forrest, in some way.

She doesn't want to pull away from the curb, tires screeching happily, while Forrest is having some sort of emotional reckoning. So they sit there, the engine idling.

"Well, that's done," Forrest says at last.

Charlie is so startled that she accidentally presses the gas pedal and the engine gives a little upset roar—it sounds like a giant has stepped on his cat's tail. She had not realized until now that they are, actually, done—or Charlie is, anyway.

She sits there with the keys swinging in the ignition, her eyes wide with wonder. Of course Charlie knows—everyone knows—that the top three most stressful life events are death, divorce, and relocation. But suddenly she realizes that she and Barbara had gone through a death and divorce together and, as of today, also a relocation. They didn't do these things as friends or family, and they certainly didn't do them together by choice, but they did them.

And now it's done, as Forrest says. Charlie and Barbara don't have to do anything else together because there isn't anything left for them to do.

# Pandemic Behavior

ON THE SIXTY-THIRD DAY OF THE PANDEMIC, I ZOOMED WITH MY
neurologist, Dr. Ventura. He was a bearded man in his early fifties
who wore wire-rimmed glasses. He looked like an older, plumper
Steve Jobs. I was at home in Gainesville, but he was obviously in the
sunroom of a beach house—in the background, palm trees were
waving their leaves wildly, making him look like a news correspon-
dent reporting on a hurricane.

"What can I do for you, Daphne?" he asked.

"I'm getting a lot of migraines," I said. "More than usual."

"How many in the last month?"

"Twelve. And they last all day." When I woke up with one, no
amount of migraine meds could banish it. I stayed in bed and the
migraine had its way with me until it decided to move on.

Dr. Ventura frowned. "That *is* a big increase for you. Has anything changed recently?"

"Well, yes," I said, "there's a pandemic and civil unrest and murder hornets."

"I meant in terms of your personal habits," Dr. Ventura said. "Are
you sleeping well? How is your diet? What about exercise?"

I didn't want to tell him that since being on lockdown, I couldn't
write and ate cereal all the time, so I gave him a fanciful description of some other girl's life, someone who ate healthily and slept

regularly. I almost told him that I went to the gym every day until I remembered that gyms were no more.

"Hmmmm," Dr. Ventura said. "Let me think about it and I'll get back to you later today."

℮ﾟ

I HAD TWO JOBS before lockdown, the bookstore and the Professor. Maybe three jobs if you counted writing my novel. I worked the morning shift in a bookstore called Your Books or Mine? I spent most of my time there processing returns for self-help books and trying to convince the owner to change the store name. They let me go when lockdown started.

I also worked part-time helping Professor Rossignol write his book. The Professor was in his late eighties and he was retired now, but he'd had a long and illustrious career in citrus grove management. He and his wife, Esther, lived in a Spanish-style bungalow near me and I went there three afternoons a week. Esther always answered the door and ushered me to the Professor's study, saying, "The Professor is ready to see you." I never heard her call him by his first name.

The Professor's book was going to be a profound (his word) mixture of memoir and textbook. I don't know whether it was profound or not because every time we sat down to work on it, the Professor would say, "Now don't rush me! Esther always rushes me."

And so I would sit patiently, pen poised, while he cleared his throat and said "Ahhhh," as though he were about to start dictating at any second. But he never did. Usually after a few minutes of throat clearing, he gave up and told me something unrelated to citrus groves.

He was an odd combination of optimist and science zealot. He had complete faith in the scientific method and felt that all failures—his own included—were the result of not properly applying it. He told me that he'd tried to make fudge for Esther for their sugar anniversary and had failed to use a double boiler to melt the chocolate, and they had to throw out the pan with the wooden spoon still stuck in it. "And I called myself a scientist!" he said. "You'd think I'd never heard of thermodynamics!"

His speech was full of exclamation points, but they were proclamatory rather than excited—imagine Cicero if he'd lived in Florida instead of Rome and wasn't so interested in politics.

The Professor was certain that science would cure my migraines soon. "The brain is really just a series of electrochemical reactions," he said. "Nothing so mysterious about it! Some chemist is probably discovering the cure even as we speak!"

Often he asked about my novel and then immediately apologized and said, "Ahhhh, forgive me for asking! You're an artist and no artist should be interrogated about their art. I'm sure it will be a masterpiece and I don't use that word lightly."

I liked him a lot for that. In college, they told us that people who ask you what your novel is about really want to know how it will make them feel and that you should say "thrilling" or "heartwarming." But in my experience, people who ask you what your novel is about really want you to say something like "It's about a young woman experiencing independence for the first time," so they can say, "Hasn't that been done to death?" (It was actually only one person who'd said that to me—a man I sat next to on a flight home to see my parents—but I felt he spoke for everyone.)

Working for the Professor wasn't a hard way to earn eighteen dollars an hour. The only hard part was that Esther hovered hopefully just outside the Professor's study and I would have to pretend to be talking on my phone when I left so she wouldn't ask me how the book was going.

There was no way I could continue working for the Professor during the pandemic. He was in a total of eight high-risk groups for COVID and Esther was in the two that he wasn't. "Don't you worry," the Professor told me on the phone. "Science will lead us through this disaster! But meanwhile, you stay safe at home. Don't even think about coming in to work."

"No," I said. "I'd feel terrible if I gave it to you."

"Ahhhhh, but you need your income," the Professor said. "I'll send you a check every week. You use this time to work on your novel."

I felt guilty about the Professor sending me a check every week for doing nothing at my house but in the end I decided it wasn't that different from him paying me to do nothing at his house.

MY ROOMMATE'S NAME was Lohania. She had long wavy black hair and the irises of her eyes were so dark you couldn't see the pupils. She was a cosmetics buyer for Macy's and she sold Havergenix cosmetics on the side, even though that was prohibited in her contract. Once lockdown started, she worked from home, and most of the time she wore a silky lavender-colored robe belted with a tasseled curtain tieback cord that looped around her waist twice. She kept her Bluetooth earpiece in constantly during business hours and apparently someone was talking to her the whole time because whenever she spoke to me, she tapped the earpiece to mute herself and then tapped it to unmute herself afterward. At five o'clock every night, she took the earpiece out and threw it on the kitchen table with a soft squeal of relief. She ate one meal a day, at lunchtime—ham-and-cheese roll-ups drizzled with honey. Otherwise, she drank can after can of Diet Coke in the morning, and then about midafternoon she switched to mango margaritas, and the margaritas saw her out. She said this was pandemic behavior, but the only kitchen equipment she brought with her when she moved in was her blender and her alternate blender so it might have been more deep-rooted than that.

We had met on CribSplit when I advertised for a roommate after my previous roommate moved out. I chose Lohania because she was literally the only person who said she didn't like sunsets on the beach. (It turned out she's allergic to sand fleas.)

When I told her I got migraines, she looked thoughtful and said, "That sucks for you."

"Yes," I said. "It does." It did. Lohania had cut to the heart of it.

Lohania and I were of one mind about COVID and that mind was filled with fear and uncertainty. We were among the first people to start hoarding toilet paper and hand sanitizer—and it was a challenge because we had almost no storage space in our tiny house. Huge stacks of toilet paper packages accumulated on tables and chairs and countertops and in corners until it looked like we were living in the ruins of an exploded toilet paper factory. Lohania used masking tape to stick dozens of packages together into furniture shapes—chairs, loveseats, a coffee table—and draped blankets over them. (Then it looked like we had tried to spiff up the ruins of an exploded toilet paper factory.)

We turned our cars into autoclaves, and anything we wanted to sterilize—clothing, handbags, shoes, Amazon packages, CVS purchases—we stuffed into garbage bags and then put in our cars for two days. We did that until a can of hairspray exploded in Lohania's car and Lohania said her car smelled like she'd just driven a bunch of old ladies to morning mass. We switched over to sanitizing stuff in the freezer, but that was hard because we didn't have a lot of freezer space due to Lohania's bags of frozen mangoes, and it was kind of disturbing and serial-killerish to be storing shoes and handbags in the freezer anyway.

Lohania hooked us up with an early supply of KN95 respirator masks through a friend who was a nail technician but we never used the masks because we never went anywhere. Even before official lockdown, we stopped going to places that would deliver their products, like the supermarket, the pharmacy, and the liquor store. Then we stopped going to places that *didn't* deliver their products, like the coffee shop and the nail salon and the bar. Then we stopped going places that didn't even *have* products, like the park and the beach and the walking trail. The result was that we didn't even go outside except to take out the garbage once a week. (Lohania did this, wearing a white lab coat she'd gotten from a skin-care convention and plastic gloves.)

For a while, we rinsed our nasal passages nightly with a saline spray but then Lohania worried that we were actually forcing germs up *toward* our brains instead of flushing them out and we stopped. We put eucalyptus oil in multiple air diffusers and kept them going around the clock, but the smell gave me even more migraines than usual and caused our asparagus fern to wilt, so we stopped that, too. We swallowed vitamin C to boost our immune systems and watched live video streams of puppies sleeping to boost our serenity and listened to Marconi Union to boost our mental well-being and slept under weighted blankets to boost our tranquility. None of it helped much. We also had Lohania's mother's prayer group pray for us to stay healthy, but Lohania told me that the prayer group had prayed for her to get a job right after college and all she got was a *part-time* job, so either not everyone in the group was praying when they said they were praying or you just couldn't put faith in these things.

We didn't know each other very well. Lohania had moved in two weeks before lockdown began and it was sort of like on *The Walking Dead* when Andrea and Michonne get stranded in the woods together as strangers and have to depend on each other for survival.

I say *sort of like that* but really it was just like that.

DR. VENTURA HAVING TO THINK about how to treat me was disturbing on a number of levels. First, *why* did he have to think about it? Wasn't this pretty much what he did all day and had done for decades? Second, it turned out we had to Zoom again, and I had to pay another forty-dollar co-pay. Third, it meant I had to take off my pajama top and put on a real shirt for the second time that day.

"I'm going to start you on an injection," Dr. Ventura said. The trees were still tossing wildly behind him. "You give it to yourself at home."

"I don't think I can give myself a shot."

"Have your boyfriend do it," Dr. Ventura said.

"I don't have a boyfriend," I said thoughtfully. "But I do have a roommate."

SOME PEOPLE SAY THAT migraines feel like bad hangovers and some people say that migraines feel like headaches that pulse and some people say that migraines feel like stomach flu in your head. But what migraines really feel like is being tied to a railroad track while the world's longest, loudest freight train thunders over you.

It starts with a bright light in the corner of your vision—very bright like someone is standing beside you and shining a flashlight in your eye. But you can't bat the light away, can't turn your head from it. Then you hear the train's shrill whistle, the dull angry clank of the bell, the roar of its engine. By then you're tied to the train track (hopefully the track is your bed and not a bus stop bench or a restaurant table) and you can only try to flatten yourself as the train rushes toward you, its light flashing and horn blaring. Finally you feel the hot breath of its arrival, feel the smoky burning exhaust fill your lungs. And then it's thundering over you.

Of course, the train—the noise and the light and the fumes—is all in your head. But that's the problem: *it's all in your head.* You can't escape it. You can only lie on the track, waiting for the roaring, shrieking, light-splintering pain to pass. And remember: this is the world's longest train. You'll be here for hours, in this exact position, in this much pain. Lifting your head (even if you were capable of that, which you're not) would result in instant decapitation. But decapitation would at least stop the pain, and sometimes you wish for it.

I ASKED LOHANIA if she'd be willing to inject me and she said, "God, no, what if I kill you with an air bubble?"

"It's not that kind of shot," I said. "It just goes into the skin somewhere."

Lohania shrugged. "Oh, well, sure."

I'd found a video online about how to administer the injection and said we should watch it together.

"Okay," Lohania said. "Just let me make a margarita first. You want one?"

"Tequila gives me migraines," I told her for the billionth time.

"Oh, that's right, you and your headaches," she said, as though we hadn't been discussing my headaches two seconds ago.

The YouTube video was of a mousy woman who looked like she would be easily bullied by small children. She explained how important it was not to drop the injector, which made me nervous because Lohania's hands shake a lot in the morning from hangovers, and a lot in the afternoon from caffeine, and a lot in the evening from alcohol. The woman in the video injected herself in the thigh to show how easy it was.

When it was over, Lohania asked if we could watch it again. She said she hadn't heard a word that the mousy woman had said because she looked so uncannily like her aunt, the one who crocheted compulsively and was addicted to Hot Pockets.

DR. VENTURA CALLED the prescription in to the pharmacy but the pharmacy said they couldn't fill it unless my insurance approved it and my insurance said they wouldn't.

I called Dr. Ventura's office and left a message and Dr. Ventura sent me another Zoom invitation.

"The thing is," I said when we were finally face-to-face, or whatever you are on Zoom, "my insurance won't cover it."

Dr. Ventura leaned back in his chair and put his hands behind his head. He talked about how the American health-care system is broken and how the high cost of insurance leads to larger numbers of uninsured people and *that* leads to more health problems all around and also Big Pharma and their history of fraud and scandals and how it's the second-most-hated industry in America (right behind tobacco) and how their single-minded pursuit of profit basically left America wide open to something like COVID-19.

When he wound down, I said again, "The thing is, my insurance won't cover it."

He looked thoughtful. "I'll have the office send you a coupon."

DR. VENTURA OFTEN PROMISED that his office would do certain things but I knew from back before COVID (when we still went places) that "the office" was in reality one fierce, overworked, frizzy-haired woman and she didn't always do what Dr. Ventura said she would. Sometimes she said, "I have no idea why he would say that. Literally no idea."

But whatever he said to her worked this time—the pharmacy sent me a text saying the shot would be delivered that day.

I HAD PLANNED TO HAVE Lohania inject me during the brief, magical, crossover time when caffeine had sharpened her brain and alcohol had soothed her nerves, but the pharmacy didn't deliver the shot until that evening. By then Lohania had already filled and emptied the blender once.

"Is now a, um, good time for you to give me my injection?" I asked.

"No problem," she said. She was wearing her hair loose, a cloud of tiny curls.

"By *good* I actually meant *sober.*"

"Girl, relax. Is that the shot right there?"

I sighed and handed it over. "Remember, don't drop it."

"Shouldn't I inject this into your neck so it gets to your brain faster?" Lohania asked.

Yes, I was allowing this person to empty the contents of a syringe into my system.

"I think arm is fine," I said.

Lohania got the intense, slightly cross-eyed look she got when she was trying to scrape the last bit of margarita out of the blender. She held the injector in her fist and cocked her arm back as though she intended to inject me by javelin throw. Then swung her fist forward and plunged the injector into my arm. Nothing happened.

"You have to press the button on the end." I said.

"Oh, yeah, I forgot." Lohania pressed it. We heard a loud click and I felt the hot sting of the needle.

We were supposed to put the used injector in an official sharps container and not just throw it in the trash where it would later impale an innocent sanitation worker, but we didn't have a sharps container. Lohania wiped the injector for fingerprints and put it in our neighbor's trash can. She said that way the impaled sanitation worker would blame our neighbors and not us. Well, unless the sanitation department took it to the next level and did a DNA analysis, in which case, we'd probably both go to jail.

DR. VENTURA SENT ME a Zoom invitation the following day and I was certain that the injections had been found to be fatal in women under twenty-five and that I had only hours to live, but when he appeared on the screen, he said, "I just wanted to see how you're tolerating it."

I frowned. "Better than I'm tolerating my roommate."

In a rush of gratitude to Lohania for injecting me, I'd agreed to appear in a Havergenix makeover live video and she'd introduced me to everyone (although I don't know exactly how many people were watching) by saying, "This is my roommate, Daphne, and she's here without makeup, which in her case means without eyebrows."

"I forgot you had a roommate," Dr. Ventura said. "Tell me about her."

He had never asked me such a personal question before. I thought about describing Lohania. About how she left a chocolate mint on her own pillow every day when she made her bed so she could pretend she lived in a hotel. About how once she'd glared at her phone and said *"Que te folle un pez!"* in such a scornful voice that I, who spoke no Spanish, could tell she'd said, *"I hope you get fucked by a fish."* About how when she walked from the shower to her bedroom, her wet footprints were C shaped because of her extremely high arches.

Instead I said, "I can't afford all these co-pays."

Dr. Ventura nodded. "We'll find another way."

THE NEXT MORNING, Lohania and I were in the kitchen, wiping down our delivered groceries—frozen mangoes and Diet Coke for her, milk and cereal for me—with sanitizing wipes.

"This sanitizing shit is killing my nails," Lohania said. "Next pandemic, count me out."

"Do you think this does any good at all?" I asked. "Because I've been reading that it doesn't."

"Could be that it does and they just don't know it yet," Lohania said. "Like penicillin and mold. We just have to keep at it."

"Penicillin and mold?"

Lohania said something, but I didn't hear what because a light flickered in the corner of my eye then and I heard the earsplitting whistle of the train.

THE PROFESSOR CALLED ME. "Ahhhh," he said when I answered.

"Hello, Professor."

"Hello, Daphne," he said. "You haven't cashed your last two checks."

"I don't feel right having you pay me for nothing."

"Nonsense!" he said. "We need to look out for each other! It's like the great freeze in eighty-nine where we lost so many orange trees. I said then that the solution would be to plant a record number of trees in the spring. Science looks forward! You work on your novel and I'll consider it an investment in the future."

"I still don't feel right about it."

"I'm sending you a check right now and I want you to cash it."

I sighed. "Thank you, Professor."

"You're not alone, are you?" he asked. "No one should be alone during such a terrible time."

"No," I said. "I have a roommate, Lohania."

"Ahhhh, *Lohania,*" the Professor said in an appreciative voice. "The Celtic *eu* for 'good' and *lou* for 'light.' 'Good light.' A beautiful name! And your own name, Daphne! Greek for 'laurel' and Hebrew for 'victory.' Just stunning! In my youth, all the girls were named Betty or Doris and to tell you the truth, it detracted some from the glamour and beauty of early love. Don't tell Esther I said that, obviously."

DR. VENTURA AND I began talking every night about seven. We didn't discuss it or confirm it. He just sent me a Zoom invitation every afternoon, and I logged in every evening and he asked me about my migraines. He was always drinking something in a tall tumbler—something he said was iced tea but that was probably bourbon. Sometimes we talked about other stuff, about the Australian brush fires and the impeachment and how one lesson COVID had taught us was that all toilet paper is not created equal.

Lohania said my talking to Dr. Ventura was like her getting a bikini wax.

"It's a way of measuring time." Lohania looked at me, her eyes like dark pansies. "Like in the olden days, when I got my bikini line waxed, I'd think, well, another two weeks has gone by and I'm that much closer to a promotion or a raise or a vacation. Dr. Ventura is like that for you—every night you realize we've survived another day in this pandemic hellscape." (She pronounced it "hell-shape"; we were many margaritas into the evening.)

"Just to be clear," I said. "By 'olden days,' you mean like four months ago?"

"Yes." Lohania sighed sadly. "I don't think we'll ever go back to that. We'll say to our children, 'You won't believe this but in my day, we had that thing *waxed*. We paid someone to get down there without a mask on and pour germ-ridden wax around and then rip the hair off with cloth strips.'"

"Lohania, that's a little pessimistic—"

"And then we'll say, 'What's more, we cleared that area so other people could get down there with their germ-ridden *mouths*,'" Lohania continued. "We'll say, 'Pre-COVID, it was all that.'"

LOHANIA HOSTED ANOTHER Havergenix makeover live video and accidentally invited one of her coworkers from Macy's and now the coworker was extorting Lohania for Havergenix night cream. It was pretty much the most exciting thing to happen to us since lockdown.

"Serves me right for staying up late surfing the web for toilet paper," Lohania said. "If I got more sleep, I'd never have messed up like that."

"Maybe you, um, shouldn't go online after so many margaritas?" I said.

"No, it's the pandemic," she said. "It's sapping our intelligence. When this shit is over, they're gonna find out everyone's brains have shrunk."

*eᔆ*

A MIGRAINE WOKE ME UP the next morning—the scream of its engine, the blinding strobe of its lights. I ducked my head as the bed shook, squeezed my eyes tight against impact. It was impossible to believe that I alone heard the frenzied sound of the pistons dumping steam, saw the glaring beams, coughed the black smoke. Then the train pounced on me with a furious sort of glee. I felt sure that my head could not take this—hours of this—without imploding. I would wake up with dents in my head, like the dimples on a partially deflated beach ball.

It finally passed at five that afternoon, and I ran my fingers tentatively over my scalp. No dents or impressions but my head still seemed unprotected, vulnerable. The sound of Lohania's blender running in the kitchen felt like the blades were cutting into the soft gray meat of my brain.

*eᔆ*

THE NEXT TIME I talked to Dr. Ventura, all I could think about was bikini waxes. I thought I might rather be having one than listening to Dr. Ventura talk about his diverticulitis.

"I haven't had a serious flare-up in years," he said. "But in college and med school, I had about twenty attacks per month."

"That's awful," I said. "I can't believe you made it through."

"I tended to get them in the late afternoons," Dr. Ventura said. He refilled his "iced tea" from an unseen bottle below his desktop. "And usually classes were in the morning."

"Are you sure you got all of it?" I asked.

"All of what?"

"All of med school. All of what they were teaching you."

"Oh, yes," Dr. Ventura said. "Mostly."

❧

ESTHER CALLED ME to tell me that Professor Rossignol had COVID and was in the hospital but not on a ventilator. She sounded calm, as though she were saying the Professor had gone to take a nap after a long day.

"I'm so sorry to hear that," I said. "I mean, I'm sorry about the hospital but glad he's not on a ventilator."

"He got COVID from a pecan pie," Esther said.

"I didn't know you could get it from food."

"It was a pecan pie baked by our neighbor," Esther said. "She left it on our stoop covered with tinfoil and I told the Professor not to touch it. I said, 'I know the pie itself has been baked in an oven but we don't know who-all handled it afterward or what their hand-washing habits are like. For all we know, it's crawling with death.' But he wouldn't listen. He said, 'We have to live our lives, just a little bit,' and now he's in the hospital."

"Please give him my best," I said. "Please tell him he's in my prayers."

"We're atheists, dear, the both of us," Esther said. "But I'll tell him."

❧

LOHANIA SAID THAT Dr. Ventura was in love with me, or else why all the Zooms?

"I don't think so," I said. "We never talk about anything but migraines and current events."

Lohania shook her head and her sheaves of hair made a slight rasping sound against her robe. She was painting over all the little shaving cuts on her legs with liquid bandage in case COVID was like necrotizing fasciitis. (We'd watched a documentary about rare diseases. In retrospect, that was probably a mistake.)

"He's legit in love with you," she said. "Any day now he'll tell you his wife doesn't understand him."

⌒

"MY WIFE ISN'T A DOCTOR," Dr. Ventura said in our very next Zoom. "So she doesn't understand what it's like."

After that he talked about his wife quite a bit. About how time-consuming her job as a software developer was. About how she screened his mother's calls, but if *her* mother called, she picked up before the second ring. About her new obsession with Impossible burgers and heart-healthy eating in general. About how she wanted to have a pool built in their backyard, when—hello!—home insurance rates in Florida are already higher than other states. ("*Twenty percent* higher," Dr. Ventura added darkly. "You should thank your lucky stars you're renting.") About how she would only give him blow jobs on his birthday and certain other nonreligious holidays.

He didn't really say that last part but Lohania said it was implied.

⌒

LOHANIA'S COWORKER UPPED her blackmail demands and now wanted free Havergenix brightening serum, too.

"It's our most expensive item," Lohania said to me. "This has gone beyond blackmail now. It's terrorism."

"Are you going to report her to the police?" I asked.

"No, I'm going to give her the serum," Lohania said, picking at her nail polish. "She should know I have my limits, is all I'm saying."

⌒

I HAD A MIGRAINE the next day so Lohania Zoomed with Dr. Ventura in my place for the dual purpose of seeing what he looked like and sounding him out for an Adderall prescription. She reported back that he was unreceptive to the Adderall but he did buy some Havergenix vitamin E cream for his wife, which helped Lohania meet her monthly quota.

I asked if she thought he was attractive and she said that some people look like Steve Jobs and it's a good thing, and then there was Dr. Ventura.

LOHANIA AND I STARTED watching postapocalyptic plague movies, one after the other: *I Am Legend, The Girl with All the Gifts, 28 Days Later, Cargo, Outbreak, Contagion, It Comes at Night*. I told Lohania that I thought we were watching them in an attempt to put a controlled narrative on our current situation. Lohania said we watched them to reassure ourselves that other people had it worse, that we couldn't go out for drinks but at least we didn't have to learn to use a crossbow.

Either way, I realized that I only liked the first halves of the movies—the initial infections, the breakdown of civilization, the inevitable slide into a new and brutal society. The endings, where the survivors left their makeshift shelters and set about the work of rebuilding the world, of reestablishing humankind, only made me feel tired.

THREE DAYS WENT BY without a migraine. Four. Five. Six.

"Stop talking," I said to Lohania.

She hit the mute button on her earpiece. "Why?"

"Because I can't *hear*." I was listening for the train.

THE NEXT NIGHT, Dr. Ventura told me that his receptionist had asked for a raise.

"I don't want to give in," he said, "but I probably will."

"Maybe you should get a new receptionist," I said. "The current one is not super friendly."

"I like that about her," Dr. Ventura said. "It keeps the riffraff out."

I paused for a second. "By 'riffraff,' you mean people with migraines?"

"I wouldn't phrase it quite like that."

"You just phrased it *exactly* like that."

"Well, some patients can be very . . . demanding."

I thought about migraines, about freight trains, about how I couldn't trust my own brain not to turn on me, about the whole days of my life that I spent in bed, about how sometimes I thought migraines would kill me because no one could have so much pain and live.

Dr. Ventura took a sip of certainly-bourbon. "Let's talk about something else. How's your novel going?"

"It's going."

"What's it about? You've never said."

I crossed my arms. "A girl who gets migraines."

"I hope—ha ha—that I'm not in it." Dr. Ventura smiled through his beard.

"There's a doctor in it."

"A neurologist?"

"Yes, of course. Because of the girl's very bad migraines. He doesn't help her, though."

He stopped smiling. "No?"

"No, not very much. He exploits her. He exploits this girl in tremendous pain," I said. "He's that kind of person."

ESTHER CALLED ME AGAIN the next afternoon. "I'm very sorry to tell you this, Daphne, but Professor Rossignol passed away this afternoon."

"Oh, Esther," I said. "I don't know what to say."

"He ended up on a ventilator after all," Esther continued in a matter-of-fact voice. "And from there on, it was very quick. At least, they tell me it was quick. I couldn't be there with him."

Something crawled down my cheek, and I touched a finger to my face. It was a tear.

"Turns out he didn't get COVID from the pecan pie," Esther said. "He got it from the electrician when he came to fix our circuit breaker. The electrician called me two days ago to tell me he tested positive." She sighed. "I'm going to miss him so. The Professor, I mean. Not the electrician."

I cleared my throat and tried to keep my voice from wobbling. "I hope the journey to his next place was swift and easy."

"I don't believe in the afterlife, and neither did the Professor," Esther said. "Though maybe we're wrong. Maybe I'll get there and the Professor will greet me and say, 'Esther, we were completely mistaken about this. I've got a nice little duplex set up for us, and your sister and her husband are right next door because it turns out that your sister doesn't annoy me here in the spirit world.'"

She sighed again. "I don't believe that, though."

I WENT STRAIGHT TO the kitchen to find Lohania. "We have to go out," I said. "Now that things are reopening."

Lohania was adding tequila to the mango-filled blender. "Oh, right," she said. "Let's drive to the beach and run around with a bunch of unmasked idiots." She had just taken a shower and her lavender robe clung to her body in wet spots. Her hair was wrapped in a towel except for one lock which curled on her forehead like the winding-road arrow on a traffic sign.

"We have to," I said urgently. "I've lost so many days to migraines and so many to lockdown. I can't lose any more. We won't go to the beach but we need to go outside."

She looked unconvinced.

"Lohania," I said. "We have to live our lives, just a little bit."

She bit her lower lip and then shrugged. "Okay. I have some orders we can drop in the UPS box on the corner. But first let me drink this." And she added an extra shot of tequila to the blender.

TWENTY MINUTES LATER, Lohania and I stepped outside onto the front porch and surveyed the night. The oak in the front yard looked like the trees that children draw, with thick stubby branches criss-crossing one another and fluffy leaves turned aqua colored by the approaching gloom. Crickets scratched at the air with a sound like maracas, and the frangipani smell was intoxicating. I felt a jolt of wonder: nature still existed! But of course it did. It had never stopped.

I thought of Dr. Ventura, who had sent me a Zoom link, same as always, and who would be logging onto Zoom right now, waiting for me, like a ham radio operator searching frequencies for a lost ship. I thought of Professor Rossignol, who roamed all frequencies at will now, who soared out over the ocean, who chased the sun over the horizon until he caught up with the golden daylight. Or maybe he didn't.

The lights of the shops up the street didn't seem welcoming—they seemed menacing, just like the deserted-except-for-zombies towns in an apocalypse movie. I felt suddenly tired. I didn't want to leave the safety of the house. I didn't want to rebuild society or establish contact with other survivors. But I reached for Lohania's hand and she laced her fingers through mine.

Together, we walked down the sidewalk, to start the work that must be done.

# Bridesmaid, Revisited

IT'S HARD TO SAY WHY MARLEE WEARS THE BRIDESMAID'S DRESS TO work today. It isn't because she has an unconscious desire to be let go from her job as a receptionist—Marlee has been *consciously* desiring that since she started working there six months ago. The job is strictly to pay the bills.

It certainly isn't because she has a fondness for the dress itself. The dress is tea length, with a shiny black sleeveless bodice and appliquéd flowers lining the scoop neckline. The full black dirndl-type skirt is printed with huge red and white roses and fluffed out with taffeta underneath. It looks like something an American Girl doll might wear to a movie premiere but even American Girl dolls have better fashion sense.

But, still, it's a dress and Marlee reaches for it. This is the kind of decision that comes from being slightly hungover and experiencing a laundry crisis while forced to get up too early. (Circumstances that have brought the downfall of many people.)

MARLEE TRUDGES OFF to the subway in the baking summer heat, the dress making her shadow an unfamiliar Christmas-tree shape.

The dress doesn't suit Marlee. It didn't suit her three years ago when Rhonda Rhinebeck made Marlee wear it back in Eden Prairie, Minnesota. Marlee's fragile prettiness is overwhelmed by dark or vibrant colors, by any sort of glitter or embellishment. Since high school, she's worn her pale brown hair in a chin-length bob so precise it looks like every strand has been individually razor cut and she has an angular face and arched eyebrows. A lot of people have told her that she would be beautiful if she wore more makeup, which is amazingly passive-aggressive and also not true—Marlee has tried wearing more makeup, believe it. But it's sort of nice to know everyone is mentally upgrading her looks without her having to make any effort. Anyway, it's hard to imagine who would look good in this dress, but it definitely isn't Marlee.

Still, she doesn't think about how it must look to other people until a man on the subway offers her a seat. Marlee is twenty-four and in good health and this has never happened to her before.

"Please, allow me," the man says, and Marlee gives him a big beaming smile, not just because she's grateful for the seat but because she's suddenly realized how funny this is.

MARLEE IS THE RECEPTIONIST at a copier company called Theron Copystar in Midtown. Her desk is on the main level, in the showroom, and the corporate offices are all downstairs in the basement. Pretty much no one ever comes in to look at the copiers and Marlee works most of her days alone, surrounded by silent machines, like the last office worker in an apocalypse. The company is hopelessly anachronistic, and sales have been in a death spiral ever since she started—Marlee attends the weekly sales meeting, so she knows—but no one seems to realize this.

Normally, the first hour of the day is when Marlee does the most work. Not Theron Copystar work, obviously—work on her podcast. She and her best friend Veronika are starting a podcast called *Mythify*. The podcast is about two friends investigating urban and scientific myths, not because Marlee and Veronika care that much about myths, but because there are already podcasts about two friends investigating every other possible subject. (Veronika has thirty-five thousand followers on TikTok who like to watch her make boxed macaroni and cheese in various outfits, so hopefully they can leverage that audience in order to sell *Mythify.*) The first episode explored the myth that a penny dropped off the Empire State Building can kill a passerby. Marlee and Veronika interviewed a chic and funny physicist named Leola Britt who told them the dropped penny would be harmless and explained the physics behind her answer, and then told amusing stories about people who've tested it. The second episode is going to determine whether your body really does replace all your cells every seven years. So far they've interviewed a geneticist named Dr. Swanson, who told Marlee and Veronika to call him Swanny. Swanny was in his late sixties, and scrawny-looking, with weathered skin and a soft white goatee that wagged when he talked. He was also the most maddening person in perhaps all the five boroughs and wouldn't answer any question directly.

"It is and it isn't," he said when Marlee asked him if it was nice out and when Veronika asked him if the coffee she'd made for him was okay.

Asked about whether cells renew every seven years, he said, "Some do and some don't." Do the majority of cells renew? "Define 'majority.'" (Wag, wag, went his goatee.) Say seventy-five percent? "It might be higher." Ninety percent? Ninety-nine percent? "I couldn't calibrate with that sort of accuracy." Well, okay, what about the seven years? "What about it?" Is that the average renewal rate for cells? "Cell renewal rates vary." Just generally speaking? "I don't like to speak in generalities. I'm a scientist." Well, then what is your specific answer as to whether the human body renews itself every seven years? "I would say yes and no." What if someone held a gun to your head? "Held a gun to my head and asked me whether the human body renews itself every seven years?" Uh-huh. "I would say there's a simple answer and a complicated answer." Pretend my finger here is a gun. The person will shoot you if you don't say yes or no. "Shoot me? In the head?" Yes. Possibly more than once. "Then I'd say the answer is yes."

At the end of the interview, Swanny asked Veronika out for drinks and told Marlee that modern medicine had made a lot of progress in astigmatism treatments (she has a tendency to squint when concentrating). The Swanny tape is basically useless but Marlee had planned to give it another listen this morning.

Instead she calls Veronika and says, "You won't believe this, but I wore a bridesmaid's dress to work."

One of the best things about Veronika is that she never needs to have jokes explained to her. She gives a delighted gasp. "Is it . . . strapless?"

"No, but it is sleeveless."

"Is it pink? Please tell me it's pink."

"No," Marlee says, "it's black and the skirt is flowered—"

"Take a photo and send it to me," Veronika commands. "Right away."

℮

MARLEE TAKES A FEW SELFIES sitting sideways at her desk but she can't get the whole dress in the frame. Luckily, right then Herb Accounting comes puffing up the spiral staircase that connects the corporate offices to the showroom.

Herb could be any age between thirty and fifty, a heavyset man with receding brown hair and too-large eyeglasses. He's oddly mountainous-looking—not in a lumberjack sort of way but in an actual mountain sort of way, with the crest of hair far back on his head being the summit and his shoulders the sloping sides and his belly (which strains against every shirt he seems to own) the spreading lowlands.

"Good morning, Marlee," he says. His glasses are slightly fogged and his cheeks are bright red, either from the climb or from speaking to her.

"Good morning, Herb," Marlee says.

Herb holds up a folder. "I've just come up to make some copies of these remittance advice documents," he says, thus betraying that he's actually come up to make personal copies of some sort. (If not, he wouldn't bother to explain what they were. Probably more flyers for his a cappella singing group.)

Marlee asks him if he'd mind taking a picture of her and he says no problem at all. She gives him her phone and he takes several photos of Marlee posing at her desk and in the showroom. The one Marlee likes best is a shot of her sitting on the Theron Maxima 3313 (David Purchasing would have an aneurysm) with her legs crossed and a slightly mocking expression.

She sends it to Veronika, who replies immediately: *I'm coming to have lunch with you so I can see for myself.*

Herb Accounting makes copies on the Theron Malvo 4530 (definitely flyers—the Malvo has the best color) and then gathers all his papers back into the folder with a quick peek over his shoulder to see if she's watching.

He comes up to her desk, gripping the folder in his damp-looking hands, and says formally, "I think you look very pretty in that dress, Marlee."

Marlee sighs sadly, knowing she will have to spend the next month avoiding him or he will invite her to his a cappella group's next performance.

MARLEE POSTS THE DRESS photo on Instagram and captions it *Casual Friday at the office.* She doesn't worry that Rhonda Rhinebeck will see it because Marlee blocked Rhonda on all her social media accounts long ago.

Marlee only became friends with Rhonda in the first place because of a good joke Rhonda made in high school. Rhonda sat behind Marlee in algebra class and one day Rhonda whispered that

Mr. McManus, the teacher, looked like Patrick Star from *SpongeBob*. It was true—Mr. McManus had a sloping pink-skinned forehead and he often threw his arms up in excitement when talking about quadratic equations. Looking at Mr. McManus after that made Marlee so happy that she didn't hear a word he said for the rest of the year. Her math grades suffered but it was pretty much worth it.

It might sound like the Patrick Star joke wasn't enough to base a friendship on, and that's because it wasn't. Marlee started hanging out with Rhonda, hoping for more jokes, and then discovered that Rhonda was basically humorless. It was very disappointing—sort of like how California must have felt when they figured out Arnold Schwarzenegger wasn't actually the Terminator. Rhonda told long, solemn stories about how she checked the Hollister clearance page or how she reprinted her persuasive essay on gun control in thirteen-point font. Even the few funny stories she had—how she forgot where she parked in the student lot and had to wait until everyone left for the day—were told so seriously that Marlee felt bad laughing.

Marlee also discovered that, once befriended, Rhonda was really, really hard to shake. Rhonda waited by Marlee's locker in the mornings and saved her a place at lunch, and she treated the most tentative plans as stone carved, and she was the very first person to like Marlee's posts on social media. She was the very first person to like Marlee's comments on *other* people's posts. Eventually Marlee accepted that she was going to have to be friends with Rhonda Rhinebeck for the duration of high school. It wasn't that bad—if you could live without humor—because Rhonda's father was an airline pilot and her mother had family money. This meant that Rhonda lived in a big beautiful house that hardly ever had parents in it. Marlee has many fond memories of different rooms in that house, memories that have boys' names attached to them. And then Marlee moved to New York to go to NYU and Rhonda went to some small Christian liberal arts college in upstate Minnesota and they saw each other less and less, and that was as it should be, in Marlee's opinion.

But the summer after junior year, Rhonda got engaged at the ridiculously young age of twenty to her future-dentist boyfriend and came over to Marlee's parents' house to show off her ring and ask Marlee to be a bridesmaid in her wedding the next June. Marlee agreed, partly because she was caught by surprise, and partly because her parents were right there, and partly because a year seemed like such a long time away. That sounds like a lot of "partlys," a lot of parts, but no part of Marlee actually *wanted* to be in the wedding.

She also had no idea that Rhonda would treat wedding preparation in an oddly joyless fashion, like a garbage can that's been kicked over and scatters cockroaches everywhere. Weren't brides supposed to be so full of loving happiness that it spilled over onto those around them? Not Rhonda. Every wedding decision was a cockroach that Rhonda had to hunt down and stomp out as fiercely as possible. And she wanted help. She wanted Marlee to visit possible venues with her and go dress shopping with her and comparison shop for florists with her and taste wedding cakes with her and discuss prewedding pampering and plan her bachelorette party. Marlee was happy to escape back to New York at the end of that summer, but Rhonda created a WhatsApp group for all the bridesmaids and named it "Bride Tribe" and beseeched Marlee and the four other bridesmaids on a daily basis for some wedding-related enthusiasm. Not much enthusiasm was forthcoming—the bridesmaids set new records in slowness when it came to returning Rhonda's messages. Marlee supposed they were all trying not to call attention to themselves. (Being a bridesmaid is like a prison sentence where you try to serve your time and keep your head down and hope no one will rough you up in the shower.)

I want your input, Tribe! Rhonda tapped out endlessly. We need to think about bridesmaid dresses right away. I want to pick something you will all love.

Now, honestly, has any bridesmaid—anywhere, anytime—ever *loved* her bridesmaid's dress? (Spoiler: no.) Bridesmaid dresses are universally unlovely, unflattering, unfashionable, and unable to be passed off as any sort of dress that is.

But Rhonda was determined. The bridesmaids' dresses were like cockroaches that had scuttled under the stove, but Rhonda was down on the floor with a wire coat hanger and a canister of boric acid. She would get them. She would. Did the bridesmaids prefer plain or something with a print? Plain, everyone wrote. I think I'll go with print, Rhonda replied. Tea length or knee? Full skirt or narrow? She said it couldn't be strapless because dentists had very conservative views on fashion. (Rhonda talked a lot about dentists and how wonderful they were and how they deserved wives of the finest caliber. It seemed to Marlee that maybe the future dentist had given Rhonda too much nitrous oxide and reprogrammed her to think it was 1950.) Rhonda WhatsApped the Bride Tribe dozens of photos of dresses and solicited many opinions constantly and even asked them to go to various department stores to try the dresses on and send her photos of how they looked.

Rhonda wrote I want the dress to be something you'll wear again and again! so many times that finally Marlee lost it and typed Pick whatever dress you like the best because I am NEVER wearing it again. Rhonda got super upset and Marlee had to apologize in a long telephone call and blame her irritability on vitamin $B_{12}$ deficiency. (But later, one of the other bridesmaids sent Marlee an emoji of a clenched fist raised in solidarity, so Marlee came to think of it as time and effort well spent.)

And yet. And yet. Here's Marlee, wearing the dress again.

*e⌇*

VERONIKA ARRIVES JUST BEFORE noon, pushing open the heavy glass doors of the showroom and coming straight to Marlee's desk. She puts her hands over her eyes and says, "Stand up so I can get the whole experience at once."

Unfortunately Bill Marketing is also standing at Marlee's desk and he frowns and says, "Surely you know better than to have friends visit you at work, Marlee."

Marlee thinks that Bill Marketing should be happy that *anyone* visits the showroom, friend or otherwise. But she's not in the mood for a lecture, so she says, "This is Veronika Nováková. She's interested in the Theron Ultima 5150."

"I'm the facilities manager for Citibank," says Veronika, who actually works part-time on the sales floor of a shop in the East Village which sells healing crystals.

It's unlikely that Bill Marketing believes Veronika works for Citibank—she's wearing black leggings, an Idle Hands T-shirt, and a faded plaid flannel shirt—but she is, as always, beautiful and exotic with her thick black eyeliner and ice-blue eyes and long blond hair bleached the color and texture of shredded cellophane. (Plus Bill has a weakness for the Ultima 5150. He loves to show off the booklet-maker function.)

So Bill leads Veronika over to the Ultima 5150 and goes into his sales pitch. Veronika nods along and says, at intervals, in her slightly Dracula Czech accent:

"That's phenomenal."

"A truly exceptional machine."

"Any office could benefit from this."

"The image quality alone is worth the price."

"Does it make espresso?"

Marlee interrupts at this point to tell Bill Marketing he has a call and should get back to his office. "I'll get Miss Nováková's contact information so you can follow up."

Veronika extends her hand. "Yes, I would *love* that," she says and Bill Marketing looks so flustered that Marlee thinks he might fall down the spiral staircase on the way back to his office. He doesn't have a call, but Marlee figures he'll have forgotten all about that by the time he gets there. She switches the phones over to voicemail and she and Veronika go out to lunch.

℮∽

OUTSIDE, VERONIKA MAKES Marlee turn in a circle.

"It's so great," Veronika says in a slow but happy voice. "Even pink wouldn't be this great. What do you suppose people think when they see you?"

"Maybe that my building burned down and this was the only dress I saved?" Marlee says. "Or that I'm having an odd kind of mental breakdown?"

"Or that you escaped from somewhere," Veronika says, "from a bridal shop or wax museum."

They walk over to Between the Bread and even standing in line, Veronika can't stop staring at the dress. "Who was the bride who chose this?"

"Her name is Rhonda Rhinebeck," Marlee says.

"That name!" Veronika winces. "Why didn't she change it?"

"She did," Marlee says. "She's Rhonda Fredricks now."

"But why didn't she change it totally, before she got married?"

"That's not really something people do in Eden Prairie."

"And Rhonda Rhinebeck, did she like this dress?"

Marlee blinks. She had never, until this moment, wondered if Rhonda liked this dress. It had only seemed like Rhonda wanted Marlee and the other bridesmaids to wear this dress in order to show their fealty. Long live Rhonda the Bride.

"I don't know," Marlee says finally. "I guess she did."

"I've never heard you talk about her," Veronika says. "Are you still close?"

"No." Suddenly Marlee can only stare at the floor, at the dirty black-and-white hexagons of tile. "I wouldn't say we're close."

Veronika says nothing but Marlee can feel the weight of her gaze. She looks up. "Seriously, do I look insane?"

"Mostly you look like my grandmother," Veronika says. "The one who lives in Mikulov."

THE DRESS NO LONGER seems quite as funny after lunch. In fact, it seems embarrassing. Marlee walks back to the office in the heat, the stupid taffeta underskirt of the dress rustling, the appliquéd flowers on the neckline making her skin itch. Why had she worn it? Why did she still even own it? She's sweaty and irritable by the time she gets to her desk. She deletes the photo from Instagram. Nobody seemed to think it was all that funny anyway, except someone who said she looked like a goth Elsa. Marlee wants nothing more than to hide behind her desk and wait out the day.

But of course, *of course,* this turns out to be some odd, exceptionally busy afternoon when an unprecedented number of customers (that is to say: three) come into the showroom and Marlee has to show them the machines. She hates coming out from behind her desk and seeing the customers' eyes widen. Also, the skirt of her dress has gotten fuller and the top shinier. That may seem impossible, but Marlee can assure you it's not.

One older woman asks her if she's an actress on Broadway and Marlee tells her yes, she just won't have time to change into her costume before the first performance and the woman asks what the play is and Marlee says *Seven Brides for Seven Brothers* and the woman gets all sort of quivery with excitement and says that's her favorite musical and Marlee says it's her mother's favorite too (which is actually true) and the woman asks what character she plays and Marlee says Alice Elcott and the woman says she's going to go buy tickets for herself and her husband that very afternoon for tonight's performance and Marlee says she'll put her hand over her heart at the end of "Goin' Courtin'" as a tribute and the woman gets even more quivery and it's the closest to happy Marlee's been all day.

As she's showing the woman out, a man looking at the Jemsa 4590 says, "Hello? Hello! Lady in the prom dress? Can we get some help over here?" And that puts Marlee in such a bad mood that she tells him the Jemsa 4590 comes with an Internal Stapler Finisher, even though it doesn't—it's an add-on and will cost him $295, and he could see that for himself on the spec sheet if he wasn't such a fucking idiot.

℮↝

A TERRIBLE THING HAPPENS that afternoon. Well, actually two terrible things. One of them, the first, is the weekly sales meeting. The meeting shouldn't come as a surprise to Marlee, since she's basically in charge of it and has actually sent out email reminders and booked the conference room, but it still does. Or rather, it comes as a surprise to realize that she's going to have to attend it wearing the bridesmaid's dress.

She delays as long as possible, but finally, she puts the phones on hold and goes downstairs to the conference room, where everyone is expectantly gathered around the table.

Marlee has to walk right to the front of the room and spend what seems like an eternity setting up the Prezi slides on one of the laptops, her dress rustling like a palm tree in a typhoon. Thomas Tech Support should be doing this, but he's a slender young gay guy who's too glamorous to ever do any actual work, and he just sits there watching. Finally, he says, "Interesting outfit, Marlee," and Herb Accounting immediately says, "I think Marlee looks very pretty today." Both comments, for different reasons, make Marlee long to go into the stockroom and stick her head in the paper shredder.

Finally, she finishes setting up and sits down at her own place at the conference table. Bill Marketing is chairing the meeting and he asks for updates from the sales team. Becca Sales goes first and says, as she always does, that she's working on the new sales brochure and it should be ready soon. She also says that her Pomeranian is unexpectedly pregnant by the neighbors' French bulldog and she's accepting deposits on puppies. Paul Sales says that he's been actively pursuing a lead with a company called Energy Realm and is expecting to hear back by next week. Stacy Sales says she'll be very surprised if that happens and Paul Sales asks why and Stacy says because they closed *three years ago* and Paul asks then why is their website still up? Bill Marketing says never mind, he has a promising lead with the facilities manager from Citibank.

"That reminds me," he says to Marlee. "You haven't emailed me Ms. Nováková's contact info."

"I have it up at my desk." Marlee makes a mental note to tell Veronika to change her voicemail greeting to something corporate for a few days at least. "I should start the presentation now," she tells Bill, "or we'll never get out of here before rush hour."

Bill Marketing looks at his watch in a startled way and Marlee leans forward to hit PLAY on the laptop while Stacy Sales dims the lights. The slideshow was created by someone who left the company before Marlee got there. Marlee is pretty sure it wasn't created specifically for Theron and it may not even be specifically about selling copiers. The same slides of an anonymous workplace every week, and the same captions: *Uncover obstacles. Share insights. Explore the metrics. Analyze the competition. Teamwork, Dedication, Loyalty.*

Marlee feels her throat close. Loyalty. Loyalty.

RHONDA HAD DRIVEN MARLEE so crazy in the run-up to the wedding—Nobody was going to wear glasses, were they? And the taller bridesmaids would remember to wear flats, right? And Rhonda did hope that they'd all had their teeth cleaned within the last three months because dentists were so sensitive to oral hygiene—that the only way she could force herself to go was by rewarding herself constantly.

On the morning of the wedding, she had bacon—only bacon, eight big strips of it—for breakfast. She got dressed at home, even though they were all supposed to get dressed in some sort of bridal dressing chamber. She refused to wear the Rhonda-mandated nude-colored pantyhose and went bare-legged. She allowed herself to feel happy about the rainy weather and how berserk it must be making Rhonda. And she drove slowly to the country club, knowing it would make her late for the morning's itinerary—hair, makeup, photos, and "reflection time," whatever that was.

When she got to the bridal dressing room, Rhonda was seated in a pink upholstered chair having her makeup done. She held up a hand to stop the makeup girl and looked Marlee over from head to toe.

"I thought we agreed on Pink Cashmere as the color for everyone's nails," Rhonda said.

"The salon was out of Pink Cashmere," said Marlee, who hadn't been. "I thought no polish would be better than going rogue with some other shade of pink."

Rhonda narrowed her eyes. "Which salon? Did you ask to speak to the manager?"

"Rhonda, I think your eyeliner is a little uneven," said the bridesmaid who'd sent the solidarity emoji. She winked at Marlee. "I think the left side is just slightly thicker than the right side."

Rhonda, diverted, shot the makeup girl a murderous look, and the makeup girl sighed.

Half an hour later, Marlee slipped away for a cigarette. It was easy. Rhonda was measuring all the bridesmaids' earrings—she had instructed them all to wear six-millimeter studs but obviously didn't trust them—and Marlee just picked up her purse and stepped quietly out into the hall. She snuck down an unpromising stairway and through a door that led to a small patio at the back of the club protected from the rain by the deck above. And that's where she ran into Rhonda's father, Captain Rhinebeck.

Captain Rhinebeck had always intrigued Marlee. He was so different from other people's fathers with their office jobs, and he looked different from those other fathers, too. Not handsome, exactly—in fact, he teetered on the edge of ugly: short and slightly stocky, with thinning black hair. But his skin was deeply tanned, as though he flew to the Mediterranean instead of the endless Minneapolis-Detroit-Chicago route, and his thick lips were sensual, his teeth startling white. He exuded a vitality and alertness that was unusual in Eden Prairie, and he had a reputation, too. Well, a vague, small reputation, held by one person—Marlee's mother—who said once that all airline pilots were womanizers.

He was standing on the edge of the patio, smoking a black cigarette that matched his tuxedo. He saw her, and looked for a moment as though he was going to defend himself, and then shrugged lazily. Silently, Marlee pulled her pack of cigarettes out of her purse. (She had moved to New York with a lot of pastel T-shirts and a fondness for wedge sneakers, and almost immediately she'd begun to wear black all the time and smoke Marlboro Lights. The transformation seemed to happen without her awareness or consent.)

Captain Rhinebeck smiled. "Desperate times, huh?" he said, blowing a cloud of smoke out into the rain.

Marlee nodded.

He took a lighter out of his breast pocket. "Come over here."

She crossed the patio to where he was standing and he lit her cigarette. Other men had lit cigarettes for Marlee—men in bars, her building super, her freshman roommate's thirteen-year-old brother—but it was different to have someone's father do it. Normally friends' fathers don't do things for you. They might pass the butter if you're having dinner at their houses or they might ask you to move your car if you've parked them in, but in general, any sort of one-on-one interaction is avoided. Marlee had friends whose fathers had never even spoken to her directly—just "Good night, girls" or "Don't forget to lock up." This lighting of her cigarette seemed both personal and illicit, like a rendezvous between spies.

She drew deeply on her cigarette and he watched her, seeming to approve. "Aren't you supposed to be doing something wedding related?"

Marlee paused. Captain Rhinebeck looked at her so attentively that she had the feeling she could say anything to him.

"Aren't you?" Marlee asked.

Captain Rhinebeck laughed and Marlee realized all of a sudden why her mother didn't like him—he was a risk-taker. He took risks and he encouraged other people to take them.

"At least you're not paying for it," he said.

That tingle of intimacy again, of risk. "I have to wear this dress, though," she said.

Captain Rhinebeck stood back and eyed her, head tilted. "You are—"

But just then the glass door slid open and Mrs. Rhinebeck poked her head out. "For God's sake!" she snapped. "We need both of you for photos!"

Captain Rhinebeck's eyes met Marlee's and some sort of connection between them caught and pulled tight. Right there, right then, Marlee decided Captain Rhinebeck would be the way she rewarded herself for the rest of the day.

It was really only a series of glances but it made the day more bearable. This is how it went: Rhonda tells Marlee to call KTMY and ask when the rain is going to stop—Marlee looks at Captain Rhinebeck. Mrs. Rhinebeck says that her cousin Linda was really terribly inconsiderate to wear beige—Marlee looks at Captain Rhinebeck. The bakery delivers a cake with a plastic swan figure on top and Rhonda cries, "Who do they think I *am?*"—Marlee looks at Captain Rhinebeck.

Always when Marlee looked at him, his dark eyes were looking back at her, and she knew they were thinking exactly the same thing. She was certain that they would meet later to talk about it and that certainty made her pupils dilate and her breath quicken. (There is no aphrodisiac even half as powerful as talking shit about someone.)

Marlee didn't know how or where she and Captain Rhinebeck would meet again, but the certainty it would happen sustained her through the afternoon and into the evening. Well, quite a few mimosas sustained her, too. But she needed them! There seemed to be no end to the wedding awfulness, the bridal awfulness: Rhonda during the ceremony, switching her gaze beadily between groom and pastor, ready to pounce if one made a mistake. Rhonda's need for a minimum of two bridesmaids to accompany her to the bathroom. Rhonda's fury when the bandleader explained that the bass player had bronchitis and that they had brought an (apparently inferior) alternate. Rhonda's extremely clear and personal unhappiness with God for allowing the rain to continue.

Truly, when Marlee came out of the second-story restroom after tugging up the hot, uncomfortable, nude-colored pantyhose (Rhonda had had spare pairs), and saw Captain Rhinebeck leaning against the opposite wall, clearly waiting for her, it felt exciting and risky, yes. But more important, it felt *deserved*.

Captain Rhinebeck smiled his lazy smile, and held up his lighter. "Do you need a smoke?"

"God, yes," Marlee said. "But the bridesmaids had to leave their stuff in the dressing room."

Captain Rhinebeck pulled a pack of Marlboro Lights from his breast pocket. "I brought you some."

He had remembered what brand of cigarette she smoked! Marlee had friends whose fathers couldn't remember her *name*. Carly, Marla, Darlene—it was all the same to them. Captain Rhinebeck was different. She smiled and let him lead her to a little alcove with a window overlooking the wet green golf course. Captain Rhinebeck cranked the hopper window open slightly and then lit a cigarette for himself and one for Marlee. They had to stand very close to each other in order to blow the smoke out the window, and occasional drops of rain came in and sparkled like tiny jewels on their hair and shoulders.

This was it, the conversation Marlee had looked forward to all day. Yet neither she nor Captain Rhinebeck said a word. And Marlee knew why: they were waiting to kiss.

But you have to understand that, even at this point, to Marlee, Captain Rhinebeck was basically a street vendor peanut. When Marlee first moved to New York and smelled the sweetly perfumed air that came from the vendor carts on nearly every corner, she'd been utterly intoxicated. People were so wrong when they said the city smelled like piss and rotting garbage! New York smelled of warm honey and caramelized sugar, like some delicious form of godly sustenance. The peanuts themselves were a crushing disappointment: stale, slightly burned, almost bitter. ("They don't taste as good as they smell," Marlee had told Veronika, who said firmly, "*Nothing* tastes as good as those smell.") Captain Rhinebeck was like those peanuts—Marlee found him sexy but she knew it was only an illusion. It was just a question of whether she was going to let him kiss her.

She decided she was. They were standing so close to each other and alternating leaning up to exhale out the window, first her face turned up and then Captain Rhinebeck's. All she would have to do, really, was keep still so that when Captain Rhinebeck drew back from the window, their faces would be almost touching. They would be kissing without even intending to, sort of. It would be the simplest accident—

Marlee threw her cigarette out the window and kissed him. Captain Rhinebeck hesitated for the tiniest of moments—still long enough to scare Marlee into thinking she'd misinterpreted him terribly—and then his mouth opened against hers and they were kissing properly. (Or improperly, depending on your point of view.) Captain Rhinebeck cupped her face with his free hand. He tasted of whiskey and smoke and coffee and basil. Marlee realized from the basil that Captain Rhinebeck had chosen the salmon over the beef Wellington option on the wedding menu—and that was a startling and unsexy realization. It made Marlee wonder if she was as overinvested in wedding details as Rhonda was. The thought almost made Marlee stop kissing Captain Rhinebeck. And the kiss wasn't that great to begin with—it had none of the excitement and zing Marlee had counted on. It was, well, disappointing. Just like street nuts.

It was then that Marlee heard the rustle of Rhonda's wedding gown. She was sure of that later—she'd definitely heard the gown even before she heard Rhonda's sudden, horrified gasp. She pulled away from Captain Rhinebeck and looked over his shoulder.

Rhonda was standing in the hallway, all seven and a half feet of her lace cathedral train looped over her arm. Her gown glowed with pearly magnificence, her skin was flawless in the light cast from the window, her dark hair gleaming in its sleek chignon. Marlee thought for a second—much less than a second—how beautiful Rhonda looked, how achingly lovely, when earlier she had achieved only a sort of standard prettiness. Even Rhonda's expression, in that moment, was hauntingly wounded, cinematically betrayed. She looked like an exquisite ghost-bride who had witnessed something so terrible that she was destined to wander the halls for all eternity, reliving it again and again.

Captain Rhinebeck glanced back to see what Marlee was looking at. "Rhonda," he said. "Rhonda, honey—"

Rhonda turned and fled back down the hall, surprisingly agile for someone who had needed so much gown assistance all day. She let go of the train, gathered her full skirt in both hands, and started down the stairs.

Captain Rhinebeck stood rooted to the spot. Marlee pushed past him to the top of the stairs. "Wait!" she cried over the banister.

Rhonda looked up, every angle of her upturned face shadowed with hurt.

"I'm sorry!" Marlee called down to her. And she was. She was sorry about Captain Rhinebeck, she was sorry about the bridesmaid's dress, she was sorry about her behavior during all the weeks leading up to this, she was sorry Rhonda wasn't from New York. She was sorry. She really was.

THE SECOND TERRIBLE THING that happens that afternoon is that Marlee starts crying in the sales meeting. Silently but undeniably crying. No one could look at her and think she has been walking in windy weather or is suffering from hay fever. Her mouth is wobbling and tears are trembling on her lower lashes. Marlee knows those tears are merely the front-runners and a thousand other tears will follow.

She pushes back her chair and stumbles out of the dark conference room toward the restroom. But she finds the restroom door is locked (no one seems able to break the building maintenance man of his habit of leaving early on Fridays) and so she can only stand there, sobbing and rattling the door handle.

Eventually, she feels Herb Accounting's hand patting her shoulder tentatively. She turns blindly and leans against him, she leans against the mountain of Herb, and he puts his arm around her. She's crying out loud now—harsh braying wails and loud hitching gasps for air. This is the worst kind of crying, the most humiliating, because it's no longer anonymous. This kind of crying incorporates the crying person's voice—her voice, Marlee's voice, the voice that is distinctively hers.

Her face is pressed against Herb's chest and this makes Marlee feel even worse. Not because Herb is Herb and sings in an a cappella group and says "Pardon my French" when he swears. Not because Herb is slightly sweaty and his hands are damp on her shoulders and his belly is pushed against her as urgently as an erection. It's because Herb's kind enough to follow a crying person out of the conference room and offer comfort, and Marlee knows, without a doubt, that he is far too good for the likes of her.

℮↦

IT TURNS OUT THAT Veronika is still in Midtown—she texts Marlee to say that she spent the afternoon shopping for Lita boots—so they meet at the subway station, Veronika carrying a large shoebox and Marlee with her swollen pink eyes. Veronika looks at Marlee carefully but doesn't say anything. She just puts an arm around her shoulder and squeezes as they walk down the stairs.

No one offers Marlee a seat on the subway this time. (Chivalry is indeed dead and apparently it died in the past eight hours.) She and Veronika have to grip a pole in the middle of the train and sway with the crowds all the way to Park Street before enough people get off for them to sit down.

They drop into seats next to each other and the skirt of Marlee's dress puffs out onto Veronika's lap. Marlee tucks the skirt more securely under her legs, hating the feel of the slick material on her hands, the rough taffeta underskirt on her legs. She can't remember ever having hated an inanimate object more, not even the 1991 Chevy Corsica hatchback she drove in high school when it broke down in an Arby's drive-thru with a hundred angry customers behind her.

Marlee leans her head against Veronika's shoulder. She should have thrown the dress away. The wedding was three years ago—she's a different person now. Actually, according to Swanny, she'll *literally* be a different person in four more years, when all her cells renew. Not only would this different person never do what Marlee had done—the person would actually be someone who hadn't done it at all.

The train picks up speed and Marlee's head bumps against Veronika's shoulder. She closes her eyes and focuses on changing, renewing. Three stops away from home now. When they get there, she'll be that much closer to being somebody else.

# King Midas

OSCAR'S GIRLFRIEND TESSA SAID THE MOST ALARMING THINGS. SOME-
times she said, "If you and I ran off together, I think your wife and
I would learn to be friends." It wasn't the running off part that was
so alarming—they had both agreed that was something that would
never happen—it was the part about his wife and Tessa learning
to be friends (something else that would never happen, Oscar was
sure). But Tessa said things like that all the time. Often right after
sex, she pulled on her underpants and then stood there (she was
magnificent, standing in her underpants) and said, "Wait, I'm trying to remember when I ovulated." If Oscar talked about anything
remotely scientific or mathematical, she said, "Hold on, let me get
my dad on the phone for you." She said she was crazy about Oscar.
He wanted to believe her.

OSCAR'S WIFE WAS NAMED Winifred, and if you were in a good mood,
you might describe her as petite and determined, and if you were
not in a good mood, you might describe her as a birdlike control
freak.

Whenever she spoke to Oscar, she cleared her throat and then
there was a three-second pause, as though she were trying to choose
which of the many ways he'd disappointed her to address. Oscar
had grown so tense about these pauses that even when she said

something totally innocuous—well, almost totally innocuous—like "I see you bought a new brand of cat food," he felt defensive and a little bit ashamed.

Those pauses had not been there twenty-five years ago when they got married, Oscar was positive. Or maybe they had been. Maybe they were just longer pauses now that Oscar had done so many disappointing things, both known and unknown to Winifred. Maybe ten years from now, there would be thirty-second pauses, and maybe ten years after *that,* they would live in disapproving silence. He almost looked forward to it.

OSCAR HAD NEVER KNOWN anyone else besides Tessa whose eyes and hair were exactly the same color. In Tessa's case, both were the color of Southern Comfort. She was thirty-three and had a seven-year-old son named Gabriel. Oscar was fifty-two, and his and Winifred's daughter was in college now. A seven-year-old seemed like almost more responsibility than he could imagine. Gabriel's father had been a drunk long-haul trucker. At least that's what Tessa said and for a long time Oscar believed it. But he later learned that Gabriel's father was a Spanish investment banker and the drunk person at Gabriel's conception had been Tessa herself.

She shrugged off this inconsistency. "I didn't mean the actual *person,"* she said. "It was a drunk-trucker type of *relationship."*

Apparently the Spanish investment banker had viewed it somewhat differently. "He wanted to get *married,"* Tessa said, as though that were some inexplicable and distasteful urge, like a sudden desire to move to Cleveland. The Spanish investment banker was now married to someone else and lived on the Upper East Side with his wife and two little children, and Gabriel went there every other weekend.

Oscar had seen Gabriel's father once, standing on the stoop of Tessa's building, a handsome slender man wearing suit trousers and a vest over a blindingly white shirt with black sleeve garters and a foulard tie. He had his cell phone to his ear and was saying, "Tessa—Tessa—" The end of each word was cut off and swallowed, like there was more he wanted to say but didn't dare.

Oscar had more sympathy for him than you can imagine.

OSCAR WAS A HUMAN-RIGHTS lawyer; Tessa was a photographer. She'd had photographs featured in *Vanity Fair* and twice in the Style section of *The Times*. But mostly she was a wedding photographer and a successful one. She had an assistant named Ricky and they worked almost every weekend, Gabriel trailing after them with an armful of tripods. Tessa claimed to hate weddings and wedding photography and she always said the word "brides" as though speaking of some abhorrent subset of humanity, like serial killers. She said the wedding photography was strictly temporary, but Oscar wondered. He thought maybe wedding photography was like organized crime, or tax evasion, or adultery—you got into it without really meaning to and the rewards were so great you stayed and the years rolled by and suddenly, there you were, not the person you'd intended to be at all. (Oscar should know.)

OSCAR LIVED EIGHT BLOCKS away from Tessa, which was convenient for trysting but terrifying in terms of accidental meetings. Oscar didn't even like to think about what they would do if he and Winifred met Tessa in the supermarket or a restaurant or the dry cleaner's. Well, he knew what *he* would do—absolutely nothing. It's what *Tessa* would do that was so worrisome. She was totally capable of winking at him, or squeezing his elbow, or even speaking to him. She would probably speak to *Winifred,* just so that later she could spend several days having a pleasurable postmortem of the conversation.

He tried to tell Tessa that if they met, she should avoid him completely, and she got all excited. "Where do you think we might bump into each other? That Italian restaurant Winifred likes?" Oh, how he regretted ever telling her anything about Winifred!

"What would Winifred think if she just, you know, saw me sitting at the bar?" Tessa continued. "Would she think, 'Now, that girl looks like a really nice, interesting person'? Or would she think, 'That girl's skirt is too short and she looks like she hasn't called her mother in a really long time'?"

"Well, maybe the part about the skirt—" Oscar began and then shook his head, unable to continue. How had this conversation gotten so far off course? Honestly, Tessa would be the death of him.

OSCAR FELL ASLEEP IN Tessa's apartment one afternoon. When he woke up, Tessa was standing at the kitchen counter in a pale yellow robe, trying to open a jar of peanut butter. The sun was streaming through the window, adding gilt edges to every outline—the floorboards, the counters, the printer, the jar, Tessa herself, were all burnished with the softest amber. Oscar felt like King Midas, at least King Midas in the early, joyful stage. Everything he looked at turned to gold.

"The world is beautiful," Oscar said, his voice croaky from sleep. "You are beautiful."

Tessa glanced up with a half smile. "That's just the blow job talking," she said, and went back to struggling with the peanut-butter jar.

OSCAR KNEW THAT when Tessa needed to send Gabriel somewhere— to his father's or a friend's house or karate lessons—she used an Uber driven by a Pakistani man named Vakeel. Vakeel had once driven Tessa home after a particularly stressful wedding where the father of the bride had drunk too much champagne and tried to put his tongue in Tessa's mouth, and Vakeel had comforted Tessa by stopping for glazed doughnuts. Because of Vakeel's kindness in her moment of need, Tessa said, they had an "intense connection," only as far as Oscar could tell the intensity of their connection did not include Tessa knowing Vakeel's last name or really anything about him. This worried Oscar a great deal.

"Oh, please," Tessa said. "Vakeel is utterly, utterly reliable. Well, except that one time."

Oscar didn't ask about that one time because he couldn't bear to hear that Gabriel had fallen asleep in the back seat of the Uber and woken up in Coney Island, or that he'd been delivered to the wrong house and spent the weekend with strangers. He could not bear it. You have to understand: Oscar's heart was a delicate thing.

SOMEWHERE—OSCAR WAS CONVINCED of this—other men had affairs with women who made them feel special and cherished and desirable. These other men were greeted at the door of their girlfriends' apartments by women wearing silk robes and smelling of the mysteries of the Far East, rather than Tessa, who often said, "Sorry about the way I'm dressed, but I haven't done laundry in a while." Other men did not have to make love to their girlfriends while that girlfriend's enormous printer rumbled in the background like a disapproving beast. Other men's girlfriends did not pause in the middle of sex to lean over and inspect the flashing screens of their iPhones. Other men's girlfriends did not say, "Wait, have I told you this or did I tell the checkout girl at Gristedes?" Other men's girlfriends did not flirt outrageously with men every which where and then fly into a jealous rage when the men spoke politely to a waitress.

Other men were fools. Oscar was convinced of that, too.

TESSA HAD THREE DIFFERENT outfits she wore to weddings. She told Oscar she'd bought them from a consignment store because she wouldn't know where to shop for clothes someone's grandma would wear. Oscar was pretty sure no one's grandma had ever worn anything like these. The first one was a pearl-gray pantsuit with lines as clean and smooth as a wineglass. The second one was a dress of the freshest-looking blue, with a swirly skirt and a bodice that cupped Tessa's breasts as sweetly as a farmer's hand cups a new egg. The third one (Oscar's favorite) was a narrow brown dress with a white collar and cuffs. When Tessa wore it, she pulled her hair back in a ladylike knot and clipped on small pearl earrings and Oscar thought she looked like a sexy librarian and he grew dizzy with desire. (But he couldn't tell her that because she'd break up with him for being too conventional.)

Oscar knew about these outfits because sometimes there would be a long wait between the wedding ceremony and the reception and Tessa would meet him at a bar on Lexington. These were the types of weddings Tessa hated most.

"Three hours!" she would say. "With nothing to do because God forbid these fuckers buy you a drink before they absolutely have to."

Tessa bought *herself* lots of drinks on these occasions, though, and Oscar worried that she might get too drunk and wind up with blurry photographs, but Tessa just shrugged and said that in that case she would use stock photos or close-ups of rings and flowers from other people's weddings and the brides would never know the difference, they were all such idiots anyway.

OSCAR AND WINIFRED were going to a fundraising dinner for the New York Foundation for the Arts. They went to something like this every two weeks or so. (It was, in fact, at a fundraiser for Children's Aid that Oscar had met Tessa, eight months ago. She had been the event photographer and was having a preliminary bourbon at the bar, and there was Oscar, sent to fetch Winifred's white wine.)

Oscar cared about the arts as much as the next person, but he felt infinitely weary as he adjusted his tie in the bedroom mirror. Winifred was wearing a stiff black dress that unfortunately reminded Oscar of a carapace. Or maybe it was just that Winifred seemed to be inhabiting it rather than wearing it. She looked suddenly fragile to Oscar as she searched through her jewelry box with her bony fingers.

"Let's skip this dinner," he said suddenly. "We can write them a check and just go out for pizza."

Winifred looked up, startled, and cleared her throat. She paused and cleared it again. Oscar wondered if it was possible she had some sort of throat disease. Finally she just shook her head, as though to wipe his suggestion from her mind, and turned back to her jewelry box.

℮

CALLING TESSA WAS LIKE calling Hydra—you never knew which head would answer. Oh, but answer she would. Tessa could no more resist a ringing phone than an old lady could resist a baby's smile.

Sometimes Oscar might get the Warm Tessa. "I was just thinking about you," she'd say softly, sleepily. "I'm so glad you called." He might get the Business Tessa, who answered her phone "Jane Street Photography" (she didn't live on Jane Street, or anywhere near it) and frequently pretended to be her own personal assistant. Sometimes she would pick up the phone but not put it to her ear and Oscar could hear a little bit of conversation before she spoke into it. This happened a lot when he got the Working Tessa, who said things like "Ricky, tell that cunt to put her veil on *now*—hello?" Sometimes he got the Parenting Tessa, who would answer and say, "Wait, wait, Gabriel, just sign my name on that, it'll be fine, I promise—hello?"

And then there was the Social Tessa, who answered late at night, or even sometimes in the afternoon, and in the background there would be music and people's voices and closer up the clink of ice cubes and the clatter of Tessa's bangle bracelets and Tessa saying, "Well, I really shouldn't have another, but okay," before she turned her attention to the phone and said, "Hello?"

Oscar didn't like to get the Social Tessa because he feared it was the Real Tessa. He didn't like to call her late at night and know she was out somewhere (with whom?), but sometimes he couldn't resist. Sometimes he told Winifred they were out of orange juice—this made Winifred's eyebrows race together in disapproval about juice overconsumption—just so he could go to the bodega on the corner and call Tessa on the way back.

Oscar would go into the bodega and buy the smallest carton of juice available and nod to the man behind the cash register, who nodded back and always said, "Thank you for your business!" in the most heartfelt way, as though Oscar's juice purchase was all that stood between the bodega and financial ruin.

And then Oscar would stand outside, on the dark street where the light came only from the shops on the first floors and the rest of the buildings towered over him like the husks of rotten teeth, and call Tessa. He felt at these moments that his life was slipping away from him. Tessa was the only thing in it that made sense. "Tessa, I love you," he said desperately.

"What?" said Tessa. "It's really noisy here. I can't hear you."

OSCAR HAD NEVER WITNESSED Tessa actually photographing anyone at a wedding, but he knew in his heart how it must go. Not for Tessa the velvety soothing tones or smooth patter of other photographers. No indeed. He was sure she used her usual voice: quick, rich, slightly impatient. She would say things like *Oh, come on* and

*Please cooperate* and *I have a much better idea* and *Is that the best you can do?* Oscar knew, because she said all those same things to him during sex.

℮⁓

OSCAR ARRIVED AT TESSA's apartment building, and she was standing on the sidewalk next to Gabriel, spraying his shirt with a plant mister and then rubbing it with a dryer sheet to get the wrinkles out.

"I know it's a little damp and uncomfortable," she said, "but it'll dry by the time you get to your father's." She rubbed the dryer sheet on Gabriel's hair and then sniffed. "There, you smell like you've had a bath."

A car pulled up to the curb and the driver got out. He was a balding man with heavy eyebrows and a five o'clock shadow that looked like it was made from metal shavings.

"Oh, hello, Vakeel," Tessa said.

Vakeel! Finally Oscar got to see him. Vakeel nodded. He leaned against the cab and gazed at Tessa.

"Now," she was saying to Gabriel. "Don't eat with your fingers and use your napkin and be sure to tell your grandma we speak Spanish at home"—Oscar had never heard her speak Spanish, not one single time—"and remember that nobody must ever, ever find out what happened to the hamster."

"I know," Gabriel said. He had his backpack on and his thumbs hooked under the straps, as though it were too heavy for his small shoulders. But his face was perfectly serene.

"Okay, then," Tessa said. "Have a good weekend. Oh, and say goodbye to Uncle Oscar."

Uncle Oscar? *Uncle?* Oscar was so startled and offended he couldn't speak.

"Goodbye, Uncle Oscar," Gabriel said to him, his eyes like black olives, opaque and unreadable.

"Goodbye, Gabriel," Oscar managed.

Vakeel opened the back door of the cab. His teeth—startlingly white—showed themselves in a quick smile. "Lucky kid," he said to Oscar. "He's got a lot of uncles."

OSCAR AND TESSA ALWAYS made love as soon as he got to her apartment. She said she couldn't stand uncertainty. ("You can do better than that," Tessa said today, crouched on top of him. No doubt about it: she would be the death of him.) Now Oscar sat on her couch, drinking wine and eating cheese and crackers in some sort of reverse-order date while Tessa moved around her apartment, wearing nothing but a Snoopy T-shirt. She had a box fan going in the window and every time she passed in front of it, her hair would billow out abruptly, like the plume of water sprayed from a garden hose.

"So I have this great new idea for an extra for my wedding package," Tessa said from the kitchen. "It's called 'The Morning After' and I go around the day after the wedding and take pictures of everyone when they're relaxed and natural and not stressed. But it doesn't seem to be catching on. I told this one bride about it, and she was like 'What makes you think I want to see my mother-in-law with no makeup on?'"

She picked up a piece of cheese from the cutting board and ate it as she passed in front of the fan again, her hair fluttering. She sat down on the couch and put her feet in his lap, the skin of her bare legs as unblemished as a bolt of fabric. She rested her head against the arm of the couch, and smiled at him. He began rubbing her feet.

Tessa's phone rang, a loud combination of whistling music and buzzing clatter as it vibrated on the table next to her. She always had the volume set as loud as possible. She picked it up and glanced at the screen. Her expression didn't change, but her eyes widened and

Oscar felt her delight—he felt it all the way through her body to the foot he held in his hands. Whoever was calling made her muscles tighten with pleasure.

"Fuck whoever this is," Tessa said, putting her phone on silent. "Rub right at my heel there. My feet are so sore from those ridiculous grandma shoes."

Oscar felt like King Midas again, but now it was like King Midas in the later stages, when he realized that everything vibrant and alive had turned into dead metal. He did not dare to drink his wine or eat his cracker, fearing the wine would be hardened liquid in the cup and the golden cracker would break his teeth.

℃∿

OSCAR AGREED TO GO look at kitchen tiles with Winifred, even though he knew in his heart that it was an expedition doomed to failure. Tessa had an all-day wedding in New Jersey, so there was no chance he could see her anyway.

At the kitchen store, Oscar chose his three favorite tiles, which Winifred dismissed in turn as too dark, too shiny, and too lifeless.

"Too lifeless?" Oscar said. "It's *stone*. It's supposed to be lifeless."

Both Winifred and the kitchen-store clerk looked at him, Winifred stonily (lifelessly, you could even say) and the clerk with immeasurable sympathy. Oscar and Winifred left the store with Oscar carrying a bag containing about twenty sample tiles to take home and hold up to their kitchen wall one at a time while Winifred got a feel for them—a prospect that made Oscar hope a fiery pit would open on the way home and swallow him.

But what actually happened on the way home, as they were walking back down Lexington toward their apartment, was that a taxi pulled up to the curb and a woman in a blue dress got out. She was in such a rush that she forgot to pay the cabdriver and had to swing back around in a swirl of blue cloth and tanned leg and hand him bills through the window. Then she ran across the sidewalk in the excited little chickadee-hops women use when they run in high heels, shoved open the door of the bar as though it were a boulder standing between her and survival, and dashed inside.

Oscar dropped the bag of tiles and there was an ominous breaking sound.

"Oscar!" Winifred said, too annoyed to insert the three-second pause. "For God's sake!"

But Oscar said nothing. He knew the bar the girl had run into. He knew the girl, too. He knew her run, he knew her mouth, he knew the dress and the way the neckline opened slightly when she reached for her drink, and worst of all, he knew the eager expression on her face. It was Tessa.

OSCAR WENT TO the bodega on the corner almost every night now. He went on the slightest pretext—to buy a bar of soap or box of matches or pack of paper clips. He could tell it was driving Winifred crazy, but he didn't care. Her pauses were getting fractionally longer and now she'd added a narrow probing look before she spoke. Oscar didn't care for it, although Winifred said nothing more disturbing than "*I* like to write things on the shopping list."

Tonight Oscar poked his head into the bedroom and said, "I'm going down to the store for some antacids."

Winifred was in bed, reading, a cardigan draped over her narrow shoulders, the knobs of her collarbone standing out like marbles. She looked up and cleared her throat, but before she could say anything, Oscar backed out and closed the door. That was the advantage of the pause, and Oscar's own personal three-second rule: if he could duck out before she spoke, he was free.

And what did it matter, now that he no longer called Tessa when he went out? He had not been able to bring himself to call after the day he'd seen her run into the bar three weeks ago. She didn't call him and he realized that she had *never* called him. Did she miss him?

Did she ever look at the screen of her phone with a flicker of disappointment? He had never seen her do that. She had always seemed happy with whoever called. Maybe that was the whole problem.

Oscar sighed and trudged through the darkness down to the corner. He'd had girlfriends before Tessa; there was no reason he couldn't have girlfriends after her. Then why did this feel so much like the end of love, the end of youth, the end of his life? He hadn't loved Tessa, had he? She was unlovable.

He opened the door of the bodega with its ominous jingle of bells (hello! armed robbers are here!) and nodded to the man behind the cash register.

Oscar thought that he and Tessa were like lines on a graph, nonparallel lines which could have only one intersection point, and Oscar had passed the point without noticing. Now his line and Tessa's line would continue into infinity, getting farther and farther apart—God, he should call Tessa's father and discuss this! That thought made Oscar feel like someone was using tweezers to dig around for a splinter in his heart. He grabbed a bottle of antacid tablets from the shelf.

The man behind the cash register seemed to have perpetual conjunctivitis, or else his eyes were just irritated by so much exposure to fluorescent light. It gave him a sorrowful, world-weary look. Tonight as he gave Oscar his change, he nodded his head toward the door. "You don't make your call anymore," he said.

Oscar looked outside at the oblong of hazy light thrown on the sidewalk by the streetlamp. It seemed like a magical circle suddenly, maybe a Wiccan one, or just one drawn with chalk by children, but still a very powerful one. One he could no longer enter. He had thought Tessa would be the death of him, but he was wrong—the lack of her was.

"No," Oscar said. "Not anymore."

# Sky Bar

FAWN DOESN'T ALWAYS FLIRT WITH AIRPORT SECURITY GUARDS THESE days. She's nearing forty and she worries that a time might come when the guards won't flirt back. But right now she's so happy and relieved to be leaving Hullbeck and only one guy is working security and he looks like sort of a fun job, so when he says, "That's a beautiful coat," she says, "Oh, thank you!" as though she'd been hoping he'd say just that.

(It is sort of possible that she *was* hoping he'd say that—she's dressed in a way that can only be described as aggressively stylish: black jeans and black cashmere sweater, topped with an ivory bouclé coat. Nobody likes to travel in denim—those seams and rivets, the red imprint of the button on your belly—so why is Fawn doing it? Because it's not something a Hullbeck person would do, that's why.)

The security guard is a short but muscular man with a close-clipped mustache and a monk's tonsure of short brown hair. He's wearing black pants and a cobalt-blue dress shirt with black epaulets and a gold badge. The silver nameplate pinned to his right shirt pocket reads CLYDE SANBORN.

They have a little back-and-forth while Fawn puts her coat and bag and shoes on the conveyor belt and hippity-hops through the metal detector. Clyde asks what's she doing in Hullbeck? (Visiting her parents.) Where's home now, in that case? (New York City.)

What does she do there? (Magazine editor.) What sort of magazine? (Fashion.) Is she blond all over?

He doesn't really ask that last one—it's more sort of implied. Fawn is a master of detecting that sort of implication. (And the answer is: yes.) But by the time she's put her shoes back on, she's forgotten all about Clyde.

Fawn is just as small-boned and delicate as her name suggests, although this was not always so. She used to be small-boned and very big. Well, maybe not *very* big, but certainly big enough that you couldn't tell what size her bones were. But her name wasn't Fawn then, either—it was Vangie. She wears her sandy-blond hair in a half updo with thick bangs she has to look out from under, and a little cat's-eye liner on her eyelids. It's a sort of poor man's Brigitte Bardot look, and it has served her well.

She's just walking toward her gate (one of the two gates at the Hullbeck airport) when the PA system squawks to life and a male voice with a midwestern accent says, "May I have your attention please? We regret to announce that the departure of Flight 1010 to Detroit will be delayed until five thirty-two p.m."

Fawn looks back toward the airport exit in confusion. She was so eager to leave that she hardly noticed the weather, but now she sees through the window that the sky is white and the horizon has taken on a blurred look. Individual snowflakes are dropping past the window like fluffy paratroopers. But it's Michigan—they can deal with a little snow, right?

The PA crackles again. "We will inform you of the new departure time as soon as possible. Meanwhile, we have provided complimentary snacks at gate two."

The offer of snacks strikes Fawn as extremely ominous. Also condescending, as though the passengers were overgrown kindergartners: *Everyone's getting cranky—break out the graham crackers!* And when Fawn cruises past the snack table once and then twice, she sees they are all desperately *inferior* snacks—packages of dry crumbly cookies and stale varnished-looking pretzels. Nothing but calories in the form of sawdust. She opts for a drink at the Sky Bar instead, and just as she claims the only vacant barstool, the PA man's voice speaks up again: "Flight 5186 to Chicago is delayed until six twenty-three."

The woman next to Fawn puts her glass down with a small thump and says, "That would have been good to know four beers ago."

Fawn looks at her, thinking that the woman is someone she could be friends with because (a) she's not from Hullbeck, and (b) she's not like someone who *could* be from Hullbeck. And indeed, she's not either, as Fawn finds out when she introduces herself. The woman is a commercial architect from Chicago. She has wild curly black hair and beatnik glasses and a beautiful retro cardigan as soft and red as a rose petal. Her name is Meredith.

They shake hands and then the bartender asks Fawn what she wants to drink.

The bartender must be over twenty-one, right? But she looks like a teenager, a fat and freckled one, with feathered hair and an embroidered sweater. Looking at her gives Fawn post-traumatic flashbacks to her own teen years. (Some people say time is like a river, but it's really much more like an accordion, constantly squeezing you back to high school.) She orders a vodka with three olives, and when the bartender hands it to her with a shy giggle, Fawn is torn between the desire to offer to enroll the bartender in Sarah Lawrence for the next semester and the equally strong desire to toss a drink in the bartender's face.

Instead she takes a sip and pulls her phone out. There's a text from her ex-husband, Joel: *I had hoped to see you this trip.*

Fawn sighs. It's so hard to hide these days, what with smartphones and the internet and all. Now everyone is instantly trackable and your ex-husband can find you with no trouble at all. But Fawn remembers how when she was in her late twenties, she had had an affair with a married man who used to call his wife from Fawn's apartment and say he was on a business trip while Fawn rustled a sheet of cellophane in the background to mimic long-distance static. Those were the days.

**It was a last-minute visit,** she texts back. A lie. She had planned the trip for months, to help her parents pack up their house before they moved to a retirement community later this month.

Immediately a little bubble with the three dots appears on the screen of her phone, meaning Joel is typing a response, so Fawn beats him to it by typing quickly *I meant to call you but I was unbelievably busy.* Two lies this time: she never meant to call him and she wasn't all that busy. Her parents had done most of the packing before she'd even gotten there.

The bubble with the three dots disappears, and it seems to Fawn that it vanishes sadly, reluctantly, like puppy faces staring when you pass a pet-shop window. She sighs and drops her phone back into her bag.

Fawn orders a fresh drink, along with another beer for Meredith. Meredith reaches for her glass and knocks over a dish of peanuts, sending them skittering down the bar.

"Well, thank you," the man next to her says. "Don't mind if I do." He scoops up a few peanuts off the countertop and pops them into his mouth. He smiles. "You girls doing okay?"

"We're fine," Fawn says coolly, because she senses that Meredith is about to say it warmly.

He holds out his hand to Meredith. "My name is Barry."

Barry looks like Fred Flintstone: big fleshy face, bulbous nose, shaggy forelock of black hair, five o'clock shadow. His body is large and diamond shaped. He is as far from Fawn's type as it is possible to be.

"You sure I can't buy you a drink?" he asks.

"No, thank you," Fawn says.

Barry doesn't seem offended. He just shrugs and says, "I'd better be getting home, anyway."

Fawn looks back at him, startled. "Home? What do you mean? Aren't you waiting for a flight?"

"Oh, no," Barry says, pushing one arm into his coat sleeve. "I live right here in town. I just came out for happy hour."

"You came to the *Hullbeck airport* just to have a few drinks?" Fawn asks. She can't get over this. It's like someone snuggling down on a couch with a big bowl of popcorn and forgetting to turn on the TV. "Why don't you go to the Turtle? Or Swanson's?"

"I was banned from those places," Barry says.

"But—but—what about Lefty's?" Fawn is not a Hullbeck girl for nothing.

"There, too," Barry says agreeably.

"What for?" Fawn asks.

Barry makes a face. "Some *people* say I act *entitled* when I drink."

Fawn is pretty sure that "people" are female staff and patrons, and "entitled" means Barry putting his hand up someone's skirt, but she can't help being the slightest bit impressed. She's never known anyone who's been banned from Lefty's.

"But how do you get past the airport security?" Meredith asks suddenly. "Don't you have to have a boarding pass?"

"Clyde lets me in," Barry says.

"Who's Clyde?"

"Me," the security guard says, appearing abruptly at Fawn's elbow. Fawn remembers him dimly from the security gate. "Barry and I went to high school together."

"Which high school?" Fawn asks nervously.

"Cooley," Barry says, and Fawn relaxes because it wasn't Hullbeck. She never wants to see anyone she went to high school with ever again.

Clyde looks at Barry. "Are you leaving already?"

"I guess not," Barry says happily, taking his arm back out of the coat sleeve and sitting down again. He orders another beer and

Clyde orders a club soda and Barry flicks a peanut at the bartender, who giggles. Stupid cunt, thinks Fawn.

From the depths of her purse, her phone chimes again.

WHEN FAWN TELLS PEOPLE that she was once married to a man who played the zither at Renaissance festivals, they always laugh and say, "No, *seriously*," and sometimes Fawn lets them think she was joking and sometimes she doesn't. Anyway, the zither thing was a very occasional sideline (there just aren't that many Renaissance festivals), and actually Joel owned and operated a small store in the Hullbeck mall called Airs & Graces. Sometimes people telephoned there thinking it was a tuxedo rental place, but it was a music store. Not the kind of music store that sold records; the kind that sold sheet music and clarinet reeds and violin strings.

Fawn had met Joel when she applied at Airs & Graces for a part-time job in high school. Joel was a slender—almost slight—man in his late thirties with gray-flecked dark hair that fell boyishly across his forehead. He had long-fingered, sensitive-looking hands and a smooth olive-skinned face and smelled faintly of Blue Juice valve oil. He was even more soft-spoken than Fawn, and he hired her the very same day she interviewed.

It was the perfect place for Fawn to work because it wasn't like working at Applebee's and having to wait on a table of popular kids, or working at the library and having to tell the popular kids to keep the noise down. The only people who shopped at Airs & Graces were piano teachers, or mothers of small children taking Suzuki classes, or kids who were in the marching band for unpopular reasons of their own. Fawn could sit on a stool behind the counter and answer the phone and ring up flute pads and bow rosin and endpoints as demurely as an old-time storekeeper. Joel worked in a small room separated from the main store by a pair of swinging doors. He spent his time in there repairing clarinet springs, replacing violin bridges, and swabbing crusted saliva out of saxophones.

Fawn worked the evening shift three days a week without incident through the fall of her senior year. Then one night in early winter, just before closing, the phone rang and when Fawn answered it, a man with a deep whisper-voice said, "What's better than two hands on a piano?"

"Pardon?" Fawn said, confused.

The man seemed to breathe down the line toward her. "Two lips on an organ."

Fawn had never had her lips on a man's *lips* at this point, let alone a man's organ. She gave a terrified squeak and slammed the phone down.

"What's wrong?" Joel asked, pushing his head through the swinging doors. "Did Tina Simpkins drop her flute in the toilet again?" Apparently, that was the worst thing he could think of.

"No," Fawn said shakily. "It was an obscene caller."

Joel looked at her face closely. "I see," he said softly. He didn't ask what the caller had said, which was good because Fawn would have died rather than tell him. He paused for a moment. "Perhaps I should walk you to your car tonight."

"Thank you," Fawn said. "That would be nice."

And so that night, Joel had walked Fawn through the food court to the mall entrance, holding her arm protectively. She looks back on it now and thinks that she and Joel must have looked like the Pillsbury Dough Boy and Pinocchio. (But in truth, Fawn wasn't that fat and Joel wasn't that petite—they were more like the Michelin Man and the Geico gecko.) Joel saw her safely to her car and waited until she got in and started the engine. He did the same thing the next night she worked, and the next, and on the fourth night, he kissed her shyly but urgently and that was how Fawn finally felt a man's lips on her lips, all because of a crank caller who was undoubtedly Barry or someone just like him.

℮⌒

THE TWO AIRPORT GATES are now like two gas stations in a price war, except that instead of dropping prices, they're delaying flights. First Fawn's flight by twenty more minutes, then Meredith's by twenty-five, then Fawn's, then Meredith's. All of it announced over the PA by a man who sounded like he should be teaching auto shop somewhere. Already it is six-thirty. Fawn dreads spending another night with her parents, much as she loves them. She can hear the siren song of her life in New York—her *real* life, as she thinks of it—calling her. She'll stay in a hotel near the airport if she absolutely must.

Meredith is so drunk now that she keeps closing one eye and squinting with the other, possibly to keep her vision from doubling. She has slumped to one side, the collar of her blouse askew, her cardigan hanging off one shoulder, her skirt riding up one thigh. It's like Meredith is slipping off the barstool while her clothes remain upright. Barry has become suddenly attentive, gently grasping Meredith's elbow and picking imaginary lint off her sweater. Fawn suspects that Barry can spot a drunk and vulnerable woman quicker than a lion can spot a limping zebra.

But Fawn isn't drunk because Fawn had learned to drink in high school. Fawn had been shy and self-conscious and a loner, but occasionally she was befriended by some pretty, vivacious girl, and that girl would take Fawn to parties, as an escort or maybe a sort of bouncer. The pretty girls seemed to know that Fawn would have no plans of her own, that she would be content to attend a party where she wasn't known or invited. A hundred nights sitting on the couch at a hundred parties had taught Fawn something most people don't know: inebriation is voluntary to some extent. No point in getting drunk and giggly if no boy wants to lure you into a darkened bedroom, so Fawn did not get drunk and giggly, or even drunk. She merely sat there with her hands crossed over her stomach and drank beer after beer with a grim determination. You can drink a lot of beer and not feel drunk, the same way you can eat a whole sleeve of Oreos and not feel full. For Fawn, beer became just a new way to measure time: six beers and her friend might be ready to go home.

℮∿

AT SEVEN O'CLOCK, Clyde throws up his hands slightly and gives a small shudder—a sort of involuntary spasm—and orders a beer.

"You haven't finished your club soda," Fawn says. She's not drunk, but she has reached that stage of alcohol consumption where she feels compelled to comment on everything.

"My shift ended just a minute ago," Clyde says. "I don't like to drink on duty."

"But you've been sitting here for over an hour," Fawn protests. "You mean you were supposed to be working all that time? Who's been running security?"

"Girl from the Hertz counter covers for me," Clyde says, blowing the foam off a beer the bartender sets in front of him.

Fawn wonders if there's a less secure, more dangerous airport in all the world. Well, of course there is—think of the Damascus airport with the warring rebel factions and the threat of surface-to-air missiles! But at least everyone in Syria *knows* the dangers; here in Hullbeck, the passengers are just shuffling along as placidly as cattle, totally unaware.

Suddenly, Barry grabs his drink and Meredith's. "Come on!" he says urgently.

Fawn wonders if maybe some terrorists got past the Hertz girl after all, and Barry is running from them, but then she sees that Barry moved so swiftly because the corner table is available. She helps Meredith off her barstool—which is harder than you might think, since Meredith attempts to turn around and climb down it like she's on a ladder—and Clyde takes Fawn's drink, and they lay claim to the corner table. So now, for better or for worse, they seem to be a foursome, like a string quartet. (Barry is even pretty cello shaped.)

But they don't make for an especially harmonious quartet, what with Meredith spending a full five minutes arguing with Barry over how many time zones there are in the United States. "Show me!" Meredith shouts. She pounds the table with her fist. "Just show me the fucking seventh time zone!"

Fawn keeps checking her phone. More texts from Joel, piled like pancakes:

**Which flight are you on? The weather looks bad.**

**If you need a ride home, just call me.**

**If you have time for dinner, I know a place with good chicken-fried steak.**

**Or I could bring sandwiches out to the airport.**

Now the problem here is that she can't say her flight is about to leave, because Joel could go online and see that all the flights have been delayed. She can't say she's past security because he could text back and say he's right on the other side. She can't say she'd rather die than eat chicken-fried steak because Joel has seen her eat chicken-fried steak—great amounts of it.

She decides to just ignore his texts, which is, after all, one of the advantages of texting. She puts her phone on silent and slides it back into her purse.

"You seem nervous about something," Clyde says to her, and Fawn's faith in his security abilities takes a teeny-tiny uptick: he does notice suspicious behavior after all.

"Just someone I'd rather not see," she says.

"Everybody has one of those," Clyde says, and Fawn finds that oddly comforting.

Fawn and Joel had married the June after Fawn graduated from

high school. Her worried parents—shocked at the age difference—
had begged her to reconsider, hinted at missed opportunities for a
girl with so much potential, tried to bribe her with college tuition.
But Fawn had plowed ahead with the unmovable sort of stubborn-
ness known only to teenagers and toddlers. She had never fit in as
a high-school student; now she would fit in as a married woman,
starting as soon as possible.

She'd worn a shiny white satin wedding gown and a lace head-
piece festooned with ostrich feathers—it looked like a cross between
a bathing cap and something you might sweep out of a birdcage.
Fawn moved into Joel's small two-bedroom brick house near downtown and they adopted a kitten Fawn named Mr. Bingley. Joel hired
a new girl to work the register at Airs & Graces and Fawn took lit-
erature classes at a community college. Soon their lives had settled
into a routine: Fawn cooked newlywed breakfasts of French toast
and packed newlywed lunches of egg salad on rye. She cleaned and
vacuumed with newlywed electronics, and baked newlywed casse-
roles with pineapple and ham, and shopped for newlywed furniture.
She wrote thank-you letters on newlywed stationery, and planned
newlywed dinner parties, and had newlywed sex on fresh sheets
from JC Penney, and felt a newlywed despair as black and sticky
as tar. After eight months of marriage, she moved back to her parents' house and took them up on that college tuition offer. By the
following September, she was enrolled at Hamilton College. Fawn
may not have been thin or popular but—perhaps for those very
reasons—she got marvelous grades.

Afterward, Joel had—had—had *bothered* her, is how Fawn thought
of it. For years and years. Cards on her birthday and flowers for promotions and phone calls on Christmas Eve. This had puzzled Fawn,
and then annoyed her. Her main memory of her marriage now is
the sinking sensation she got each evening when she returned to the
little brick house. She would open the door and be greeted by a puff
of warm air (Joel had thyroid issues and their thermostat was set at

seventy-six) and the smell of Mr. Bingley's litter box and the swelling notes of the Shostakovich CDs Joel loved—as if Michigan winters weren't long enough without Russian symphonies forever crashing in the background! To this day, Fawn doesn't like Shostakovich, or cats, or overheating, or Joel.

℮↷

FAWN HAS BEGUN TO HAVE that feeling familiar to bar-goers everywhere: that the night won't end until she has sex with someone. She looks over her companions, eyelids flickering. Barry is out of the question, but she looks at Clyde. He's resting his elbows on the table and talking to Barry about a friend of theirs who recently switched from briefs to boxers and then injured his scrotum on an ergonomic kneeling chair. "He had to sit on a package of frozen peas for two days," Barry says. Clyde shakes his head and clucks. His biceps swell against his shirtsleeve like the curve of an eight ball. Yes, Fawn decides: underneath her, Clyde would feel just fine.

Meredith begins pinching peanuts off the sticky table with great concentration and putting them into her mouth.

"Don't eat those," Fawn says to Meredith. "They're dirty." She and Meredith have gone from strangers to bar-friends to mother-and-child in the space of two hours.

Meredith looks up, startled, and pops another peanut in.

"No," Fawns says sternly. It seems that now they have moved on to owner-and-dog. But if there's one thing Fawn knows about, it's how and when not to eat.

In the months after she left Joel and before she went to college, Fawn had dieted and exercised herself down to her current size. It wasn't accurate to say she *lost* weight—it was more like she *chased* the weight off her body the way a farmer would chase a stray dog off his property. And like a suspicious farmer, Fawn still patrols the borders of her body, a shotgun propped in the crook of her elbow, ready to shoot any fattening food that tries to sneak back in. Of course, sometimes, foods do get past her—crunchy golden French fries, freshly baked sugar cookies—but there are ways of dealing with trespassers.

She had graduated from Hamilton with an English degree and moved to New York and got a job at a magazine as a marketing assistant where she sat in a windowless closet all day updating spreadsheets. From there, she had scrabbled her way up the editorial ladder, learning how to dress from photo-shoot stylists. She changed her name from the awkward and unsophisticated Evangeline Fyan to Fawn Evans and now nobody calls her Evangeline—let alone *Vangie*. (Except that lots of people do, like her parents and her cousins and family friends. Name changes are never as immutable and decisive as you want them to be.)

Meredith and Fawn go up to the bar to buy the next round and suddenly Meredith's shouting at the teenaged bartender. "You didn't fill that glass!"

"Ma'am—" the bartender says.

"You didn't fill that glass!" Meredith is so enraged that she's spraying saliva. "You call that fucking *full*? It's not even close!"

"Ma'am, I just poured the bottle into the glass," the bartender says patiently. "You watched me do it."

"I saw no such fucking thing!" Meredith shouts. Somewhere along the line, she has lost the top two buttons on her blouse and now it looks like her breasts are about to spill out onto the bar top.

"You tell her!" Barry calls from their table.

"Oh, fuck off, Fred!" Meredith snaps over her shoulder. Fawn feels a moment of joyful connection: she's not the only one who thinks Barry looks like Fred Flintstone!

Barry blinks in surprise and, turning, Fawn catches his eye, tilting her head at the bar, a signal that he should take over the drink ordering. She grips Meredith's elbow, saying softly, "Come with me." She gives the bartender her warmest smile—although it is almost painful to give the bartender anything—and steers Meredith down the hall to the restroom.

It's been years since Fawn has had to pull someone back from the brink of drunk-and-disorderly in a ladies' room, but she discovers—happily—that it's a skill you never completely lose.

First, she leads Meredith into one of the toilet stalls and sticks two fingers down Meredith's throat. (This is a route that Fawn's fingers are more than fleetingly familiar with—the sometimes-necessary evil to get what you've put inside back on the outside.) It works on Meredith the way it has always worked on Fawn: the hack, the gag, the rush of stomach-darkened fluid. Fawn holds Meredith's hair back while Meredith vomits three times, a glut of murky beer with peanuts floating in it.

Fawn hits the flush lever with her foot and steers Meredith out of the stall to the sink. Meredith makes a dreadful moaning sound, as though a snarling Gorgon has appeared before her, but Fawn ignores that. (This sometimes happens—it'll pass.) She produces a teeny bottle of mouthwash from the little cosmetic bag she carries in her purse and orders Meredith to rinse and spit. Fawn tears open a makeup-remover cloth and wipes away the mascara smudges under Meredith's eyes. She untangles Meredith's hair with a small hairbrush and cleans the flecks of vomit from Meredith's cardigan with a small packet of stain remover. She uses a safety pin to close the top button of Meredith's blouse so she won't be wowing any ticket agent with unintentional cleavage. A little swipe of rosy lipstick and two ancient aspirin from a tarnished tin swallowed with a cupped handful of tap water, and Meredith is as good as new. Sort of.

Fawn leads Meredith out into the hall and wheels her around to face the huge clock on the wall. Together they watch while the second hand makes one slow circular sweep, and then Fawn asks, "Did you feel like you were going to throw up?"

Meredith shakes her head.

"Good," Fawn says encouragingly. "If you can go sixty seconds, you can go a whole flight."

This is a tried-and-true formula, more reliable than the three-minute egg. But nevertheless, Fawn slips the tin of aspirin into Meredith's coat pocket. She might need it later.

e~

JUST BEFORE NINE O'CLOCK, the PA crackles and the man's voice comes back on. Apparently, they all know each other well enough now so that he can dispense with the formal wording because he just says, "Folks, all flights are canceled for the rest of the night. I repeat, no one's flying out tonight. Please see a ticket agent about getting on a flight tomorrow."

Everyone seated at the bar and at the gate groans. People grab their carry-on luggage and head back toward the airport exit and the ticket counters. It's as though the crowd swarms together and takes the shape of one giant footsore, slope-shouldered, weary traveler. Fawn and Meredith go up to their gates and wait in line for flight reassignment. Fawn is rebooked onto a 7:00 a.m. flight, Meredith one at 8:40.

Then they go back to the Sky Bar and finish their drinks with Barry and Clyde while the chubby bartender comes out from behind the bar and begins wiping down the tables. The airport has gone from crowded to deserted in a matter of minutes. Barry says Fawn and Meredith are welcome to sleep at his house and play some Xbox. Fawn is fairly sure this is code for one of them playing Xbox while Barry has sex with the other one, so she declines for both of them. But Barry offers to drive them to the Holiday Inn and it turns out he's giving Clyde a ride home anyway, so they all leave the Sky Bar together. (The bartender gives a startled squeak when Barry passes behind her, and Barry smirks at Fawn over the bartender's shoulder.)

Unlike the other travelers, they are as animated as new converts leaving a revival meeting. Meredith wants to know if it's true you can jump a snowmobile over a stream, and Barry wonders if maybe enough time has gone by so they won't recognize him at the Turtle, and Clyde asks Fawn if her bouclé coat will shake itself when it gets wet, and they are almost to the exit doors when a soft voice says, "Hi, Vangie."

Fawn looks up automatically. She can't help it. You can leave the past behind but some part of you remains there, like a rough sharp splintery tree branch sticking out along the path and snagging your sleeve.

Joel is standing alone near the exit in a puffy blue down coat with a fur-trimmed hood pushed back. His hands are in his pockets and his face is smooth and unlined. He's still that curious combination of boyish and elderly.

"Oh—Joel," Fawns says in confusion. "How—how long have you been here?"

"Not long at all," he says in a casual voice that makes her sure he's lying. "I just came out on the chance your flight was canceled and you needed a ride."

"Well, thank you," Fawn says. "But I'm riding with these—people." She was about to say, *These guys.*

These guys and Joel eye one another up for a minute. Fawn cannot imagine what a single one of them is thinking.

"Why don't you all go ahead," she says finally to Barry. "I'll catch up in a minute."

"Are you sure?" Barry asks.

Fawn nods. Barry gives Joel a little wave, and he goes out through the sliding glass doors, Clyde and Meredith trooping along behind him.

"It's good to see you," Joel says to Fawn.

"You, too."

"You look so pretty."

Fawn is saved from answering that because Barry comes running back in. She's so grateful to him for rescuing her that she gives him her most dazzling smile, but Barry only says excitedly, "The parking lot's empty! We can do doughnuts!"

Fawn had never liked the kind of doughnuts you do in parking lots as much as she liked the other kind of doughnuts, the ones with frosting and sprinkles and jelly centers. In high school, she could never see the appeal of driving around in dark crowded cars when you could stay home and eat.

"I'll be there in a minute," she says softly, and Barry races back out, the automatic doors closing behind him.

Fawn looks at Joel and then looks at the floor. She pulls her gloves out of her coat pocket and puts them on as slowly as possible. Joel clears his throat. The silence between them is spreading like the snow melting off Joel's boots.

Finally, Joel speaks. "How are your parents?"

"Oh, well, they're moving," Fawn says. "You know. To a retirement community. It's an adjustment. In lots of ways. Good and bad." She keeps adding phrases, hoping they will add up to a reasonable conversation.

He nods. "Tell them if they need any help, they can call me."

Time has reversed Fawn's parents' opinion of Joel—they often tell her how he calls to check up on them. Now she suspects they wish she'd stayed married to him.

"And how are things with you?" she asks.

He shrugs. "Same as always, I guess. Though I'm sorry to tell you that Mr. Bingley died."

Fawn looked at him, surprised. "Seriously?"

Joel nods his head sadly. "He passed just this fall from lymphoma. I'm sorry, I know it must be a shock to you."

It is a shock. Not that Mr. Bingley is dead; it's that he had been alive until so very recently. Her marriage to Joel had felt as fleeting as a goldfish's trip across its bowl, and yet—for twenty years!—Joel and Mr. Bingley had continued on in some form of plodding existence with a Russian soundtrack.

"Look, I really should go," Fawn says.

"Well, I was hoping we could have a drink or something," Joel says.

Fawn bites her lip. "That's probably not a good idea."

"But I thought, after what happened last time—" Joel begins.

What happened last time! Is there a worse phrase in the English language? Well, maybe. *The bank is foreclosing* isn't great, and *North Korea just launched a missile* is pretty awful. But *what happened last time* is the worst because it almost always refers to an event of which the participants have wildly differing interpretations. It refers to the kind of thing that happens when two people who used to be lovers page through their old yearbooks together and end up in a tangle on the sofa. Or when two people act in community theater together and get a little wild at the cast party. Or when two people go for an evening walk and one of them is worried about her aging parents, and upset about the cost of her kitchen renovations, and depressed about having her cover-line ideas shot down at a brainstorming meeting, and the two people end up having mistake-sex on a freezing-cold bench in the Hullbeck Nature Center, right down by the fucking replica wigwam, which is *what happened last time.*

Fawn had thought that she and Joel would make love like old friends, but the problem with that is that old friends get together and have endless dinners that irritate the restaurant staff, or they have two-hour phone calls where they discuss nothing but how it feels when you hear a Stevie Nicks song on the radio. Old friends don't have sex with each other; that's how they remain old friends. Joel had emailed and texted her for weeks and weeks afterward. It had been impossible to make him understand that Fawn sharing her body with him was no more meaningful and intimate than her sharing the name of her editor at *The New York Times Book Review.* (Actually, it was *less* intimate than that, because Fawn never shares the name of that editor with anyone.) In twenty years, Joel has never been able to figure out why Fawn had liked him when she was overweight and awkward, and why she dislikes him now that she's slender and pretty. He doesn't seem to understand everyone has standards—some people just hardly ever get to apply theirs.

"Last time was three years ago," Fawn said. "It's not going to happen again."

"But—" Joel starts.

"I have to go," Fawn says firmly. "My friends are waiting for me."

"Friends?" Joel says. "Didn't you just meet them?"

"Yes and no," Fawn says, thinking how true this is. She stands up a little straighter. She is not going to touch him, not even to shake hands. "Anyway, goodbye, Joel."

She walks toward the sliding doors, feeling the weight of his eyes on her. She resists the urge to shrug her shoulders, to flick the weight of his gaze off like confetti after a New Year's Eve party. Why is she so eager to be free of someone so gentle and kind? Is it fair to dislike someone solely because he reminds you of an earlier, awkward stage of your life? Probably not. But nobody ever said life was fair.

OUTSIDE, THE SKY IS as purple as a grape Popsicle and the snow is falling softly and thickly. Sometimes Fawn has thought that the rain falls more slowly in Hullbeck, and it appears that the snow does, too, in large luminous flakes that look like the fading stars of fireworks. Michigan is beautiful, just beautiful. How had Fawn forgotten that?

In the parking lot, an old Pontiac Firebird is spinning in circles, engine roaring, rear wheels skidding and throwing up plumes of snow. Even from where she stands, Fawn can hear the happy whoops and cries of the car's occupants. Fawn suspects that Barry's life skills may be somewhat less than stellar, but his doughnut-driving skills are excellent: the blank white surface of the parking lot is covered with looping tire tracks, each as perfectly formed as a young girl's penmanship.

Fawn crosses the access road outside the airport—she sees Joel's car parked at the curb—and scrambles over the median to the parking lot, waving to the Firebird.

The Firebird spins over to her, although Fawn remains safely on the median—she doesn't trust Barry's driving *that* much. But as soon as the car comes to a stop, she jumps down beside it. Meredith hops out on the passenger side and pulls the lever to make the bucket seat tilt forward. "Come on, Fawn!" she says, her face alive with drunken happiness. Her hair is one hundred thousand dark sprigs of curly parsley.

Fawn slides into the back seat next to Clyde. Meredith gets back in and slams the door. "Put on your seat belt," Clyde says to Fawn. His voice is slightly chiding, as though doing doughnuts in a parking lot were some sort of regulated activity with safety standards and she's failing to live up to them. But in the next second, he puts his hand on the inside of her thigh and pulls her leg next to his.

Barry shifts gears and guns the accelerator. The car shoots to the middle of the parking lot and he turns the steering wheel all the way to the left, yanking the hand brake, and just like that, the car is floating. Weightless. Adrift. It's like the feeling Fawn gets when sleep finally comes for her after a long night of insomnia—the lift and drop of surrender.

The car's wheels grip the asphalt again and it lurches to a stop. The inside of the car smells like Budweiser and wet wool, and the windows are fogged with humidity. Ted Nugent is blaring on the radio. Barry straightens the steering wheel and hits the gas. The car races toward the other side of the parking lot. He jerks the hand brake.

The car spins its rear wheels out to the right and Fawn feels that weightless feeling, that buoyancy again. She hopes it continues forever—she wants to do doughnuts here all night. It's just like high school. Only now it's fun.

## ACKNOWLEDGMENTS

Thank you to my agent, Kim Witherspoon. No finer agent exists. It's that simple. To Maria Whelan. Thank you for being my fortress against the world so many times. And to Felicity Rubinstein. It's not your job to make me feel happy and believed-in all the time, but you do a very good job of it anyway.

Thank you to my editor, Jenny Jackson. You never fail to meet me in the middle of the wobbly rope bridge of book writing and help me to the other side with wisdom and kindness. To Maris Dyer. You are my go-to work person and now my go-to friend. To Michelle Kane. I can never thank you enough for introducing me to the term "refresh blister" and for caring as much about this book as I do.

Thank you to Robert McCready, Jason O'Toole, Martin Harvey, and Lauren Bright Pacheco, who shared their expertise with me on everything from road tests to podcasts. You were generous beyond measure.

Thank you to Jennifer Close, Rebecca Gale, and especially Patrick Walczy for reading early drafts of these stories so willingly and so well. You have all taken up residency in my head, which is wonderful—and in my life, which is even better.

Thank you to my family. To my mother, Suzanne Heiny. I hold you always in my thoughts. To my brother, Christopher Heiny. You are the best problem solver there is, for problems both real and fictional. And to my husband, Ian McCredie. Maybe there are more articulate ways to say this, but I don't know them, so: thank you, my love. For everything.

## A Note About the Author

KATHERINE HEINY is the author of *Early Morning Riser*, *Standard Deviation*, and *Single, Carefree, Mellow*. Her short fiction has appeared in *The New Yorker*, *The Atlantic*, and many other magazines. She lives in Havre de Grace, Maryland, with her husband and children.